REVISITED

WILLIAM O. ANGELLEY

REVISITED
William Angelley
Copyright 2023 © William O. Angelley
All rights reserved

ISBN: 9798374813777
Also available in eBook
V03012023SC

Front Cover Design: Sukhchain @multiwaygraphic
Back Cover, Interior Book Design, Publishing Assistant:
The Author's Mentor, www.theauthorsmentor.com

www.AngelleyBooks.com

PUBLISHED IN THE UNITED STATES OF AMERICA

❖

For Jules. I will miss you always.

❖

Early Reviews for *Revisited*

5-HUGE-Stars for this fast-paced thriller with a surprising twist and a well-developed plot that turns "past lives" research on its head.

Batya Dulos,
Editor, RunRabbitBooks

This one really got me thinking. Science and religion explode in this fascinating paranormal thriller. I find myself hoping the author takes Devon into her own series. Think of the tales she could tell with her research!

Emil Jersey,
Best Selling Fantasy Author
Malcontent, #1 Amazon Bestseller

ONE

IF HE'D KNOWN THEY WERE GOING TO SLEEP THROUGH THE whole thing, he never would have brought them here. But he didn't know. He also didn't know that the course of his life was about to change. So, he just drove.

A wire mesh covered the rock wall that rose above the oncoming traffic lane to James Masten's left. There was no such border to his right. On that side, nothing separated his car from the deep abyss a few feet away. The road was dangerous, and he was uncomfortable. He gripped the steering wheel with both hands until his knuckles were white.

As Masten ascended the switchbacks up the mountain, his attention was split between the narrow, two-lane blacktop in front of him and the images around him. The scenery was stunning, almost too much to process. Steep, green, mountain ridges were separated by narrow canyons. Moist fog layers hung low in each of the valleys. The greens were dark and dense, like a rainforest. Everything around him looked wet, but the road was

1

dry. It seemed like something from another world, but it was the central coast of California. He'd pass through an occasional patch of fog lingering over the highway, which made him slow a bit. From his high vantage point, it felt like he was driving through the clouds.

Masten continued until he reached the summit. When he encountered a straight and flat area on top of the mountain, he relaxed a little and allowed himself more speed. It was a nice break.

He released a long breath and took his right hand off the steering wheel. He shook it trying to get the circulation back. Then he grabbed the wheel again with his right hand and gave his left the same treatment before dropping it onto his knee. He continued driving with just his right hand. A deep breath led to a yawn. Exhaling, he moved his shoulders around a little and settled back into his seat. He scratched his left knee through his blue jeans. A second later, he was compelled to scratch his right. Equal time.

Masten looked over at his wife, who was sleeping in the seat next to him. A quick glance in the rear-view mirror revealed his daughter to be sound asleep as well. He was aggravated. The whole reason he made this drive was to show the two of them the views. He had a little more time to relax though before the descent—or so he thought.

His reprieve was interrupted by a loud pop. The steering wheel began to shake, and the car pulled hard to the right toward an upcoming cliff. Masten cursed and tried hard not to panic.

With both hands gripping the wheel, he fought to pull the car back to the left, but the car fought just as hard to pull to the right. Masten knew that the S-shaped trajectory he was following was extremely dangerous on this road. He pressed the brakes. It took everything he had to resist slamming them. He was on the edge of losing control, both of the car and of himself.

He wrestled the car for what seemed like an eternity. Then, almost as suddenly as the whole event started, it stopped. It took him a few moments to realize that the car wasn't moving anymore. Masten maintained an iron grip on the steering wheel.

His heart raced, and his eyes darted in every direction. His breathing was shallow and quick. A long minute later, he regained his faculties, put the car in park, and turned off the ignition.

Masten exhaled and looked over at his wife. Her face was ashen. He then looked over his shoulder at his daughter who was staring at him wide-eyed from the back seat.

"What the hell happened?" she asked.

"I think we had a blowout. You guys okay?"

"Jesus," his daughter replied, "that scared the shit out of me."

"You and me both," he responded, ignoring her language. "Are you okay?" he asked as he turned and looked at his wife. There was no response.

"Kate, are you all right?" he asked again.

Her right hand was clutching the passenger door panel and he could see her legs shaking. She still didn't respond but was finally able to manage a small head nod.

"What happened?" Kate finally asked.

"I don't know. I guess we hit something in the road. I didn't see anything."

"Shit," his daughter shouted as she reached down into the floorboard to retrieve her phone.

Masten shot her a look this time, but he could see that her hands were shaking too.

"Okay," he said, hitting the steering wheel with both hands, "I guess I'll change the tire."

"Do you even know how?" his daughter asked.

"We're about to find out. You guys stay here."

Masten opened the door and stood up. He took a moment, found his legs, and began to walk. The front and back tires on the driver's side were fine. He then walked to the front passenger's side. That tire was flat with a large gaping hole between the top and the bottom. He pointed at it, trying to inform his wife and daughter, but neither noticed, so he continued to the back. Reaching the rear of the car, he opened the trunk with a key fob and stopped to look around. It struck him that during his

3

panic he hadn't even noticed where the car had ended up. It was sitting on a patch of dirt that was just to the right of the road's narrow shoulder. Only a few feet separated the nose of the car from the rim of a deep canyon.

Masten saw a row of scrubby trees growing below the steep drop off. A little more, and the car would have gone over. He rubbed his face and tried to shake off the chills. Then he turned his attention to the tire.

The spare was bolted into a sunken compartment beneath the removable floor of the trunk. As he fumbled with the finger-tight bolt, Masten felt the adrenaline working its way out of his system. He dragged the tire out of the trunk and laid it on the ground. He wiped the black gunk off his hands by rubbing them on the bottom of his untucked blue, flannel shirt. *It'll wash.*

When he leaned back into the trunk to retrieve the jack, he was startled by a strange noise. It sounded like a scream, but it was sudden and short. Then he heard it again. He thought it was probably an eagle or some kind of large bird, so he didn't react. When he heard the noise for the third time, he stood up and spun around. Only then did Masten realize he was hearing the screeching tires of an approaching car.

A large SUV was careening out of control and heading straight for him. He barely had time to process what was happening. Without thinking, Masten dove for the ground and rolled toward the dirt patch, but inertia carried his body over the side of the cliff. He began to flail. He managed to catch the trunk of a small scrub tree with one hand and used his feet to push against the branches below. He caught himself at a point where his head was partially above the edge of the cliff. His eyes were right at the level of the road. Then, things began moving in slow motion.

The SUV crossed the exact spot where Masten had been standing and plowed directly into the rear end of his car. The tremendous force of impact launched his smaller, lighter sedan forward. He watched in horror as the car left the ground, flew over the edge of the cliff, and began a long downward trajectory into the valley below.

4

The SUV, like a cue ball on a pool table, lost most, but not all, its energy in the impact. It rolled forward until the front wheels crossed over the edge of the cliff. The nose pitched downward. Then further downward. The sounds of scraping dirt and gravel accompanied the slow disappearance of the SUV over the side.

Still flattened against the cliff wall, Masten was frozen with shock. As one of the branches began to give way below, he was forced to snap out of it and scramble for better footing. He climbed as high as he could in the scrub tree and reached around in desperation for something on the surface he could use to pull himself up. He found a rock embedded deep in the dirt, and praying it would hold his weight, grabbed the rock with one hand and used the rubber soles of his sneakers to inch up the tree. When he was high enough, Masten grabbed the rock with the other hand and hoisted himself back onto the road.

He was overcome by violent shaking. When he was able to stand, he peered over the cliff. Masten could see two piles of smoldering wreckage below. His car had hit the ground nose first and was silent. The SUV had flipped upside down and landed square on its roof, causing the alarm to go off. He could hear the repeating, honking echo through the valley. There were no other sounds. Masten became nauseated. He leaned forward, put his hands on his knees, and retched.

By the time the nausea turned to dry heaves, he was on all fours. When the heaving stopped, Masten rolled onto his back and tried to focus. It took some more time, but he found himself able to stand. Physically in shock and mentally overloaded, he looked around. He was alone on the highway. Masten saw the spare tire still lying beside the road. It was the only remnant left of the life he'd been living just moments ago. That life was gone now—in a mere flash. He fell back to the ground and heaved again and again in between screams and sobs.

Two

"JIM, YOU WANTED TO SEE ME?" DEVON MENDEZ KNOCKED on the office door frame.

"Devon!" Masten motioned with a hand. He sounded happy to see her. "Come in, my dear. Have a seat. You're here early, especially for a Monday." He reached for the top button of his starched white shirt. "You'll have to excuse me. I haven't put my tie on yet."

Devon entered the room and sat down in one of the ordinary office chairs in front of Masten's ornate oak desk. She sat her designer handbag on the floor next to the chair. She adjusted herself a couple of times, trying to get comfortable; like a kid sitting in the principal's office.

Masten's office was plain and decorated only with stacks of papers lying along the edges of the walls. She remembered a time when he had the usual family pictures adorning the desk and walls, along with framed diplomas and other accolades hanging about. The pictures and frames were all gone now. She

6

knew why, so she never mentioned it. She'd known Masten since she was a child. He was her godfather, which meant very little to her, but was a big deal to her parents.

"Tell me," Masten said, "how have you been?"

"I've been doing fine." Devon was a little disoriented, or confused, she couldn't tell which, by the whole meeting, and Masten's cologne wasn't helping.

"Good, good," Masten said, like a father who just heard about an excellent grade. "You know, it's been a while since we've spoken, but I've been following your progress. I promised your father I would." Masten pointed at her when he said that. "I also saw that you passed your board certification with flying colors. Very impressive. Your parents would be proud."

"Thank you," Devon was still unsure why she was there.

"So, Devon," Masten said, raising his glasses and rubbing his eye with a knuckle, "I'll cut to the chase. It appears that you've decided to pursue research instead of practice." Masten's hand moved from his eye down to his mouth.

"Yes," Devon responded. "I've been working with Dr. Warnick for the past year, and I think he's looking into something fascinating."

"Past lives?" Masten asked, looking down his nose and over his glasses. His tone shifted.

Devon was a little stunned by the question. "How'd you know?"

"Look," Masten said. "I told your father I would watch out for you if anything ever happened to him. That includes guiding you in your career path. This one, dear, is a dead end."

Masten slid a file across his desk and tapped it a few times with his finger. "What is this?" Masten was half asking, half demanding. "You understand we are one of the premier research facilities in the world, don't you?"

"I do, yes," Devon responded, shifting in her seat.

Masten continued, "And I'm the person who has to approve the funding for all of the projects that come out of this medical school."

"This is simply my research proposal, Jim. Dr. Warnick is

very supportive of the idea."

Masten sighed.

"Are you skeptical of the premise?" Devon asked, "because I can …"

"I *am* skeptical of the premise. It seems nonsensical."

"I assure you, it's not," Devon responded, trying not to sound too defensive. "Scientists have been studying young children who claim to have memories from past lives for more than forty years. There are countless examples of kids knowing things they couldn't possibly know otherwise."

"Come on!" Masten said, dragging out his words. "These kids are making this up. It's fantasy. It's overactive imaginations, or someone looking for fifteen minutes of fame." Masten tossed the file across the desk at Devon and pointed a condescending finger. "You ought to know better, *Doctor* Mendez. What would your father think? And more than that, what would your mother think? She and my Kate were two of the most devout women I've ever met. You know your mother would never approve of this."

Devon took a breath and let it out. Her mother died of cancer when she was still a teen. *That was a low blow.*

"Look, Devon," Masten said. "I'm trying to help you, but you're not making it easy for me. I don't want to turn down one of your funding requests. That wouldn't reflect well on you. But I can't approve this!"

Devon felt the blood run from her head.

"Well, what about Dr. Warnick's work?" Devon objected.

"Devon," Masten said, rubbing his balding head. "He's old, he's tenured and he's working off funding that was granted to him years ago by some kooky benefactor. His work won't continue much longer."

Devon looked down. She could feel her lips going numb.

"Can we just make this go away?" Masten pleaded. "No one needs to be the wiser."

"I promise you it's not fantasy! I can show you. There's a five-year-old girl up the coast in Monterey. Her mother reached out to me yesterday. Her story is compelling, and I'm trying to set up a meeting. Come with me and see for yourself. If you're not convinced after the meeting, I'll drop the whole thing."

Masten sighed, leaned back in his chair, and pushed his glasses up. His lips moved left then right.

"A chance, that's all I'm asking for," Devon pleaded before Masten could respond. "Come with me to Monterey."

"All right," Masten acceded. "But I expect this whole business to be over when we get back."

"Yes!" Devon responded. "I'll let you know when I get it set up."

"Please do." Masten pointed at the door. The warmth of the beginning of the meeting was now gone. "You can close that behind you."

THREE

WHEN DEVON LEFT THE OFFICE, MASTEN LEANED BACK IN HIS chair and closed his eyes. Her proposal seemed outlandish. Yet, he couldn't help thinking, given his own work with Devon's father, not completely implausible. Masten let his mind wander back to that day five years ago—before the crash.

❖ ❖ ❖

"Jesus, Jim! What have we done?"

The two men stared at the dead body in complete shock. The eyes were gray and pallid from three days' worth of decomposition, but they were now open. The rest of the body, shriveled and purpling, lay perfectly still on the table. The smell was something akin to raw chicken that had been left in the fridge for about a week too long.

"David, I ... shit!"

The men jumped back when the dead man's eyes cut in the direction of Masten's voice. The man's cranium was open and there was an array of machines at the head of the table. One was connected to a long, thin needle that was inserted deep into the dead man's exposed brain. The needle, no bigger than one used for a common flu shot, terminated at a specific spot in the brain stem just between the areas known as the pons and the medulla oblongata.

The tiny needle was an electrical probe. Its purpose was to deliver an even smaller electrical current right to a specific area. The frequency of the current was controlled by a computer attached to the needle through wires no larger than fly-fishing tippet. The computer worked its way through hundreds of thousands of possible electrical frequencies, the span of which had been decided prior to beginning the experiment. It was like a computer hacker working through all possible combinations of numbers and letters of a password within a given range.

A sophisticated electroencephalogram system was also wired into the dead man's brain. If a particular frequency sparked any EEG activity, the computer would halt the frequency scan. On this particular subject, the scan halted about a minute before his eyes opened.

Raising the dead was not the point of the project. Dr. David Mendez was not Jesus, and neither was Masten. And the subject lying on the table was not Lazarus. He was a fifty-eight-year-old white male who died from untreated lung cancer.

The goal of the project was researching some portion of the nature of consciousness. The irony of researching consciousness with a dead body was not lost on Masten or Mendez, but the brain was, after all, to a large extent, an electrical device.

Most scientists believed that the brain's electrical processes were generated internally through the interactions of sodium and potassium with chloride electrolytes. Mendez didn't disagree with such provable observations, but many years of research on the structure of a certain primitive part of the brain led him to hypothesize that this area acted as nothing more than a receiver for *external* electrical signals. As far as Mendez could tell, this tiny area neither generated, nor responded to, the chemically based signals generated around it.

The research being conducted was designed to test Mendez' hypothesis. A living brain involved not just electrical impulses, but also chemical signals, conducted by various neuro-transmitters. Generating chemical signals in a dead brain was not feasible, but it was also not within the scope of Mendez and Masten's work. They focused only on the electrical. Their study was analogous to testing the battery and starter system of a car with no gas. They weren't trying to run it; they were just checking the viability and routes of the electrical currents involved.

In the process of analyzing the incoming currents, however, Mendez and Masten also discovered, much to their surprise, that there was an *outgoing* electrical current coming from this minuscule area of the brain.

Therefore, another, more sensitive probe was placed near the dead man's head, but not inserted into the brain. This probe was simply a receiver. It had been zeroed out to all possible impulses in the room. The point was to be able to pick up on any new signals generated when the brain was energized.

Almost simultaneously with the activation of the current through the small needle inserted into the brain, the receiver probe began picking up a tiny outbound signal. The machine attached to the receiver probe began lighting up.

One of the receiver system's primary functions was to log the frequency recorded by the receiver probe. The machine did its job. The outgoing signal was pegged at precisely 1.1009 Hertz, just as it had before. It was down on the low end of the Delta frequency band, much lower than the "active intelligence" range of around 13 Hertz.

The dead body in the room was the fifth subject whom Masten and Mendez had studied, and every one of them produced the exact same outbound brain frequency. As fascinating as that was, the more puzzling part of the study was the inbound frequency that was required to essentially "wake" the dead. That was different for each subject. The difference was slight in pure numerical terms, but oceans apart in terms of precision electronics.

The first subject's receiving frequency was 1.2070 Hz. The number was rounded to four digits for ease of analysis but was actually taken out to twenty-two digits by the computer. The second was 1.2214. The third was 1.2156. The fourth was 1.2178. And the frequency that animated the present subject, which was something that had not happened before with the other four subjects, was 1.2251. The first four subjects appeared to remain dead during the experiment. Only the brainwaves activated. The reanimation of a days-old dead body was an unexpected shock.

"What the hell is going on?" Masten asked.

The body remained still and the face catatonic. The eyes were lethargic but open and slowly responsive to the stimulus of movement.

"I don't know," said Mendez, who was clearly upset and agitated. "Did we get the numbers?"

Masten checked the screens of both machines. "Yes," he said. "They're recorded."

"Okay, then," Mendez commanded. "Let's shut it down."

"But David—" Masten began to protest.

"Shut it down now!" Mendez shouted.

Masten shot Mendez an aggravated glance but did as he was told. He flipped the switches on both machines and extracted the needle from the dead man's brain. He then began the tedious task of removing the numerous EEG sensors from the unexcavated portions of the subject's head.

To their relief, the body was "dead" once again. The eyes remained suspended in their last open position. There was no more movement. Masten placed the small circular portion of skull back over the hole created from its removal and secured it with several staples. He then pulled a thin white sheet up and over the dead man's face.

While Masten worked, Mendez removed the clear plastic shield covering his face and crossed the room. He sat down next to his nephew and research assistant, Steven Eddinghill. Mendez, Masten and Eddinghill were the only three people in the featureless room. Their blue scrubs contrasted starkly with the white walls and stainless-steel fixtures. Masten noticed that Mendez was leaning forward and rubbing his temples. He looked sick.

"This project will never see the light of day." Mendez finally said. "We've gone too far."

"David, I have to disagree," Masten objected, removing his rubber gloves and tossing them into a nearby trashcan. "This work is revolutionary. Do you realize what we have done?"

"No!" Mendez said sharply. "We've done nothing. We've done nothing but perhaps show that Mary Shelley was way ahead of her time."

"David," Masten said, summoning his best advocacy, "we've proven your theory that the human brain is a receiver at its core, but also a transmitter. Aren't you curious as to who or what is sending and receiving the transmissions on the other end?"

"Not in the least, Jim," Mendez said without hesitation. "You know as well as I do that all of this is most likely nothing. It's just static electricity being thrown off when we add a current to a decaying device. It was a hypothesis of mine. Nothing more. But this … *thing* …tonight ends it. I can't even count the ethical boundaries we've just blown through. I'm not in that business. This is over."

Eddinghill was listening, shifting his gaze between the two men as each spoke.

"I understand, David," Masten said, "but hear me out." He backed up and leaned against the wall, putting some space between himself and Mendez. The gesture was calculated spontaneity, like a salesman trying to draw in a tough client.

"The outbound currents are all the same, but the inbound currents are all different. If you think about it, that tells me that we are all experiencing this world on our own frequency. Our own individual input. Our souls if you will. But we all report our experiences in this world to the same place on the same channel. What we've done is show that every moment of every life that has ever existed on this planet is being recorded or communicated to something or someone somewhere." Masten paused. "Who's recording that, David? And why?"

Mendez sat, staring at the floor. Masten couldn't tell if he was receiving the argument or not. The silence hung for a few long moments, until Masten couldn't take it anymore.

"David!" he shouted. "Connect the dots! We've just proven the existence of God! This will change the world! This will change life and human behavior forever!"

Mendez's head shot up; his face was puckered. The look was an unmistakable questioning of Masten's sanity. Mendez glanced away for a moment then looked back.

"Jim!" he said, his voice raised and firm. "It's static. Nothing more. You're looking at a woefully incomplete data set and drawing illogical conclusions based upon what you want the data to reveal. That's it! You're seeing what you want to see. You're not seeing what is being shown to you, which is practically nothing!"

"Quite the opposite, David," Masten objected. "I think *you* are ignoring the obvious conclusions because you don't want to face the possibilities they bring to light. You're seeing only what *you* want to see!"

Mendez sounded dejected. "Jim, this project is over. It's my project, and I'm calling it off. I can't say it any more plainly than that."

Masten paused for a moment. He was stunned by the seeming finality, but still excited about the possibilities the research revealed.

"Let's do this, David," he said, working his best negotiation skills. "Let's sleep on it." He bumped himself off the wall and began pacing. "Hell, let's take a week or two. There's no rush. Just let it sink in. I'm due for a vacation. Labor Day is coming up. I'll take my family on a trip. I've been promising them that for two years now. When I get back, let's talk again. How's that sound?"

"I'm happy to talk to you in a week or two, Jim," Mendez said. "But I can tell you …"

Mendez tapered off and returned his gaze to Masten for a moment. The look in Masten's eyes was one Mendez hadn't seen in years, not since Masten was an early post-doc intern. The look was all dreams and no sense.

"Take that time with your family, Jim," Mendez said, not finishing his thought. "Enjoy them. You'll never get this time back. I'll keep the data, and we can talk when you return. Look, I have a house in Paso Robles. It's in the wine country. It's not much, but it's yours if you want it. I'll get you a key. You could use it as a base of operations. Go there. Go somewhere else. Go to both places. Just take them somewhere, Jim."

"Sounds like a plan," Masten nodded. "I will. And thank you!"

As Masten walked out of the room, he turned and said, "Think about it, David." He removed his blue cap and pointed at Mendez. "I'm not asking for anything other than an open mind."

Waving him away, Mendez said, "I have an open mind, Jim." He smirked and pointed back at Masten. "What you need is an open checkbook. Don't skimp on that vacation. They're the only family you've got." Mendez laughed at his own joke. "Now go have fun!" He turned his attention to his nephew.

"Steven," Mendez commanded, "let's get this mess cleaned up and get that body back in the locker."

FOUR

DEVON LEFT MASTEN'S OFFICE AND CALLED HER OLD FRIEND Ashley Bandini. The two had been friends since the first day of medical school, eventually completing their psychiatry residences together. Devon needed to talk.

"Ashley!" Devon shouted into her cell phone. "Can you work me in?"

"Dev," Ashley responded. "It's barely nine o'clock. How bad can it be?"

"I'll tell you when I get there," Devon answered and hung up.

❖ ❖ ❖

Ten minutes later, Devon was sitting on a sofa in her friend's office. She filled Ashley in on the earlier meeting with Masten.

"I know he's trying to look out for me," Devon said. "But sometimes he can be such a dick! He has zero people skills!"

"Well," Ashley replied. "He's been through something unimaginable. Just be thankful you have someone looking out for you."

"I know," Devon admitted.

17

There was a long pause.

"Is that all that's on your mind?" Ashley asked.

"No," Devon said. Another pause. "I've been thinking a lot about my dad lately. I mean, I think about him all the time, but this week for some reason, I can't stop seeing that day. It's stuck in a loop in my head. I see it over and over and over."

"That's perfectly understandable," Ashley said. "You've been through something unimaginable too. You don't just get past that."

"Well, I'm certainly not getting past it," Devon said. "It's been four years and it may as well have been yesterday." Devon paused. "I keep seeing him fall—the way his feet moved, his hands and arms reaching for something, but nothing was there. Then, he just disappeared over the cliff—and that was that."

Devon stopped speaking for a moment and wiped a tear from her eye. Ashley let the silence do its work.

"And more than all of that," Devon continued. "I keep seeing the monster that pushed him. Only—I didn't really see him push anyone. I just saw him walking away—from a distance. I couldn't even describe him to the police. Fat lotta help I was."

"There's nothing more you could've done," Ashley said. "You were too far away."

"I know," Devon said. "But knowing doesn't seem to help."

"Have you ever thought about hypnosis?" Ashley asked.

Devon looked surprised. "No. Why?"

"Well," Ashley said, "Maybe with hypnosis, you could remember more than you think. Maybe you could recall something about what he looked like or something else you saw."

"I guess," Devon mumbled.

"What's the harm?" Ashley responded. "You remember or you don't."

"I know," Devon said, "but I've never been a big hypnosis person."

"You've never practiced psychiatry!" Ashley replied. "You're a researcher. How would you know?"

Devon bristled at the statement, even though it was true.

"How long would it take?"

"About an hour. It depends on you."

"When would we do it?"

"I have an opening later today," Ashley said. "We can do it right here."

"Let me think about it," Devon said. "I'll call you in a few hours."

Devon rose from the couch and gave her friend a hug. As she was about to walk through the door, Ashley called out, "Hey Dev! I forgot to ask. How was your date?"

Devon rolled her eyes. "Same as always. Same food. Same stories. Different guy. I swear to God I'm going to die alone."

As Devon closed the door, she heard Ashley shout out, "Hang in there, babe!"

❖ ❖ ❖

Devon returned to her office and called the woman in Monterey. Her name was Peg Schroeder. Peg didn't answer, so Devon left a message. She didn't have much else to do when she hung up, so Devon stared at the ceiling and thought about the possibility of hypnosis. *If I was too far away, I was too far away. How would hypnosis help with that? It was just a guy. He wasn't big, he wasn't muscular. He was just there, walking away. Why would anyone want to kill my dad? He was a scientist. A researcher. But it's not like he was working on some secret government project. He was a neurologist. He studied brains and neural pathways. Is that worth killing for?*

Devon continued in the loop for the next half-hour. She decided hypnosis might be worth a shot. She called Ashley and agreed to meet her at four-thirty.

Five

A SMALL GROUP OF PEOPLE SAT IN METAL CHAIRS ARRANGED in a circle on a lush green lawn, nestled among redwood trees and picturesque flowers. The scents of the flowers and pines, and the sound and sight of the ocean just beyond the nearby bluffs, created a soothing atmosphere.

A chapel made of glass, wood, and stone provided a beautiful backdrop for the gathering. It was a small but stunning chapel. The inside was a long, narrow rectangle, with polished wooden pews abutting short stone walls. The stone walls created a foundation for glass walls and a glass ceiling accented by dark redwood beams so that a person sitting in the chapel had a near unobstructed view of the forested exterior, the landscaped grounds, and the Pacific Ocean. The chapel's design and location made it one of a kind and was the reason why it was a premier wedding venue booked months in advance.

The group seated just outside of the chapel, however, was not there for a wedding. They were gathered for their weekly morning prayer service. As they conducted their quiet service, a man and a woman inside worked polishing the pews in the main nave. Once that task was complete, the two would set about mopping the floor. It was hard work, but the couple found it enjoyable. Plus, the church leadership was generous, and the work allowed them to feed their family regularly and rent a small apartment in nearby San Pedro, where their three young children could attend school without the constant threat of violence. These were not luxuries they had in the Republic of Honduras.

Another man arrived, entered the chapel and made his way to a small office. There, he switched on his computer, then made a cup of coffee in the nearby kitchen. He waved and offered a friendly hello to the couple working in the church. They returned the greeting.

To this dozen or so people, it was just the beginning of another day. None of them had any idea that the night before, Ricardo Colusa had been hard at work on these very same grounds.

❖ ❖ ❖

Colusa now sat on a white rock looking out at the Pacific Ocean. The sun was up, and the tide was halfway between low and high. It would peak in a few hours. There was a tiny inlet to his left, where the seawater washed in and out of a small cave behind him. The sound was rhythmic and calming, as the water moved in and out of the cave. A chilly breeze was blowing in from the ocean and Colusa could smell the odor of fish and sea algae. A formation of pelicans flew by from just beyond the bluff to his right. In the distance, he could see a giant cargo ship, most likely making its way back to China or Hong Kong.

Colusa hiked to this spot using a small trail leading down from the cliffs above. He liked both the seclusion and the view, but mostly he liked the vantage point it provided. He could see everything he needed to see, and he could be out and gone in a matter of minutes.

Above and behind Colusa at the top of the bluffs was the town of Rancho Palos Verdes, a small but wealthy suburb of Los Angeles. A few miles around the shoreline to his left were the ports of Long Beach and Los Angeles. Colusa had arrived there two days earlier, checking into a cliff top resort. He needed some time to put things in place.

Colusa was, by any standard, unremarkable. He was average height and thin, but not skinny. He was not muscular. Approaching middle age had cost him quite a bit of his hairline up front. It also cost him some eyesight, which resulted in the need for glasses. Colusa chose plain black frames. Nondescript, just as he liked things.

He didn't speak to anyone, and no one spoke to him. Colusa was the sort of person who could come and go unnoticed from almost any setting. He was an invisible man.

Most people would find Colusa's life depressing. Most days, he did too. But he learned long ago to turn his mundane presence into an advantage. Whether it was a gift or a curse, his ability to pass unnoticed and unremembered from place to place made him excellent at his job.

Colusa had killed many people, and he'd made a great deal of money doing so. He was careful. In and out. No one anywhere knew his name. No cop or investigator had ever gotten close to him, and like the rest of the world, they didn't even know he existed. Most times, the authorities didn't even know there was a person behind the killing. The deaths were chalked up to causes other than murder or went unsolved. This morning would be no different.

No one found Colusa; he found them. His jobs came from long hours of monitoring certain internet chat rooms. They were the sites that formed the Web's deepest, darkest underbelly. The attendees' IP addresses were scrambled and bounced all over the world until they were untraceable. No one used names or any other kind of identifying information. They were anonymous, and Colusa felt completely at home there.

Many of the discussions in the rooms focused on drugs, illegal weapons, child pornography, and sex trafficking—the things one might expect to be buried deep in the dark web—but none of that was of interest to Colusa. He waited and watched for posts by people looking to have other people killed. He didn't care about the reason. When he saw such posts, he would reach out and test the legitimacy of the inquiry. He also tested the means. Serious inquiries only.

If the job was real and big enough, Colusa required a twenty-five-thousand-dollar deposit into one of his numbered, offshore accounts. If the job didn't pan out, Colusa kept the money. If it did, the amount would be applied against the full cost of services.

Once the earnest money was deposited, the requester would send the details to Colusa through a highly encrypted and highly secure server. If he decided to take the job, the remainder of the money was due up front. Once paid, the deed would simply be done. There was no further communication.

Colusa's current project deviated from his normal practice in that it was more complex and involved progress payments. His role was the same, but there were phases to this job—four phases, to be precise. An old man had been the first. He finished that four years ago. He was now working on the second. The third would come in five days, and the last the day after that. He didn't know who hired him, but he respected the patience and diligence.

Colusa wasn't bothered by the timeline, the phases, or the plan. In the end, he would be paid more than five times his usual rate. And, he'd already been paid well. What did bother him was the waiting around and the requirement of some continued client communication. That, however, was prearranged and occurred only via text through disposable phones and burner lines. Colusa was presently awaiting such a text. If it came, he would move forward. If it didn't, he would quietly leave town. Either way, he kept the money he'd been paid. That was the deal.

The text came. Colusa looked at his watch. It was nine-thirty a.m.—the appointed time. He pulled out his phone and dialed a number. Within seconds he heard the sounds. There were two deep, rolling booms, followed by a yellow plume of fire that quickly turned to billowing black smoke. He could see it all in the distance from where he sat. The church was gone.

Colusa imagined that anyone inside the building was

instantly obliterated and knew they were the lucky ones. Anyone outside would likely be badly burned, though it would be severe shrapnel wounds from the flying glass and wood shards that would cause their deaths. Colusa knew the scene was horrific. He could feel it. He didn't know who was in or near the chapel, and he didn't care. He simply offered himself a moment of congratulations for another job well done.

Colusa sat and watched the smoke plume rise then settle into the cool morning sea air. He could see that most of the trees on the chapel grounds were on fire. In less than a minute, he heard the sirens begin to approach. Soon, there would be fire trucks, ambulances, and police cars all converging on this one space. The roads would no doubt be blocked as well. He stood and walked back up the trail to his car.

He passed two fire trucks on the way back to the hotel. He packed the few things he had brought with him and drove to the airport. His plane left in three hours. He'd catch up on some reading while he waited.

Six

"OKAY, DEVON, JUST RELAX." ASHLEY'S VOICE WAS CALM and soothing. She spoke in a slow, almost monotone voice. "Remember—you are in complete control. You can stop anytime you choose, okay?"

Devon closed her eyes and nodded. She was reclined on Ashley's sofa with her fingers interlocked, hands resting on her chest. She tried having her hands by her side, but there was too much tension. It wasn't working. This position was much better.

"I want you to focus on the rain," Ashley continued. "Can you do that?" Ashley had a small set of speakers that piped in the quiet sound of rain.

The room had three windows to the outside. The blinds were lowered and mostly closed on each. The lights were dimmed, but not off. The room was cool and quiet, except for Ashley's voice and the sound of rain.

"The rain is relaxing," Ashley said. "Just listen to the rain."

Devon took a deep breath then exhaled. The grip of her interlocked fingers loosened as her body sunk deeper into the sofa.

"Imagine an open window near you," Ashley added. "There is a white curtain covering the window. It moves in and out with the gentle breeze blowing the rain. Just watch the curtain and listen to the rain."

Devon's fingers loosened more as Ashley allowed a few moments to pass. "Clear your mind of everything but the rain." Ashley could see Devon's body slide deeper and deeper into a state of relaxation.

Ashley allowed a few more minutes to pass. She could see that Devon was now completely relaxed. She decided it was time to break the silence.

"All right, Devon," Ashley said. "I want you to keep thinking about the rain, but I also want you to go back to that day. The rain will keep you calm. Trust the rain. Can you do that?"

Devon gave a slight, almost imperceptible nod, but Ashley saw it.

"Take me to that day and tell me what you see."

Devon shifted a bit on the bed. "I'm coming out of my father's house. I stayed there the night before because we had dinner, and it was too late and too far to drive home. He insisted.

My father lives near the ocean and near cliffs above the ocean. He walks early every morning on a trail along those cliffs. I want to bring him a cup of coffee. I have a cup for me in one hand and a cup for him in the other.

I walk out the door and see him on the trail in the distance. I'm still standing on the porch. I see my father falling."

"Do you see a man near him?" Ashley asked.

"Yes," Devon answered. "I can see him. He's walking away. He's moving away from me. He crosses a street and turns a little to the side, but he's far away now."

"Can you describe the man?" Ashley asked.

"Not really. He doesn't look up. He just disappears beside a house."

"Tell me what you can," Ashley said.

"He looks younger than my father, but not taller. He's thinner, but not thin. He's wearing light colored pants – maybe

26

khaki. It's hard to tell. His shirt is blue, with long sleeves. I think he has dark hair, but I think I see some scalp on the top of his head."

"What happens next, Devon" Ashley asked.

"I drop the coffee cups on the porch and run to where my father fell."

"What do you see?" Ashley asked.

"No!" Devon responded, shaking her head and re-clasping her hands.

"It's okay, Devon," Ashley responded. "Just relax and focus on the rain." After a few moments, Ashley asked, "Can you tell me what you see now?"

"No. No more," Devon responded.

"Let's focus on the man again," Ashley pushed. "Do you remember anything else about him?"

"No. No more," Devon repeated.

"Okay," Ashley said. "Let's come back now."

"Black glasses!" Devon blurted. "He was wearing black glasses."

"Good," Ashley said. "I want you to focus on the rain again. Just the rain. Listen to the rain. Forget everything else. Just listen to the rain.

Devon began to calm down. Her body relaxed and the shaking stopped, but tears still fell down her face.

"Watch the curtain, Devon," the doctor said. "Watch it blow in and out. In and out. Listen to the rain. The rain is soothing, calming."

Devon took a deep breath and exhaled.

A few moments later, Ashley said, "I want you to focus on the light in this room. Don't open your eyes. Just let the light pass through your eyelids and see that there is light in this room. Focus on the light."

Using a small remote control, Ashley raised the light level from its dim setting. Devon made several facial movements and turned her head toward a window in the office.

"Focus on the light," Ashley said. "Take some time, and just focus on the light."

"All right, Devon," Ashley said, a few moments later. "It's time to come all the way back. I'm going to count to three, and when you hear me say three, you will be fully awake, okay." There was a brief pause. "One, two, three."

Devon blinked hard a few times and looked around. She sat up from the bed and wiped the tears from her eyes. She looked nauseated. Stunned.

Ashley had to call Devon's name several times before she responded with a slow and eventual nod. Devon covered her eyes with her hands and sobbed for a few moments before she spoke.

"Jesus, Ashley!" Devon shouted as she threw her hands down. "What the hell was that?"

"You made more progress than you think," Ashley said. "Do you remember anything?"

"No." Devon wiped the continuing tears from her eyes.

"Well, apparently your guy was wearing khaki pants a blue shirt and had black glasses," Ashley said. "And he wasn't a big guy."

"What?" Devon asked. "Seriously? I said that?"

"You did."

"Jesus!" Devon whispered. Her eyes darted around the room. She looked at her watch, as if she needed to be somewhere, but she didn't have any place to be. "Look, I have to run, Ashley. I'll call you tomorrow. Thank you for the help. Really." She jumped off the sofa and ran to the door.

"You know you're never going to find him, right?" Ashley called out.

Devon stopped and turned. "Find who?"

Ashley smirked. "Your father. You and I both know that's why you do what you do. This stuff we just did may help you find his killer. I hope to God it does. But your father's gone, sweetie. I think it's healthier if you learn to accept that."

Devon was silent. A little stunned.

"I'm sorry, Devon." Ashley said. "I didn't mean to upset you."

"No. No. It's fine. I guess I just never heard it out loud

before. It is a little disturbing, isn't it."

"A little?"

They both laughed, trying to break the tension.

"Well, I have to go."

Ashley didn't want to leave it like that. "I love you, girl!"

❖ ❖ ❖

Devon couldn't get away fast enough. She sped down the hallway and tapped her foot for the one-floor elevator ride down. When the doors opened on the first floor, she darted out. Devon ran across the small parking lot, got into her car, and began to cry again. Sitting alone in her car allowed her time to try and shake it off. She checked her phone. There were too many emails to look at, but there was also a voicemail. It was from Peg Schroeder in Monterey.

SEVEN

DEVON WALKED UP TWO FLIGHTS OF CONCRETE STAIRS UNTIL she reached the second floor of her run-down apartment complex. She didn't grab the gray metal pole to her right. *God only knows what grows there.* When she reached the landing, she turned right and walked to her door, which she knew by the cheap, gold, craft-store numbers tacked just above the peephole: two-one-seven.

Pulling the key from her pocket, Devon opened the door. The reality awaiting inside was dismal—unclean carpet, a dingy couch, and a kitchen just one step ahead of a hot pad and a tiny sink. In the other room was a bed with covers that had no doubt been recycled from the red-light district a few blocks away. But it all came with inexpensive rent.

Devon pretended not to notice. The apartment's positives were a nice workstation, albeit on a folding card table, and a strong wireless signal. She sat down at the small, simple desk and powered up her laptop. She threw her phone on the table and debated whether to return Peg's call tonight or tomorrow. She decided on tomorrow.

She scrolled through her emails and some news. There was report that had broken earlier that day about a church exploding in Rancho Palos Verdes, which was about twenty miles south of her. She knew the place well. Her father lived—and died there. Devon read the article and various others describing the damage, the investigation and the victims. It sounded horrible.

After an hour, Devon gave up and leaned back into the uncomfortable wooden chair. The chair didn't lean, so she essentially just slid her legs out in front of her and scooted forward on the seat. She pushed her long dark hair back over her forehead repeatedly with both hands. A few seconds later, she transitioned into measuring the length of her hair between her fingers. She could use a trip to the salon.

Standing up, Devon placed her hands against the top of her hips, then leaned back and twisted until she heard and felt a satisfying crack. She felt ready again—though for what, she didn't know. There was absolutely nothing interesting, or fun, or happy, in her dump of an apartment.

The earlier session with Ashley left her in a funk. So did the meeting with Masten. Devon stood and paced the floor for a bit. She needed a drink but had nothing on hand. Grabbing a jacket, she went back downstairs. There was a seedy looking joint down the street she'd noticed several times in the two months she'd lived in the apartment. It felt like a perfect fit tonight.

The stench of beer and cigarettes that hit her when she pushed the door open only served to invigorate Devon. The loud music, however, was a bit of a culture shock. It was bad country. She guessed the tunes were all at least twenty years old but didn't know for sure. Devon never really listened to country music, though she did watch the PBS documentary on it. Hillbilly music. It was originally made by and for sad, desperate people. *Maybe I should listen more.*

An empty barstool on the far left had her name on it. Devon made her way there and perched on the high seat. The bartender appeared and took her order. "Vodka martini, straight up with two olives." The drink appeared a few minutes later.

A small kerfuffle to the right caught her attention. A tallish, blondish guy about Devon's age, was adjusting a backpack and a briefcase. When the bags were situated to his satisfaction, he took the open barstool next to Devon and climbed aboard. He grabbed the bottom of the seat and bounced it forward a couple of times until he and the stool were right against the bar.

The man sat on the stool, looking around until the bartender yelled out for his order. The pressure was on. Devon noticed that he looked panicked, like he wanted a drink but had no idea what to ask for.

"I'll have a beer, please," he finally answered.

The bartender rolled his eyes.

"We got like fifteen of them, brother," he said. "What do you want?"

The man read the label on the tap closest to him and ordered that. Devon could see that he had no idea what it was. A few minutes later, a pint glass with a light amber beer was placed on the sticky, wooden bar in front of the man.

"You wanna start a tab?"

The man reached into his back pocket, pulled out his wallet, and handed a credit card to the bartender, who walked over to a small touch screen, tapped in a few entries, and placed the card in a nearby glass.

Devon watched as the man took a sip of his beer. He put the glass back on the bar and twisted it back and forth from the rim. After a few moments, the man looked at Devon and said, "You know? How is it that a guy who pours drinks for a living can make a highly educated man feel like such an asshole? It's truly an odd superpower."

Devon smiled and looked back up. They couldn't hear the television hanging above the bar in front of them, but closed captioning ran across the bottom of the screen as several ex-athletes in beautiful suits ran through the week's sports highlights.

Devon looked over at the man. "So," she paused, "you're highly educated?"

The man chuckled a little. "Well," he said, "probably more than that guy." He pointed a thumb at the bartender. I'm Todd Hawthorne." He held out a hand for Devon to shake.

"Devon Mendez." She responded without taking Hawthorne's hand.

Hawthorne looked at Devon's half empty glass. "Tough day?"

"Yep. Martini tough," she said. "I'll have another," she said pointing to the bartender. Then she turned back to the big screen above the bar.

The bartender nodded and walked away. Hawthorne turned back to the television too but couldn't help sneaking subtle glances at Devon from time to time.

She was striking, with long, dark brown hair and a dark olive complexion. Her face wasn't too thin, and her features were full, healthy, and very well put together. Nothing about her seemed fragile, and yet, Hawthorne thought he detected a sense of brokenness in her.

As she waited, Devon tapped her fingers against the bar top. It sounded a little like a horse running. She looked down from the screen when her drink arrived and thanked the bartender, who gave her a long smile before moving to an older man down the bar.

Devon started tapping her fingers again as she sipped her drink. Hawthorne didn't notice because he was thumping the side of his glass in between twists. He started thumping more.

A beat developed, and Hawthorne's glass thumping synchronized with Devon's finger tapping, although neither noticed. An older man inserted himself between the two of them, waiting on the bartender. After a couple of minutes, he commented, "You two make quite the rhythm section."

They both immediately stopped. Hawthorne's eyes widened in embarrassment, but Devon began laughing out loud. Her laugh was bigger than she was.

"I guess we do, don't we?" she said, acknowledging Hawthorne.

The bartender motioned for the man at the bar to move

toward him, and Hawthorne and Devon were alone once more.

"Sorry," she said, still chuckling. "I guess my tension is contagious."

"Maybe," Hawthorne said, offering a wry look, "but you do drive a beat."

The comment made them both laugh.

"So, Todd," she said, taking a sip of her martini, "why are you drinking alone?"

Hawthorne's reaction was muted, but also very clear.

"Don't be offended," she said, swatting a hand in the air. "I drink alone a lot."

Devon's abrupt, honest, straight-on engagement made Hawthorne relax and drew something similar out of him.

"If you lived in the shithole I live in, you'd drink alone even more," he said.

"You haven't seen my shithole," Devon replied. It sounded wrong and both looked away in awkward silence.

Hawthorne broke the ice and asked, "So, what makes this a martini tough day?"

"You were listening, huh?"

"Well, I was sitting right here," Hawthorne responded. "So, what's up, if you don't mind my asking?"

Devon took a last swig and motioned to the bartender for another.

"Are you really that bored?" she asked, raising an eyebrow.

"I'm sitting here alone, aren't I?"

Devon conceded the point with a nod but demurred anyway. "I'm not gonna tell my sob story to some random person sitting in a bar. And, honestly, it's not that interesting."

"Try me," Hawthorne said.

"No," Devon responded. "Let's keep it light. Standard bar room banter." Devon took another sip. "So, tell me Todd, what do you do for work?"

"I'm a reporter," Hawthorne answered. A journalist, actually. I write for the *L.A. Tribune*."

"Are you doing okay, sir?" the bartender interrupted.

Hawthorne looked at his half-empty beer glass and decided to join the lady. He'd earned it too.

"You know," he said, "this is not going down. I think I'll have one of those." He pointed at Devon's martini glass.

"So, what do you write?" Devon asked, as the bartender walked off.

"Investigative pieces," Hawthorne explained. "It's usually city corruption, political scandals, local corporate graft—that kind of thing."

"So, are you on a story now?" Devon asked.

"I was," Hawthorne said. "Or I thought I was. I got pulled off this afternoon." The bartender sat Hawthorne's martini in front of him. Devon spoke as Hawthorne took a big swig.

"Pulled off?"

"Yep," Hawthorne said, drawing the word out and popping the *p*. "Apparently, this one was better suited for Margot Keller. I really hate that bitch. She's better at sleeping than writing if you know what I mean."

"Yeah, I get it," Devon said.

Hawthorne winked, pointed, and made a little gun clicking sound with his tongue. Devon laughed a little.

"You don't drink much, do you?"

"Hey, I can be as rowdy as the next guy," Hawthorne said, his words starting to slur.

"Uh huh," Devon responded. "So, what was the story you were pulled from?"

"Oh, same shit," Hawthorne said. "Some administrator skimming off the county retirement fund. Nothing mind-bending, but my pay is based partially on my print, so it sucks when I lose a story, and I haven't ever had a *really* good story."

"That does suck," Devon said. "Especially when the folks paying you are the ones taking you off of the story."

"Exactly," Hawthorne exclaimed, raising his hands into the air. "You're a good listener."

"Well …," Devon said, cocking her head sideways.

"So, tell me about you, Devon Mendez," Hawthorne said, taking another drink and pointing at the bartender for the next.

35

"What's your story?"

Devon drew in a deep breath and let it out slowly. "I am a psychiatrist, a medical doctor."

Hawthorne yelled, "I knew it!"

His reaction was so animated that he slipped off the stool and banged his elbow on the bar. "Shit!" he yelled. "Right on the funny bone! And totally not funny." He moaned and grabbed his elbow.

"Let me have a look," Devon said.

She examined Hawthorne's elbow and moved it up and down.

"Does that hurt?" she asked.

"No," Hawthorne responded. "Just the spot where I hit it."

"It'll just be a bruise tomorrow," Devon concluded. "Nothing broken."

He climbed back onto the stool and grabbed his new drink. "Thanks, Doc," he said, taking a sip.

"You may want to take it easy with that stuff," Devon cautioned.

Hawthorne nodded and looked away, a little embarrassed. After a pause, a light went on in Hawthorne's head.

"Wait a second!" he almost shouted. "That's why you're such a good listener! You're a friggin' shrink!" He pointed and shoved against the bar, almost knocking himself off the stool again.

"Well, I guess technically, but not really," Devon corrected. "I'm more of a researcher. Truth be told, I'm actually an investigator myself."

Hawthorne took another drink. *This stuff is strong.*

"Really?" Hawthorne sounded skeptical. "What do you investigate, Dr. Mendez?" There was an emphasis on the word *doctor*.

"Oh, lord," she said. "You wouldn't believe me if I told you."

"Try me," Hawthorne responded. "I just sang you my sad song. You can at least tell me what you do."

Devon took another drink and a deep breath. After a pause,

she decided to go for it.

"I investigate past life experiences."

Hawthorne looked at her with raised eyebrows, but an otherwise blank expression. Then he began to laugh. Hawthorne finished his drink and motioned for another.

"I'm sorry, I'm sorry," he said as he waved a hand. "A few of these and I'm … well, I'm this. Anyway, you do *what*?"

Devon adjusted herself and ordered a third martini.

"Some young kids, around the age of three to six, claim that they remember being someone else in another life," she explained. "Many of them give details that are not only accurate, but also impossible for the kids to know. They can sometimes identify specific people and places and causes of death that are verifiable. Some even have a strange sort of clairvoyance that allows them to see things that happened to the people around them in their prior lives, even if it didn't involve them. So, it's not just memories. It's almost like they're tapped into an all-seeing eye. It's quite fascinating, and controversial, but well … that's what I research."

Devon paused, waiting for the next burst of laughter. Hawthorne didn't laugh though. Instead, he looked contemplative. The martinis had slowed the information flow, but he was processing, nonetheless.

"So," he asked, "where do you find these kids? Where are they?"

"All over, really," Devon answered. "Malaysia, India, Vietnam, Thailand. There seem to be fewer in the Western countries, honestly, but that may simply be a function of cultural cover-up. Maybe the religious views in the West suppress the acceptance of such possibilities. That's actually one of the things that I'm interested in right now."

Hawthorne nodded along.

"I have one current case that's local," Devon continued. "A five-year-old girl up in Monterey."

"California?" Hawthorne asked, trying to grab the bar for support.

"Yes," Devon replied. "I'm going up for an interview

hopefully this week. It's sad for the family. The dad died not too long ago. Leaving a mom and two kids."

Hawthorne took another drink.

"Anyway, I want to talk to this girl soon. She claims to have died in a car wreck. Her mom at the time, in her previous life, died with her. The girl still has nightmares about falling. She said she remembers hitting the ground and dying."

Devon pointed at Hawthorne. "That one is weird, I have to tell you. Most people wake up from falling dreams before they hit the ground."

"Very weird, Dr. Mendez," Hawthorne agreed as he took another sip. "Very weird. And I may need a playbill to keep up."

Hawthorne burped and clapped an embarrassed hand over his mouth. His eyes shot toward Devon, who didn't notice any of it. She was still pondering the replay of the voicemail in her head.

"So, what is this young lady's name?" Hawthorne asked, swaying a little.

Devon winked and leaned in. "It's classified."

Hawthorne gave a nod of gravitas that only a drunk person could offer.

"No, really," she said, laughing at her own bad joke. "I can't reveal the names of my clients. It would be unethical. Not to mention that the girl's mom would kick the shit out of me if word ever got out."

They both laughed.

"But," Devon added, pointing at Hawthorne, "I can tell you that she says she used to be named Claire."

"Claire," Hawthorne repeated with a little flair. "I like it. It's traditional. It conjures images of starched white cotton dresses buttoned all the way to the Adam's apple." He paused, then nodding and looking up, said, "Claire. Yep, that's her."

"Stop," Devon said, swatting at Hawthorne. "It's just a name."

"Hey, a person's name says a lot," Hawthorne said, holding up both hands. "Take mine for instance—Todd." He said it again for emphasis, rolling his eyes. "Todd. It's utterly meaningless. On its best day, it's only a half a step above what two cave-men would grunt to one another around a fire. Seriously! Who names their child Todd?"

Devon giggled at the drama. "Well, I like it. And it seems to fit you."

"Oh, Jesus," Hawthorne said. "Take that back."

"No really," Devon responded. "Todd. It's simple. Maybe a bit understated, but strong."

Hawthorne raised his eyebrows and paused. "Devon," he said pointing. "Now that's a name. It conjures up mystery. Intelligence. It's a definite leading lady name."

"Shut up," Devon said, swatting again. "I'm glad you like my name, but nothing's happening here, bucko."

Hawthorne held up two hands again. "Well, it's time for me to go, my friend. I've enjoyed meeting you, but I think your intentions are turning questionable."

"I'm sorry?" Devon asked.

"Or maybe mine are," Hawthorne winked and pointed at her. "Either way, it's time for me to stagger home."

"Well, it's been nice meeting you *Todd*," Devon said with a little extra emphasis.

"See you soon, *Dr.* Mendez."

Hawthorne cut an unbalanced path towards the exit.

Devon stared at her empty martini glass for a moment before the bartender asked if she wanted another. She waved a hand to indicate she was good, closed her tab and walked back to her dismal room. It somehow felt less dismal, though. She had no idea who Todd Hawthorne was, but he seemed sweet.

EIGHT

DEVON WOKE UP DEHYDRATED AND SUFFERING FROM A monster headache. When she sat up, she grabbed the bed's head rail as the room began to spin. She gave it a moment before trying to stand, then carefully made her way to the bathroom and braced herself with both hands resting on the cheap countertop.

Devon stared straight ahead into the mirror. She hardly recognized the girl looking back. The whites of her eyes were now red. Large bags had collected underneath. Her face was puffy, and her tongue was dry. Her long hair was always tossed in the morning, but now it looked and felt brittle and gross. She grabbed a handful of her hair and pulled it around to her nose. It reeked of stale cigarette smoke from the dingy bar. Devon recoiled at the smell and let go.

She turned on the cold-water knob and filled her hands, drinking a couple of sips before dousing her face. The shock of the cold water woke her up some, but the queasy feeling persisted. She had neither the strength nor the stability to shower yet, so she walked to the kitchen and made herself a cup of coffee, then sat down on the couch and stared at a spot where the floor met the wall.

Slowly, like individual light switches being flicked on, memories from last night's outing came back to her. She remembered talking to a guy. *What was his name?* She recalled his longish hair and kind eyes. He seemed engaging but not cheesy. She didn't think he'd hit on her.

Devon made her way back to the bathroom where adrenaline and caffeine sustained her through a shower. While washing the stale smoke out of her hair, she remembered she needed to call Peg Schroeder back. Her daughter's story was fascinating.

She rinsed and thought. Lathered again and thought, then rinsed again. *How could a five-year-old, or anyone for that matter, remember the transition from life to death as it happened in another life. That was a new one.* She turned away from the showerhead and let the water do its work on the rest of her.

She dressed, then caught a glimpse of herself in the full-length mirror. A bath towel on her head was twisted into a giant turban. She'd forgotten to dry her hair. Part of her didn't care, but a bigger part knew it would be an unsalvageable mess if she didn't do it now.

As Devon blew and brushed her hair, it dawned on her that Peg's call was a welcome break from the anxiety she felt about her father's death. It also dawned on her that she had to teach a class at nine. She'd forgotten about that. She looked at the clock by her bed. It was seven forty-five. She picked up the pace. She'd call Peg on the way to school.

❖ ❖ ❖

When Devon arrived in the classroom, most of her students were already there. She was teaching part of a six-week block to first-year medical students that included psychopathology and psychopharmacology. They met Tuesdays and Thursdays. As she stood, trying to steady herself against the rectangular black tabletop, she realized that she was probably better suited at that moment to teach a class on the negative effects of psychoactive substances. Alcohol, to be specific.

Devon looked at her phone, waiting on the last few

stragglers. She began speaking precisely at nine. At precisely nine-twelve, Devon had to excuse herself. She returned about five minutes later looking paler and feeling much emptier, but no better.

Endurance was the only thing that carried her to the end of the class. Thankfully, no one had any questions, at least any they were willing to ask.

When the last student left, Devon turned out the light in the classroom and headed to her office. She did her best not to stagger, but none too successfully. She hoped no one saw her.

When she reached her office, she went straight to the long, white, plastic stick hanging from the edge of the window shade and twisted it a few times. The outside light dimmed to a much more civilized level. Devon left the overhead light off and sat in her chair. She put her head down on the desk, forehead resting on forearm.

Devon wanted nothing more than to go home and crawl back into bed, but she had another class in two hours and knew she had to rally soon. Tapping the spacebar on her keyboard a couple of times lit the screen, but the light hurt her eyes and she turned away. Laying her head back down on the desk, Devon gave in to her desperate need for more sleep; but troubled sleep sometimes produced disturbing dreams.

❖ ❖ ❖

The coffee maker was old and slow, but through a long series of gurgling spurts and hisses, it eventually filled the glass carafe. Devon dressed as the ancient machine did its work. As she buttoned her top, she studied a couple of old pictures that sat on a dresser. One was her at fifteen, wearing a blue dress and a small faux diamond necklace. It was taken at her quinceañera. Her mother, God rest her soul, wanted her to wear the matching tiara. Devon refused. It was too much.

The second was taken at a family gathering when she was around eleven. Everyone important to her was still alive and all of them were in the picture. Her mother and father, her abuela and abuelo, aunts and uncles and so many cousins that they almost didn't fit in the photo. She was standing in the back on the right. She kissed two fingers and touched them against her mother's face. Then she left the room.

When Devon returned to the kitchen, the smell was welcoming—an aromatic sign of a brand-new day. She took two large cups from the cabinet and filled both. She walked to the front door and set both cups on a small table. She pulled open a double set of heavy drapes hanging in front of a large window. Bright sunlight filled the room. Devon opened the door and turned, grabbing the two cups.

When she stepped onto the porch, Devon looked up and took a deep breath. The sun felt good on her face. She looked right; toward the trail she knew her father walked. Devon saw him in the distance, but something was off. His hands were in the air and his feet were moving as if he were trying to dance. Devon squinted, trying to make sense of what she was seeing. The movement of a man walking away caught her attention and she looked at the man for a second. She looked back at her father just in time to see him go over the cliff.

Devon gasped and dropped the mugs onto the porch. Each shattered when they hit the concrete. She began running toward the trail. Her heart pounded as she drew closer and closer to the spot. She looked over the side and called her father's name. There was no response. She moved to a new place on the trail and called louder, screaming her father's name now. There was still no response. When she moved again, she caught a glimpse of her father's shoe. She got on her stomach and crawled to the edge so she could look further over the side of the steep cliff. Then she saw him. He father's contorted body was lying in a narrow pit at the bottom of the canyon. Devon shrieked. "Oh my god!" The words came several times.

A few neighbors heard the commotion and came outside. Several tried to help Devon up, but she could only manage to sit. She couldn't control her hysteria, and no one could assist with that.

A team of sheriff's officers arrived soon thereafter, along

with a couple of teams of EMTs and rescuers. As the teams worked to get down to her father, Devon was hustled away in an ambulance. Still hysterical in the ER, Devon felt a small needle enter her arm just below the shoulder. A few moments later, she lost consciousness.

❖ ❖ ❖

Devon raised her head from her desk and tried to re-orient herself. The hypnosis session with Ashley had apparently brought the whole event back in vivid detail. She couldn't help but play it out a couple of more times in her head. *Who was the man she saw walking away and why would he do that?* Then, something clicked in her head.

Devon reached for her phone and scrolled through her contacts. She stopped when she found her cousin, Steven Eddinghill. She pressed the screen and called the number. Eddinghill didn't answer, so she left a hasty message asking him to call her as soon as possible. She put the phone down and thought through her question. Her phone rang a minute later, but it wasn't Eddinghill. It was Peg Schroeder. The two had been playing phone tag. Devon called her right back.

NINE

MASTEN DIDN'T KNOW IT, BUT HIS TO-DO LIST HAD BECOME much longer overnight. Arriving early to the office, usual cup of coffee in hand, Masten sat down at his desk and waited for his computer to boot up. In the meantime, he rifled through a few papers in his inbox. He hadn't been there five minutes when a knock on the door caused him to look up. Dana Phillips, the Dean of the medical school, came in carrying a stack of files she could barely manage.

"It's the same old story, Jim," she said. "Budget cuts. We can't fund all these research projects anymore. The committee needs you to take a look and decide which ones to keep and which ones to scrap. We need to shave at least five million off the budget."

"Five million!" Masten repeated. "Did somebody lose big in Vegas?"

"AI," Dana responded, expressionless. "The university is shifting boatloads of money into artificial intelligence. It leaves the rest of us scrambling, but that's life in the fast lane, right?" She shook her head and shrugged as she left Masten's office.

Masten stared at the daunting stack for a moment, then turned to his computer screen. He went first to his emails. There was nothing pressing. He clicked his internet browser and scanned the news, but it looked about the same as the day before. None of the headlines were very interesting. He scrolled down a bit to waste some time and was struck by a headline near the bottom of the page: "Explosion at Mariner's Chapel, at least 12 Dead." The story described an explosion that had happened the morning before across the bay in in Rancho Palos Verdes. There was no word yet on the cause.

Masten read the article a second time, closed out of his browser and sized up the stack of folders in front of him. This was not going to be an easy job. Careers were at stake. He respected all legitimate research, but he'd been around long enough to know that it all cost money.

He decided he would read each folder through once and come up with some sort of cost versus potential yield metric upon which to judge each project. Five million was a deep cut, and he wanted to make sure that he preserved the university's best options going forward. He would put each folder into one of two stacks: Maybes, and Definitely Nots.

He steeled himself and picked up a file. It was entitled, "Benefits of Low-Level Radon Exposure." Masten almost laughed out loud. Radon was a silent killer. This was an easy no. The file was placed in the reject stack.

The next file was even less plausible than the radon premise. If this was the best that was going on, Masten thought, five million might not be that hard to cut after all. He shook his head as he tossed the file onto the reject stack.

The next file up was entitled "Acrylamide Versus Coffee: Is Juan Valdez a Friend or Foe?" Masten threw it straight onto the reject pile and took a sip from his cup. The toss was frustrated and hard.

The next file was titled "Snap Judgments: Why a Single Data Point Is Never Enough." He scanned the opening pages and quickly recognized the premise, which reminded him of a well-known, at least in academic circles, paper written by psychologists Daniel Kahneman and Amos Tversky years earlier. Their study explored why people, even trained scientists, fell into the trap of concluding that a small amount of information about something was reflective of the whole amount of information on the matter. It was a little like the parable of the three blind people touching different parts of an elephant and arguing to one another about the description of the whole animal.

At least this was in his wheelhouse. Masten placed it in the Maybe file. He wanted to read the materials more carefully and perhaps talk to the researchers to make sure they weren't simply hiking down a previously blazed trail.

As Masten reached for the next file, his eyes caught the word "Revisits" on the small folder tab at the top of the folder. This was Devon's project. She'd sent it to him a few days earlier. Masten sighed, shook his head, and tossed the file onto his desk, but not in any of the other stacks. He wondered how she'd gotten so far out into the weeds—but he knew the answer. Losing everything.

As if on cue, Masten heard a knock on his door. It was Devon. She looked off. Disheveled.

"Are you alright, dear" Masten asked.

"Yes," She answered, trying to maintain some semblance of professional poise. "It's just one of those mornings. Slow start. Anyway, I heard from the woman in Monterey. She can see us tomorrow at one. I wanted to make sure you were available before I responded."

Masten pulled up his calendar and pretended to scroll through his events. There was nothing on it, but Devon had no way of knowing. He didn't let on, but he was excited to get out of the office and away from the never-ending stack of inane research proposals that cluttered his desk.

"I have a call, but I can move it," Masten lied. "Hopefully Her Majesty has something interesting for us."

Devon didn't know what to make of the comment. It was sarcastic, but with a casual delivery.

"I'm certain she will," Devon said. "Pick you up at seven?"

"I'll be here."

TEN

HAWTHORNE WASN'T IN MUCH BETTER SHAPE THAN DEVON when he woke up. He managed to open his eyes but couldn't manage much else. It was odd, if one stared at the center of a rotating ceiling fan, the blades and movement combined to make a big, single circle shape. But if one focused only on one blade, it would just go round and round and the circle shape disappeared. The single blade looked like it moved slower than the whole circle.

Hawthorne lay on his bed, switching back and forth between the two views of the ceiling fan. His phone rang, jerking him from his epiphany. He recognized the number. It was his boss. He remembered why he'd gone on the drunken bender in the first place. It was *that* asshole.

Hawthorne watched the phone as it rang. He didn't have anything to say. Besides, it was too early for any civilized human to be calling another anyway. When the phone stopped ringing, he sat in anticipatory silence. A minute or so later, he heard the telltale, two-tone chime of a newly received voicemail.

In an act that was part rebellion and part delay, Hawthorne

ignored his phone and went to the kitchen to get a cup of coffee. He took his time before returning to the inevitable.

"Todd," the voice said. "It's Ben. Listen, I've got Keller on the county retirement thing, but something else has come up. I need you up in Carmel ASAP. We've just gotten word that the governor may be announcing a run for the presidency during his annual tournament in Pebble Beach. I want you there and on it. Call me back."

Hawthorne went from struggling to sober in less than a heartbeat. As he listened to the message, his eyebrows raised, and he leaned forward to make sure he was hearing correctly. This was an enormous break, or at least it seemed to be. A moment of insecurity made him pause. Why wasn't Keller taking this story? If Ben liked her so much, why wasn't he giving the story to her? What was the catch? Was this a bullshit story? Was Ben just trying to get him out of town?

Competition was a shitty business. Tibetan monks, he once heard, didn't compete for anything, which probably kept them sane. They would all be mental too if they had to compete for their lot in life—to be best at ringing a big bell with a giant stick, or best at staying silent the longest, or best at chanting complex things without screwing up the words. Those guys had it figured out.

Hawthorne took a deep breath and shook his head. Pulling up the voicemail on his phone he touched the dial-back icon. The call was answered before the first ring had even finished.

"You got my message?" Ben asked in his usual curt manner.

"I did. When do you need me there?"

"Yesterday," Ben said.

Hawthorne nodded before he responded. Everything with Ben needed to be done yesterday.

"Okay," he said. "I'm on the next flight out."

"I'd drive," Ben said. "You won't make the nonstop out of LAX and the rest of the flights will run you all over hell and gone."

"I'll check," Hawthorne said, "but I'll be there by this afternoon. When does the tournament start?"

"Day after tomorrow," Ben said. "But this is big. You'll need a full day of background."

"I'm on it," Hawthorne replied, and clicked his phone off.

This sounded big. This was a story. Maybe Ben wasn't such an asshole. Hawthorne scowled. No, he definitely was. But maybe he wasn't totally unfair. Either way, Hawthorne was determined to deliver. He opened his laptop and started looking at hotels. He would leave in a couple of hours.

ELEVEN

COLUSA LANDED IN SANTA FE, NEW MEXICO, AROUND TWO in the afternoon. A few minutes after the plane reached the gate, he heard a soft ping. Unbuckling his seatbelt, he stood up in the aisle. Because the plane was small, he'd gate-checked his roll-on, but he grabbed the black backpack tucked underneath the seat in front of him.

When the people in front of him cleared out, he walked off the plane, grabbing his bag on the way, and exited the tiny, adobe-style airport. A black car was waiting for him just outside the door. The driver held a small, white sign with block lettering: MR. JONES. Colusa approached and gave him that name.

The driver circled around the small parking lot until he reached the road that led to the airport exit. To Colusa's right, a yellow sign with blue lettering embedded within a reddish adobe structure read, "Welcome to Santa Fe. Established 1610. Altitude 7199 Feet." The right side of Colusa's mouth turned up in a sort of smile. He doubted he'd be welcome for long.

Just past the sign and to the left was an auto salvage yard. He had called ahead and arranged for one of the employees to receive a box for him. At precisely two-twenty p.m. that day, the box was to be placed outside of the salvage yard entrance on the gravel shoulder beside the road.

The car stopped when they reached the box. The driver got out, placed the box in the trunk, and swapped it with a smaller box Colusa pulled from his backpack. A little money could always get one what one wanted. In less than two minutes, the car was back on the road and headed into the small town.

To his left and right, Colusa could see snow-capped mountains against a bright blue sky. Short scrubby trees and brush dotted the brown landscape along the highway. A few minutes later, the car exited the highway and merged onto one of the main roads leading into town. Out Colusa's left window was an expansive cemetery.

The car pulled up to a light and stopped in the left turn lane. When the green arrow came, the car in front of them did not go. It was an arthritic old Subaru driven by an even older woman with close-cropped gray hair. Colusa's driver honked, and the Subaru crept forward. Colusa's car made the turn just before the yellow arrow turned red. When there were two lanes, the driver sped past the oblivious woman.

The road narrowed as the car entered an older part of town. Santa Fe's famous Plaza was to the right, and the buildings along the road were earth-toned adobe structures accented by coyote fencing constructed from the trunks of small piñon trees. None of the buildings were more than two or three stories high.

A few minutes later, the car made a left then a quick right into the valet area of Colusa's chosen hotel, a magnificent Santa Fe style building constructed of adobe and adorned with large dark wooden beams and posts. The grounds were beautifully landscaped with pine, fir, and cottonwood trees. The building looked old, as if it had been built in the late eighteen hundreds, but it carried its age well.

When the car stopped under the porte cochere, a young man wearing black pants and a white shirt opened Colusa's door.

"Good afternoon, sir," he said.

Colusa remained seated. The driver got out and explained to

the young man that Colusa wanted his bag taken to his room, and that he would be back later that evening for the key. Sunset in the desert was not far off, and they needed to hurry to get just the right light. The valet understood. Santa Fe was accustomed to hosting photographers, painters, and artists of all kinds. The young man checked the guest registry for Mr. Jones and nodded.

"Yes, very well, sir."

The driver handed Colusa's roll-on bag to the valet, along with a twenty-dollar bill. The valet thanked him and walked through the hotel doors, rolling the bag behind him. After a quick turnaround, Colusa's car was on the move again.

For a good portion of the remaining trip, the car backtracked the route from the Santa Fe airport. Instead of taking the main highway again, however, the driver took a couple of different turns and a round-a-bout, heading off on a less-traveled road into the desert. There was scrub brush in the near distance and mountains in the far distance. A couple of miles down the road, the car slowed and turned right down a bumpy dirt path. It was not developed enough to be called a road.

The ride became much more dynamic. Both Colusa and the driver bounced in their seats as the car pressed forward into the desert. Colusa looked behind him and saw only a sand-colored cloud of dust. Twenty minutes later, the driver stopped.

"I think you will like this place, sir," he said.

The driver got out and opened Colusa's door, at the same time motioning that Colusa was free to emerge. Colusa took his time but stepped out of the back seat. He stood, stretched, and had a quick look around. The view was incredible. To the east, blue hues were descending on the distant peaks and were beginning to fold onto the town itself, as had happened like clockwork for the last four hundred years. The lights below glowed against the darker backdrop. The scene made Colusa pause.

After a few moments, he turned around. The western view was even more spectacular. The brilliant yellow sun had sunk behind a far-away mountain and transformed into a soft, pastel orange. The clarity was stunning. To Colusa's left, the first star appeared in the sky. The rest of the horizon was essentially a rainbow. There were pinks, purples, reds, greens, and oranges that seamlessly merged into a singular breathtaking landscape.

"We'd better hurry, sir," the driver said. "The sun sets quickly."

"Yes," Colusa said. "My box, please. I think just over there should be fine." Colusa pointed to an area just beyond the car.

"Yes, sir."

The driver retrieved the box from the trunk, carried it to the spot identified by Colusa, and set it down.

"Shall I help you unpack?"

"No," Colusa answered. "I've got it." He patted himself down for a moment then looked up. "Although," he asked, "do you have anything I could use to cut the tape?"

Within an instant, the driver held out a small pocketknife.

"Thank you," Colusa nodded.

Colusa cut the sides first then down the middle. The driver stood about five feet away with his hands clasped behind his back. Colusa pulled up all four flaps of the cardboard box and reached deep inside. The driver was staring off into the distance toward the peaks to the west, waiting for his next order.

As Colusa leaned over and rifled through the items in the bottom of the box, he said, "That sunset's really something, isn't it?"

"Oh, it is," the driver agreed. "I like to come out here and …"

Colusa put two small caliber bullets into the driver's forehead. The driver dropped to the ground, his mouth and eyes wide open.

Colusa passed the body on his way to the car. Removing his backpack from the back seat he returned to the box, loaded its contents into the backpack, and walked back to the car. He tossed the backpack into the passenger's seat and reached for the keys in the ignition. They were not there.

Annoyed, Colusa walked back to the driver's body and patted the man's pants pockets. The keys were on the right side. He retrieved them, then returned to the car and started the ignition. After some maneuvering, Colusa turned the car around on the dirt road and made his way back to pavement. He followed the lights into town.

With the help of his phone, Colusa navigated back to his hotel, though he knew he couldn't pull in. There would be too many questions. He continued driving until he reached an intersection with Canyon Road, turned right, and pulled into a large dirt parking lot. He parked in the farthest spot from the street and ignored the honor system payment meters.

Colusa wiped the car down, threw the keys in the floorboard, grabbed his backpack, and walked the half-mile to his hotel. No one thought twice when he walked up, backpack strapped over one shoulder, and said, "I'm Richard Jones. You took my things to my room earlier."

Colusa was shown to a small private casita adjacent to the main building. The bellman asked if he would like a fire in the kiva. Colusa declined. He dismissed all assistance and dropped onto the turned-down bed. It had been a long, few days.

He had been to St. Louis, Cleveland, Denver, and much to his annoyance, a small town in west Texas called Lubbock. He visited churches or synagogues in all of those places. His instructions were the same for each. He was to demolish the building, preferably with some worshipers inside. The scheme took a lot of planning, a myriad of logistics, and a lot of travel.

Money, more than connections, allowed Colusa to get the necessary explosives on site. Patience allowed him to effectively utilize them. Each site required at least a day to round up and place the hardware and link it to a specific cell phone number. Everything was in place in the other four cities. After some much-needed rest, Colusa would turn his attention to his last target.

TWELVE

DEVON WAS RIGHT ON TIME. MASTEN WAS RUNNING LATE, but at least he texted. Wednesdays were about as bad as Mondays. She handed him a coffee when he climbed into her car. They took the 405 north until they were in San Fernando, where it turned into the Five. The traffic was already building, but lightened up a little, at least in their direction, when they reached Castaic. Just outside of Wheeler Ridge, everything turned flat. Farmland here and there, interrupted by desert.

Devon and Masten were silent for most of the first stretch of the drive. Part of it was the early hour and part of it was the nagging awkwardness of the meeting. Masten had made clear that he was not interested in the least. He was just placating her because he was her godfather and her father's best friend. Her nervousness made her break the ice first.

"I think you'll like Peg. She's an ophthalmologist—UCLA grad."

Masten grunted and nodded. Devon didn't respond. She looked forward and drove on.

Masten was never one for small talk, but even he started to

feel uncomfortable in the silence.

"So, how are you doing?" he asked. That seemed to be all he ever asked.

"I'm fine," she answered. She realized that she sounded like a sullen teenager who was asked how their day at school was.

Masten got it and pressed. "Have you given any thought at all to other areas of study you would like to pursue?"

"Besides this? No." Her answer was curter than she intended.

"Well, come see me when we get back," Masten said. "I have a stack of proposals a mile high. I can plug you into which ever one you want."

Devon didn't answer. They rode in silence for a while. The landscape was still just flat and mostly brown. When the Five intersected with Highway 46, they pulled off at a Truck Stop. They were back on the road ten minutes later, business done and fresh drinks in the cup holders. A green sign indicated they were headed to Paso Robles. It made Devon think of a question. She was looking for anything.

"Paso Robles," she said. "Did you ever sell that house there?"

Masten looked over at her. "No," he said. "I haven't done anything with it. I haven't even been back since ..."

"Yeah," Devon interrupted. "That sign just made me think of it."

There was more silence for a bit.

"You know," Devon said, trying to push the boulder forward. "I never knew anything about the place. My dad never mentioned that he owned it."

"Believe me, you're better off. The house was a dump back then. I can only imagine what it's like now." Masten allowed himself a quick chuckle.

Devon smiled.

"Your dad was a good man," Masten volunteered. "He knew what he stood for to a fault. And he was very proud of you."

"I miss him every day."

"I hear you," Masten answered.

"Never in a million years would I have thought that I would be an orphan before I was thirty."

Masten looked over and stared for a moment. "Twists and turns," he said. "Life is full of them. I know better than anyone."

Devon nodded. She knew he did. They rode in silence for much of the remaining trip, but at least a little ice had been broken. Beyond Paso Robles, the road signs indicated that they were on their way into Monterey. There was more awkward small talk here and there, but no more work talk.

THIRTEEN

COLUSA SLEPT IN, AT LEAST FOR HIM. HE AWOKE AT SEVEN-thirty and searched the room for a coffee maker. There wasn't one. He rolled his eyes and sighed in frustration. He couldn't stand places that pretended to be too highbrow to include a simple coffee maker in the room. Such hotels thought they were being classy. Colusa thought they were being cheap pains in the ass.

The practical effect was that he had to get dressed without showering, walk to the lobby in the main building where he passed several other "morning people," get his simple cup of coffee, then reverse course back to his room. Colusa thought it wholly uncivilized.

Coffee now in hand, he removed the old school room key from his pocket, inserted it into the keyhole and pushed the heavy door open. Grabbing the television remote, he sat down on the bed and pressed the power button. He flipped to a morning news show and stared at the screen while he sipped his hard-won coffee.

When the caffeine kicked in, he showered, dressed, and left

his room. Breakfast was a grab and go offering from a fruit bowl next to the damnable coffee pots in the lobby. He was working on a banana when he left the hotel. At the corner, an orange hand on a sign across the street turned into a green walker signal.

The uneven sidewalk led him past several small shops and art galleries. A couple of blocks later he came upon the open, park-like space of the Plaza to his left. But Colusa wasn't headed toward the Plaza. Instead, he turned right. His destination was about a block down.

The Cathedral of St. James was an extraordinary building. The structure was built in the late eighteen hundreds on the site of two prior churches: one from the early seventeen hundreds and one dating to around 1685.

The façade featured a large square bell tower. Round stained-glass windows accented ornate archways leading to the entrance. Traditional Corinthian columns supported the archways.

When he reached the entrance, Colusa pulled the handle on a large bronze and wooden door and stepped inside, expecting to walk into the sanctuary. Instead, he passed through an area where everything was for sale. Candles, angels, books, carvings, copies of paintings, and general knickknacks were all just a cash register away. Colusa smiled at the irony. He was not a religious man, but he had read enough to know that Jesus threw the moneychangers out of the temple.

The interior of the cathedral was more stunning than the exterior, with beautiful stained-glass windows lining each wall to the left and right. Large wooden beams supported intricately painted arches towering over rows of simple wooden pews that spanned from the rear to the front.

Another thought crossed his mind as he entered the grand inner sanctum. It was the same thought he had in the various other cities he had visited. Why were the followers of a simple carpenter who rejected all materialism, so hell bent on raising such expensive and intricate centers of worship? He understood the basic human desire to offer up the best, but it seemed to him like the point was being missed.

Colusa shrugged. It was what it was. He turned to the task of scoping out the structure of the cathedral. He studied the detail, with a particular focus on the areas that would be vulnerable to explosive forces.

When he had created mental notes about the inside, he left the building and wandered around the exterior. His research was interrupted by the ranting of a noisy protester who seemed off his meds, and perhaps in need of some help. A couple of police officers approached the man and began to talk with him in low tones.

When he finished scoping the outside of the church, Colusa decided to take in the Plaza on his way back to the hotel. The Plaza was a small, square park surrounded by streets on all four sides. A couple of the streets were cordoned off with decorative metal poles and loosely hanging chains. Tall, old-growth cottonwood and oak trees shaded the grassy areas and the various park benches dotting the perimeter.

Colusa strolled to the center of the park and saw a large, cubical plinth surrounded by small pine trees set inside a black iron fence. There was nothing resting on the base, however. It was just an empty cube. He wondered what was there before and made a mental note to check it out.

North of the cubical base, Colusa saw a covered stage. There was no activity that morning, but Colusa wished that there were. He would have loved nothing more than to take a seat on a nearby park bench and spend the morning listening to music.

About as soon as he had the thought, the blowing breeze brought the breathy, but soothing sound of an Andean pan flute his way. He looked around and noticed it was coming from a busker across the street. Colusa crossed and walked beneath the city-block-long portal of the Palace of the Governors. It was supported by large, rough-hewn wooden beams. Known as a covered patio in Anglo-settled America, this particular *portal*, pronounced por-*tal*, as he learned from his research before arriving in Santa Fe, was a traditional hub of local commerce.

From what he could see, business was booming. Native American artisans sat on the ground with their backs against the cream-colored adobe building and their wares lying out on colorful, Southwestern blankets. Many of the blankets held turquoise jewelry. A few had ornate wooden carvings. Others had folded blankets displayed, for those who wanted to take home a woven souvenir. At the end of the portal were several collections of dried red chile peppers attached to long pieces of string that looked like overgrown Christmas ornaments. Colusa learned from a tourist pamphlet that these ornaments were called ristras.

Intriguing as the wares were, Colusa passed all the vendors without making a single purchase. He packed light and didn't want to have to contend with the logistics of lugging anything new home, although he was tempted by the thought of draping one of the blankets over the back of the sofa in his home library.

When he found the source of the pan flute, he stood and listened for a few minutes. The sounds were coming from an older man dressed in what appeared to be Incan garb. For all Colusa knew, the guy had been born and raised in the Bronx, but he played his instrument well.

Colusa listened for a few more minutes and dropped a couple of dollars into an overturned hat laying on the sidewalk in front of the man. He completed his walk around the Plaza and made his way back to the hotel. It would be lunchtime soon and he needed to do some research. He wasn't a fan of spicy food, so he found a website that helped him identify alternatives to red, green, and Christmas. It was still early, but Colusa set his phone alarm for three a.m. He wanted to make sure he had time to do his work before his seven-fifteen flight the next morning.

Fourteen

IT WAS ONE-THIRTY WHEN DEVON AND MASTEN PULLED UP in front of the house. There was no path to the front door, so they walked in the street to the driveway and up toward the house. A brick path started near the garage door and curved around to the porch.

Before she pushed the doorbell, Devon checked herself for presentability and ran a hand through her hair. Masten looked at her with a sardonic stare.

"All set?" he asked.

Devon felt self-conscious and shifted her eyes, then looked at the ground. *Someone's grumpy from the drive!*

"Well, let's get this going," Masten said, flicking a hand toward the doorbell.

"Oh, yes, of course, sorry," Devon reached up and pushed the small, round button.

A few moments later, the door opened.

"Hello," Peg said.

"Dr. Schroeder," Devon said, as she held out her hand. "I'm Devon Mendez. Good to meet you in person. Thanks for seeing us."

63

"Yes, yes," Peg said, as she shook Devon's hand. "Welcome."

"This is Dr. James Masten," Devon gestured.

"How do you do?" Masten said.

Peg glanced at Masten, nodded, then looked back at Devon.

"Well, please come in," she said, and led them through the entryway. There were pictures on the walls and several tables of a boy and a girl at various stages of development. "We can talk here in the kitchen. Can I get you anything to drink?"

"I'm fine," Masten responded.

"Oh, no thank you, ma'am," Devon said. "I still have tea in the car. Speaking of which ...?"

Peg interrupted her. "Yes, down this hall, second door on the left."

"Are you sure I can't get you anything?" Peg asked, breaking the awkward silence with Masten.

"No, thank you, I'm fine," Masten responded.

Peg sat down and drummed her fingers on the table.

"So," she said. "Devon tells me you're the head of her department."

"Well, strictly speaking, no," Masten answered. "But I'm the Vice Dean for Research at the Medical School. I control the funding for her program. I'm along today just to observe."

"Oh, goodness," Peg said, raising an eyebrow. "Well, we'll try to do our best."

Devon walked back in the room. "Okay," she said, rubbing her hands together. "Sorry about that."

"Oh, no problem," Peg stood up. "Let me get Callie. Hang on just a moment."

"Dr. Schroeder," Devon interjected.

"You can call me Peg," she interrupted. "I'm not that formal."

"Okay, Peg," Devon said. "If it's alright with you, I'd like to speak with you first."

"Sure," Peg sat back down. "What would you like to know?"

With a notepad on the table and a pen in hand, Devon took Peg through a series of basic questions.

"When was Callie born?" she began.

"September 5, 2017," Peg answered.

"Oh! It's almost her birthday," Devon said.

"It is," Peg answered.

"She was born here in Monterey?" Devon asked without looking up, as she wrote down the birthdate.

"Yes," Peg answered. "At the Community Hospital."

"And I'm sorry to ask this," Devon grimaced, "but when did your husband pass?"

"January 23, 2020," Peg responded in a more somber tone.

"So," Devon dragged out the word as she did the math in her head, still looking down at his notepad, "Callie was two and some change?"

"Yes."

Devon looked up just in time to see Peg's finger rub the side of her nose then drop back down to the table. She heard Peg draw in a quick deep breath and release it.

"I'm sorry," Devon said. "I know this is difficult."

"It's fine," Peg said quickly.

"Alright," Devon said, as ready to change the subject as Peg. "Let's talk about the incidents with Callie, and when they began to occur."

The first instance Peg could recall was when Callie was about three.

"Like I told you on the phone, it had been about a year since Callie's father died, maybe a little less," Peg said. "She was so young. I'm not even sure she really processed the loss. But that was the first time I heard her refer to herself as Claire."

"Do you know anyone else named Claire?"

"No," Peg answered, shaking her head. "No one."

Devon made a quick note. She then asked about Callie's development.

"Callie's speech came in pretty much on schedule," Peg responded. "She was babbling by six months. She said her first words by ten months and could complete simple sentences by eighteen months. That aspect of her was ordinary. She wasn't a savant, but she wasn't behind either. She was just a normally developing child."

Devon nodded and made more notes.

"The exception came one afternoon following a nap," Peg continued. "Callie approached me and described a dream she had. It involved falling. I told her that dreams about falling were common and that people always woke up before they hit the ground. I told her it was just a normal dream."

Devon put her pen down and stared directly at Peg. "What did Callie say?"

"She said she didn't wake up," Peg responded. "She said she hit the ground and died."

Devon let her eyes drift for a moment then picked up her pen again. She made a quick note and once again paused.

"Okay, what happened next?" Devon asked.

"Well, nothing for a while," Peg recalled. "And, honestly, I didn't think much more about it. I didn't hear anything else for several months. Then one day out of the blue, maybe two or three months ago, she started crying for no apparent reason. I asked her what was going on and all Callie could say was, 'I miss Foot Foot.' I had no idea what she was talking about. Callie never had anything, alive or not, named Foot Foot."

Devon pursed her lips and nodded. She hadn't heard that one before.

"Okay," Devon said. "You mentioned on the phone that Callie said something about her mother dying as well, and that they were in a car accident when Callie, or Claire, excuse me, was thirteen?"

"Yes," Peg nodded.

"Has Callie said anymore about that?"

"No," Peg answered. "Not that I've heard."

"Okay." Devon tapped her pen against her pad, considering the next question. She noticed that Masten seemed disengaged from the conversation. He was looking at the ceiling, scratching his throat with the backs of his fingers, and shifting in his chair as if he couldn't get comfortable. Devon read this as a bad sign for her project.

Peg picked up on it as well and tried to deflect a bit. "Well," she said. "Should I get Callie now?"

"Sure," Devon said. "I'd love to meet her."

Peg left the room and returned a few minutes later with her daughter.

"Dr. Mendez," she said. "This is my daughter, Callie."

Devon stood and extended her hand. She offered a big smile and said, "Hi, Callie. I'm Devon, and this is Dr. Masten."

Callie's eyes and head wandered the room for a moment until Peg pulled out a chair and told her to have a seat.

"Sweetie, Dr. Mendez just wants to talk to you for a few minutes," Peg said. "Is that alright?"

Callie nodded. She was clearly uncomfortable and self-conscious. Devon did her best to make Callie feel better.

"Like your mom said, I'd just like to talk with you for a few minutes," she said. "That's all. Then you can go back to playing, okay?" Callie nodded again.

"So," Devon started with her questions, "I understand that a long time ago, your name was Claire. Is that right?"

Callie nodded yes.

"That's pretty cool," Devon said, trying to sound cool herself. "Will you tell me about your memories of being Claire?"

Callie looked at her mother then froze.

"It's alright, sweetheart," Peg said. "You're not in trouble. She's just asking some questions. You just tell her what you remember."

"I don't know," Callie said. "I was Claire. That's all I remember."

"Did you have a mom and dad?" Devon asked.

"Yeah," Callie responded.

"What did they look like?"

Callie tilted her head up slightly. Her eyes rolled up and to the left. She paused there for a moment, then dropped her head again.

"I don't remember," she said.

"Your mom said you had a dream about dying when you were Claire," Devon coaxed. "Can you remember anything about that?"

"I remember falling," Callie said. "I had big butterflies in my stomach."

"Butterflies in your stomach?" Devon asked.

"Yeah," Callie answered. "It kind of tickled, like when we go over a big bump in the road. I feel them at night sometimes, too."

"Kind of like a roller coaster?" Devon asked, jotting down notes.

"I don't know," Callie shrugged. "I've never been on a roller coaster."

Devon looked up. *Touché.* She smiled. She was impressed by the humble honesty of the answer, and by Callie's engagement in the questions.

"Can you tell me anything else about that day?"

"My mom fell, too," Callie said. "I couldn't see her when I was falling, but I could hear her."

"What was she saying?" Devon asked, her eyes now fixed on the child.

Callie looked a bit stunned. "She wasn't saying anything. She was screaming."

Devon put two fingers on her jaw and nodded. There was a short moment of silence as she processed the chilling detail.

"Do you remember your mom's name?" Devon asked.

Callie crinkled her face and again looked up and to the left. "Katrina, Katherine, Kim," she mumbled. "Something like that."

"Okay," Devon said. "How about your dad? Do you recall his name?"

Callie studied the air and her brain for a few moments, then shook her head.

"I don't know," she said. "I remember he was happy that day. He had just found something big at work."

Masten was beginning to sweat, and his face was pale. Peg instantly recognized his distress.

"Are you okay, sir?" she asked.

"I'm fine," Masten said as he adjusted himself in the chair.

Devon looked at Masten for a moment, then turned back to Callie. "How old were you when you died as Claire?"

"Thirteen," Callie answered.

"Just a few more questions, okay?" Devon said. "Do you remember where you lived when you were Claire?"

"We lived by the ocean," Callie said. "I could see it from my backyard. Kind of like here."

"Great!" Devon responded, nodding with approval.

"But that's not where I died," Callie added.

Devon's expression froze for a second. Her eyes darted left then right and stopped back on Callie.

"Okay," she said, drawing the word out. "Where *did* you die?"

"It was in the mountains," Callie said. "It was foggy and green, and it smelled kind of like my mom's bathroom air freshener."

Devon made a fist and tapped the side of it lightly against her mouth. She was trying to come up with the next question.

"I can remember a lot when I'm in the bathroom," Callie interjected, "because of the smell." Callie caught herself and giggled, putting her hand over her mouth. "The smell of the air freshener," she laughed. "That's what I meant."

"I understand," Devon laughed, too.

"Actually, I may need some air." Masten interrupted the brief moment of levity. "May I step out for a moment?"

"Of course," Peg pointed. "That door there will take you out to the back deck."

"Thank you," Masten said as he rubbed his face and stood up. He walked to the back deck and grabbed the railing with both hands. He leaned forward a little and took several deep breaths.

"Is he alright?" Peg asked Devon.

"I honestly don't know," Devon responded. "Maybe I should go check on him."

"I think so," Peg agreed.

Devon stood and walked out to the deck. "Jim, are you okay?"

"I'm fine!" Masten snapped back. "Go back inside. I'll be there in a minute."

Devon sat back down at the table and sighed as she shrugged.

"He says he's fine," Devon said to Peg. "Let's keep going, I guess. I don't want to take up too much of your time." She turned again to Callie. "Do you remember your last name when you were Claire?"

Callie thought for a long moment, then shook her head. "I don't."

"It's okay," Devon said, putting her hand into the air. "There aren't any wrong answers. I just want to know what you remember, and if you can't remember, that's perfectly fine."

Callie nodded.

"Can I go now?" Callie asked. "I'm really tired."

"Yes, of course," Devon said. "I'm glad I got to talk to you. You are a very smart girl with a very good memory."

"Okay, bye!" Callie said as she bounded out of the room.

When Callie was gone, Peg looked at Devon. "So, what do you think?"

"It's quite compelling. I can't imagine having memories like that as a child. It must be tough for both of you. For now, I'd say just keep listening to her and let her tell her story. Just keep being supportive. It sounds like she's trying to process something awful, wherever it's coming from. And if it's okay, I'd like to come back again in a few weeks and spend more time with her."

Peg considered, and said, "That would be fine."

"And in the meantime, if she says anything else that we didn't hear today, would you please call or email me?"

Devon handed her a card, even though Peg already had her information. It was more to look professional than anything.

"Okay," Peg said, taking the card between two fingers.

"I also want to do some research and see if I can find out any independent information about what she's said," Devon added. "How about I call again in a week or so and we can set something up?"

Masten heard the session ending and walked back in.

"My apologies," he said. "I don't know what happened. Must have been something I ate."

"It's okay," Peg said as she moved them both toward the front door. "Well, Dr. Mendez, I'll talk to you soon. Thank you both for coming."

When Peg finished, Masten and Devon were again standing on the front porch. Devon waved and said goodbye. Masten turned and walked down the steps. Peg closed the door. Her son, Max, would be home from school soon.

FIFTEEN

THE DRIVE BACK TO LOS ANGELES WAS UNCOMFORTABLE.
Devon went over the details out loud. Masten offered no
response. He just looked out the window and shrank lower into
his seat. A long and awkward five hours later, Devon dropped
Masten off at his car, which was still in the university parking
lot. The two then went their separate ways.

Masten pulled out of the university lot and onto the street
only to be greeted by a red light. After an eternity, the light
turned green, and he advanced two blocks before encountering
another red light. The sequence continued. Red light, after red
light, after red light. *Who programmed these lights? They should
be fired, or beaten, or both.*

Arriving at his house twenty minutes later, Masten pulled
into the garage and lowered the big door behind him. He entered
the kitchen from the garage and paced for a couple of minutes
before drawing a glass of water from the kitchen faucet.

When the glass was empty, Masten put it in the sink and went
back to the garage in search of a clear plastic container that was
stacked on top of several other similar plastic containers. He

brought it back into the kitchen and removed the lid. The smell immediately hit him. The faint air of his wife's perfume was eternally embedded in a black, cotton scarf that she used to love. He held the scarf to his face and took a deep breath. Years of memories flooded back in a split second.

Masten began to cry. He hadn't opened this box in almost three years. It was a painful time capsule that he could never let go, but that he couldn't visit very often either. The tears continued as he rummaged through the box. He picked up a small, stuffed rabbit that he'd set at the foot of his daughter's bassinet the day he and Kate brought her home from the hospital.

Foot Foot, was what the rabbit would come to be called. Foot Foot knew nothing but love and great adventures for several years but, as Claire grew older, he was finally laid aside as nothing more than a parent's keepsake. On this day, though, Foot Foot was a direct path back through time.

Masten reflected on old birthday photos and pictures from family vacations and other occasions, both special and ordinary. Tucked beneath Foot Foot was a framed picture of Masten and his wife on their wedding day. Before the crash, it had a place of honor on the mantel above their fireplace for many years. Below that photo was one of he and his wife lying on a photographer's floor next to a very young Claire. They were kissing her, and she was kissing Foot Foot. He kept a smaller version of the same picture in his wallet.

Masten pulled out a few pieces of paper with crayon drawings on them. One resembled a dog eating the sun in a field of giant flowers. Masten recalled that Claire drew the picture on a rainy Saturday when she was four. A small painted rock with glued-on googly eyes lay in the box beneath the paper drawings.

There were other memories too, although they were not in the box. The fights with his wife, that came and went and occasionally stretched their marriage to its thinnest possible strand. The fights with Claire, once she was old enough to realize that he wasn't actually a superhero. Fights about the lights constantly left on, the laundry left on the floor, and the nagging about dishes and trash. The incessant arguments with his daughter about homework, grades, and her future. There were no keepsakes for those things, yet they completed the big ball of life he'd once had. And it was a ball that disappeared as fast as a pin popping a balloon.

Masten sat down in front of the box, put his face in his hands, and allowed his emotions to overtake him. He sobbed uncontrollably for several minutes. He finally cycled through to a pause and took a deep, choppy breath. He stared at the box for a few minutes and pondered how three lives, with all the love, all of the memories, and all of the joy; a lifetime of wonderfully connected moments large and small, could fit into the same sort of box that he kept his extra bed sheets in. Masten felt as if the entire perceivable universe was set on some giant cosmic roulette wheel and given a good hard spin.

He closed his eyes and tried to think about something else, anything else. It didn't work. The first image that popped into his head was a medical examiner in blue scrubs, flanked by a state trooper.

❖ ❖ ❖

"Sir, I know how hard this is," the young doctor said, "but we're going to need you to identify the bodies."

Did she really think she knew how hard this was? He'd been married longer than this woman had been alive. And there was no way she had a child. *She didn't have the first clue how hard this was.* He gave a numb nod and followed the doctor into a featureless room.

He saw two metal tables side by side, both with white sheets covering human forms. The trooper moved in behind him as the doctor directed him to the head of one of the tables.

"I'm only going to roll back enough for you to see the face, okay?" she said.

Masten stood frozen as the doctor gently rolled the first white sheet down about a foot. Masten collapsed at the knees when he saw the bruised and bloodied face of his wife facing upward on the table.

"That's her," he whispered as he started to sob. His hand instantly went up to cover his mouth, and he sputtered a bit as he held back a full-on breakdown.

"Okay, thank you," the doctor said.

The trooper moved Masten to the next table.

"No!" he begged. "Please, no."

"Sir," the doctor said. "It will just take a second. I am so sorry."

Masten became nauseous and buckled at the knees. The trooper held him up by the waist. The doctor rolled back the sheet and revealed his daughter's face. Her mouth was open slightly, with one eye open, and one eye closed. Masten let out a piercing scream then vomited in one chaotic spasm. His legs went out from under him, and the trooper held him by his torso. A second later, he fainted.

He woke up flat on the floor with a foam cushion under his head. It took him a few minutes to reboot, as if he were a computer that had been turned off and back on. His consciousness returned slowly. When it finally did, he noted that both sheets were back in place and the doctor was kneeling in front of him with a small cup of cool water.

It took a full five minutes for Masten to start coming back. All the while, he could hear the doctor and trooper talking to him, but he couldn't process anything they were saying. Moments later, the sharp, foul smell of ammonia brought him all the way back.

"Sir," the doctor said as she tapped his cheek with her hand. "Dr. Masten, can you hear me? Sir, I am so sorry."

Masten had reached the point of no expression. He nodded before the lights went out again.

"Get a crew down here, stat!" was the last thing he heard the young doctor say.

❖ ❖ ❖

REVISITED

When he awoke, Masten was on the kitchen floor. The experience of that unimaginable day was still enough to cost him his consciousness. It was getting late, and he was exhausted. It had been a long day. He walked upstairs and undressed down to his boxers and a white t-shirt. He sat down at a small desk in his bedroom, opened the center drawer, and pulled out a small hardcover book filled with hand-written notes and thoughts he had jotted down over the years. Most of it was written in black ink. He opened the book and thumbed through a few pages. He stopped when he came to an entry he'd made five years earlier in blue ink.

If there is a lesson to be taken from this apparently random existence, it is that the true value lies not with the extraordinary, but with the mundane. Claire tucking her toes under my leg while watching TV on the couch. A silly drawing brought home from school. A laugh while cooking together in the kitchen. A hug and supportive shoulder to catch tears. There is no fame, no fortune, no success that can equal the most basic of interactions with the people we love.

Maybe that was all still true, but it was a lot less meaningful. The other absolute truth, which Masten now knew, was that it could all be extinguished in an instant. Whatever illusion of permanence that seemed to accompany being alive was just that—an illusion.

Masten closed the book and placed it back in the desk drawer. He clicked the light switch off and followed a well-worn path to his bed. He crawled in and prepared for another fitful night with his closest friend. Anger.

Sixteen

DEVON ARRIVED BACK AT HER APARTMENT AND WENT straight to bed. It had been a long day and the conversation with Callie upset her more than she realized. She had researched dozens of such cases and interviewed quite a few children, but Callie seemed different. Her story was more palpable. Perhaps it was because she lived nearby, and no translator was needed. Perhaps it was because she claimed to recall the exact moment of her prior death. Whatever it was, it was unsettling and kept Devon from falling asleep.

If Callie's story was true, Devon thought, *most people's ideas about what comes after this life are wrong.* She stared at the darkened ceiling for a moment then recalled a quote from Sir Isaac Newton that was a favorite of her college physics professor: "Nature is inexorable and immutable; she never transgresses the laws imposed upon her, or cares a whit whether her abstruse reasons and methods of operation are understandable to men."

Devon thought about two things. First, the quote was a fancy way of saying that there is a truth, and the truth is not at all affected by anyone's beliefs. *We can blind ourselves with beliefs, but at the end of the day, it is what it is.* Devon's second thought was that Nature is perhaps the most faithful servant of God the universe has ever known. *It always follows the laws.*

But what are the laws of death? Devon wondered. *Callie's experience would indicate that we recycle somehow. We live one life then move into another. If the observable laws of physics are any indicator, the event happens as predictably as a ball dropping to the ground when thrown into the air.* "Can that be true?" Devon asked out loud. *If it is,* she thought, *when does the cycle end?*

Devon's musings were interrupted by the sound of her phone's ringtone. It was her cousin, Steven. She got to the point after briefly catching up.

"Listen, I didn't remember until yesterday, but I totally left the door to my dad's house open the day he died. There wasn't anything big missing that I saw, but I wanted to check with you. Do you remember anything being gone?"

"I don't recall anything, but all I took were files. I haven't looked at any of them since. I have them all in storage though. You want me to check?"

"That would be great," Devon said. "No big rush. It's just been bugging me."

"No worries," Steven responded. "It's not far. I'll look in the next day or so."

"You're the best. Give my love to your folks."

Devon hung up and rolled into the covers. She'd just gotten comfortable when her phone rang again. *Jesus.* She didn't recognize the number, but she answered anyway. It was local.

"Hello?"

"Devon?"

"Yes," she answered.

"This is Todd Hawthorne—from the bar the other night."

Devon pulled her phone away from her ear and looked at it briefly before responding. "How'd you get my number?"

"Good to hear your voice too," Hawthorne quipped as a little blood ran from his head.

"I didn't mean it like that," Devon said. "I'm sorry. This is just a surprise. A nice surprise, but ..."

"I'm an investigative reporter," Hawthorne answered. "You'd be amazed at what I can find out."

"Oh!" Devon responded. "Well, that's a little unnerving."

Now it was Hawthorne's turn to back-pedal. "No, no, no. I'm not stalking you. Maybe this was a bad idea. I'll ..."

"It's fine, Todd," Devon interrupted. "I'm glad you called. What's going on?"

"Nothing," Hawthorne said. "Absolutely nothing. I'm in Monterey to cover a story about the governor."

"Well, that sounds fun," Devon responded.

"Not really," Hawthorne said. "Covering politics is like covering a scandal at the local high school. Always high on drama. Usually low on gravitas."

Devon chuckled. "So, you got bored and decided to call me?"

"A little yes, a little no," Hawthorne answered. "I am one hundred percent bored, but I was thinking about you before that." He grimaced a little after he said it.

"Well, I wish I'd known," Devon said. "I just got back from Monterey a couple of hours ago."

"Oh, yeah," Hawthorne laughed, "Claire."

"You really don't like that name, do you."

"It's a fine name and I'm sure she's a sweet kid," Hawthorne said. "Maybe I should talk to Claire too. Help vet her story."

"Yeah, right," Devon said. "Somehow I don't think her mom would be interested in letting Callie talk to a reporter."

"Callie?" Hawthorne asked.

Devon winced and cursed to herself. "Claire," she corrected. "I meant Claire."

Hawthorne played along and left it alone.

"Well Todd Hawthorne," Devon said, "I think it's time I turned in for the night."

"Me too," Todd said. "I have a big day of chasing politicians around the golf course tomorrow."

Devon laughed and said goodbye. When she hung up, she

cursed herself again for the slip.

Hawthorne put down his phone and wrote the name Callie on a small pad next to his hotel bed. It was more out of habit than anything. He clicked the lamp off and went to sleep.

SEVENTEEN

THE PAPER DIDN'T GIVE HIM MUCH OF A BUDGET, BUT Hawthorne found a good rate online for the La Maison Sur La Mer hotel in Monterey. The place was small and a little frilly for his taste, but he could smell the ocean from his room. At least he thought it was the ocean. In truth, it was a combination of heavy bleach and a musty odor from years of sea winds blowing in.

The bed was comfortable though, and Hawthorne slept well. He was still foggy and waking up when his phone rang.

"Hello," he said in a gruff voice that would make a chain-smoking truck driver proud.

"Todd, it's Ben. Listen, the governor has moved his golf game and announcement back a few days. We just got word."

"Jesus, Ben!" Hawthorne responded, trying not to raise his voice too much. "I just got here last night. What should I do?"

"Just hang tight. The situation seems a little dynamic and I want you there first when it happens. It may be as late as Sunday, but it could be earlier. I'll keep you posted."

Ben hung up and Hawthorne rolled over and groaned.

"What the hell am I going to do until Sunday?" he said out loud.

He couldn't fall back asleep, so Hawthorne lay there breathing in the air. His first thought was food, but he didn't feel like going anywhere. He decided to table the motion and come back to it in a while. Maybe he could rally later.

He rolled over and saw the name on the pad he had written down last night. *Callie.* He thought back to the bar and his call with Devon. *This girl is in Monterey. Devon was up here investigating Callie, or Claire, she said it was. Devon said she investigated past life experiences and there is a young girl here who claims to recall one.* It seemed far-fetched to Hawthorne, but if this girl were legit, it might make a good story, and he desperately needed a good story. He raised his eyebrows and turned down the corners of his mouth. He needed more information, though, and there was only one place to get it.

He rolled and leaned over the side of the bed. There was a black backpack that he had dropped against the wall. After some stretching, Hawthorne grabbed the top strap and pulled it closer. He unzipped the main compartment and pulled out his laptop.

Once the computer was on the bed, he rolled onto his back and worked himself into an upright position. He turned on the computer and began to think. *What else was it she said in the bar? The girl's dad had died not long ago.* It wasn't much, but it was a start.

Search engines gave results that were too broad for the limited set of information, so Hawthorne used the database he had through the newspaper. He searched the obituary section of the Monterey Messenger for all deaths of men in the past three years, where two children and a wife were left behind. The resulting list was long. He input a sub search for the name Callie.

There was only one result. The obituary was for Daniel Schroeder, who died of cancer about two years earlier. He left behind a daughter named Callie, a son named Max and a wife named Peg. Hawthorne knew he'd found the girl. She was the only one who fit the search.

Continuing with the database, Hawthorne located Peg Schroeder's address in no time. The question now was how to go about this? *The direct approach is usually best*, he thought, but what would the angle be?

Hawthorne crawled out of the bed and walked to the window. The view was nothing special. His room overlooked a parking lot and some trees. The ocean view rooms were on the other side of the building. He got what he paid for, he guessed. He continued to think, but the answer was not coming to him. He had time, but no plan. He decided to take a walk.

❖ ❖ ❖

Hawthorne hustled down two flights of narrow wooden stairs. The railing and the stairs were painted white. When he reached the bottom, he pushed open a small spring-hinged gate and stepped out onto a paved patio next to the street. His hotel was on Cannery Row. At least that's what the seemingly endless signs indicated. He'd heard of Cannery Row. It may have been an old movie. Maybe a book. He couldn't recall, but from what he saw, people were interested in it.

He walked along the street, more engaged in his thoughts than his surroundings. He passed families, couples, and individuals. All of them were from somewhere else and all of them were compacted onto this one small strip of road. Hawthorne couldn't think. He recalled something about a rooftop bar at his hotel, so he turned and walked back.

The concierge told him how to get where he was going but informed him that there was no bar service at the time. Hawthorne didn't care. He took the elevator and stepped out onto a large wooden deck that overlooked Monterey Bay. The deck was accented by various kinds of native flowers and succulents meticulously maintained in large pots.

Hawthorne took a seat in a deck chair. He spent some time listening to the sounds and taking in the smells, but all the while, he was thinking about Callie and the possible story there.

He finally concluded that there was only one way.

EIGHTEEN

PEG SCHROEDER AND HER TWO KIDS STROLLED DOWN THE beach. It was a Thursday evening ritual that dated back years— well before either Callie or Max was born. Peg and Daniel ended most days strolling hand in hand on the sand. Just walking. When Dan died, it was one of the few connections to routine that she had. So, she kept it going.

The repetitive sound of the crashing waves was soothing. To the left was nothing but open sea dotted with a few fishing boats. Straight ahead, the land curved around to form Monterey Bay. In the far distance, the lights of Santa Cruz began to shine. As they walked, the verbena to the right looked thick, like green moss covering most of the dunes that flanked the long strip of flat sand.

They could smell the salt, the fish, and the plants, all at once. The sand beneath their shoes was moist and pliant but not wet. Peg walked barefoot, carrying her shoes with two fingers. The ever-present seagulls made sure that the crashing waves weren't the only sound to be heard.

Callie was about twenty yards in front of Peg and Max. She ran out to the shallow water's edge and waited for the waves to come in, then raced the tide inward, trying—but not too hard—to avoid getting her feet wet. Callie repeated the pattern many times.

The beach was about a half a mile from their house, and on weekday evenings, parking on the wharf near Del Monte Beach was not difficult. The walk had become a bonding experience for the small family since Dan's passing.

Sometimes Max and his mother talked. Sometimes they didn't. Today was mostly silent, but Peg could tell that something was on Max' mind.

"Callie said something really weird today," he opened, as a seagull sped overhead.

"Oh yeah?" Peg said. "What was that?"

"She said she died in a car wreck, when she had another mother and father."

Peg stopped walking and looked at Max, then turned her head toward the water. After a moment, she resumed walking. Max followed her lead.

"She's been saying things like that for a while now," Peg said. "Honestly, I'm surprised you haven't heard it before. I don't know what it is. I thought for a time that it was related to your father, but I think she was too young when that happened."

"It was kinda weird," Max said.

"Ha, tell me about it," Peg replied. "I talked to her pediatrician, and he said it wasn't uncommon for kids to have odd fantasies as they develop. He said it wasn't that different from pet rocks or imaginary friends."

"But a car wreck?" Max asked. "That's pretty dark. And it's pretty specific."

"I know, right?" Peg responded, more animated. "Her doctor mentioned a clinic in Los Angeles that specializes in studying kids with odd…" Peg waved her hand as she struggled for the word, "perceptions."

"What do you mean?" Max asked.

"Apparently, it's not that unusual for some young kids to have …" again Peg trailed off, "memories, or visions of what they claim to be other lives. It's strange as hell, and it's the absolute last thing I need right now. But what she says seems really odd. I don't know what to make of it."

"Did you call the clinic?"

"I did," Peg answered. "I also met with a couple of their doctors at our house yesterday while you were at school. They talked to Callie too. I kept her home. We'll see what comes of it, I guess."

"You didn't tell me that," Max objected.

"I know," Peg said. "I probably should have, but I know you're struggling too." Peg raised her eyebrows. "Newton told me about the bullying incident."

Max looked hurt and angry at the same time. "He shouldn't have done that."

"He's your oldest friend, Max," Peg said. "He's just looking out for you. Besides, what does he weigh now, two-fifty? There are worse guardian angels."

Max nodded. His mom was right. Newton Thorley had lived across the street from Max since before either of them could walk. He was everything Max wasn't—big, athletic, confident, popular, and black. Max read books. He spent his time in his head or immersed in words that provided information about the world outside his own.

Both young men were smart, but in strikingly different ways. Newton was a conqueror. Max was an observer. But their history together ensured that none of their differences mattered. Max helped Newton with Math. Newton helped Max with life.

Peg and Max walked along in silence for a while, until a larger than usual wave crashed in and soaked Max's sneakers and high white socks. Peg saw it coming and moved back toward the dunes. Up ahead, Callie stood still and let the wave overtake her. The force of the water knocked her down and drenched her clothes. The returning tide dragged her onto the waterlogged sand.

"Callie!" Peg shouted, breaking into a run. When she and Max reached Callie, Peg picked up her daughter and moved her family farther inland. There was no dusting off wet beach sand. Instead, Peg simply turned Callie around and started walking back toward the car. Max found no joy in the squishy, soggy march.

Callie didn't stay close for very long. A large gathering of seagulls was milling around on the sand ahead and she couldn't resist the urge to crash the party. She ran straight into the middle of the group and the birds started flying. She circled around in several directions until every last bird had taken off from the beach.

"Mommy, come look!" she yelled, motioning with one arm, and looking down at the sand. When the seagulls were gone, Callie began exploring the other wonders nearby. Peg and Max walked up without quickening their pace.

Callie pointed. "They look like little arrows in the sand!"

"Yeah!" Peg responded, pretending excitement.

"Those are seagull tracks," Max chimed in. "They're actually the reverse of what they look like. What appears to be the front of the arrow is the back of the seagull's foot. So, it looks like the arrow is pointing in one direction, but the bird is really walking in the other."

"That's funny," Callie said, processing the information from her brother. "Oh, and look at this!" Callie shouted, pointing down again. "What is that?"

"That," Max said, "is a sand dollar. It's a kind of sea urchin. You see a lot of them on the beach here. Most are the skeletons of ones that have died, but this one looks like it's still alive."

"Don't touch it!" Peg cautioned, as Callie reached down. "You might hurt it and you wouldn't want to do that."

"No," Callie said rubbing her hands together. "I don't want to hurt it."

"Well, let's just leave him alone," Peg said. "We need to get back home anyway. It's almost bedtime."

As they approached a long concrete pier, the sand near the end of the beach had areas that were almost black. The three moved farther away from the water, through the darker sand, toward a small staircase that led from the sand up to the pavement of a sidewalk.

Max took a bad step near the top of the staircase and fell over the side into the sand, landing on his back.

"Dammit!" He shouted.

Callie's eyes widened as she put her hand over her mouth in response to the next level language coming from her brother. She'd never heard him speak like that before.

"Oh my god, Max, are you okay?" Peg asked as she extended a hand down.

"I'm fine," Max responded, more embarrassed than hurt.

"That was quite a trick," Peg said, trying not to giggle.

"Yeah, do it again!" Callie shouted. "Do it again!"

Max shot them both a grumpy look as he dusted himself off.

"He fell over the side like Dr. Mindy," Callie said, looking at Peg.

Peg laughed for a second then stopped. She grabbed the tip of her nose.

"Like who?" she asked.

"Dr. Mindy," Callie responded. "He fell over a cliff and died. A bald man with glasses pushed him."

Peg snapped her head toward Max and offered a WTF look.

"Callie," Peg asked after a long moment, and not really wanting to hear the answer. "Who is Dr. Mindy?"

"I don't know," she shrugged. "He worked with my dad in Palace Birdies. He's dead now. Can we go home?"

The three successfully reached the top of the stairs on the second try. They passed a small blue building with restrooms designated for men and women. They stepped off the curb of the sidewalk and into the lot where their car was parked.

"Try not to get sand everywhere," Peg said to Callie.

"Okay," Callie answered, as she climbed into her booster seat, getting sand everywhere.

Peg sighed as she thought about the fact that she still had to give Callie a bath, get her changed and put her to bed. The walks were wonderful. Getting home from the walks—not so much. Peg needed a drink.

NINETEEN

HAWTHORNE SAT IN HIS CAR, DOWN THE BLOCK FROM PEG'S house. He'd been there for twenty minutes. He rang the doorbell a couple of times earlier, but no one answered, so he decided to wait. He was in the middle of going through his story for the tenth time when a blue sedan pulled into the Schroeder's' driveway. Looking through his rear-view mirror, Hawthorne saw the garage door roll up. The car pulled forward, then the garage door rolled back down.

This was his chance. He knew he was hitting them late, but he needed to make this work. He backed down the street and stopped in front of the house. He got out of his car and walked to the front door. When he reached the porch, he took a deep breath. He pressed the doorbell and stepped back. Peg appeared a minute later.

"Hello, Mrs. Schroeder," he said. "My name is Todd Hawthorne. I am a colleague of Dr. Mendez, who you met with yesterday."

"Yes," Peg said. "Dr. Mendez and another man were here."

Hawthorne ignored the comment about the other man. He

didn't know who Peg was talking about. "I'm trying to help Dr. Mendez and wondered if I could have five minutes of your time to help clear up a few loose questions she had."

"Um, is there any way you could come back tomorrow?" Peg said. "I wasn't expecting anyone, and I need to get my kids to bed. It's a school night."

"Well, I have to be back in L.A. tomorrow, but I can wait," Hawthorne said. "I don't mind at all. I'll just be out here if that's okay. I don't even need to come in. We can talk on the porch when you're done."

"I guess," Peg said. "Can you give me fifteen minutes?"

"Sure," Hawthorne answered. "Not a problem at all."

It wasn't fifteen minutes, but Peg came back a little later and invited Hawthorne in. "We don't need to talk on the porch," she said. She motioned for Hawthorne to sit on a sofa in a formal living room just inside the front door. Pictures of Callie and Max decorated the walls and tables. Most were just of the kids. Some included Peg and Daniel. The reality made Hawthorne pause for a beat, but he continued.

"If you don't mind, let's start from the beginning." Hawthorne led by laying out the very little information he heard from Devon in the bar. "I just want to make sure I understand the story, since I'm the grunt who has to write everything." He rolled his eyes and played the underling card well.

Peg talked him through everything from start to finish, including the new details about Dr. Mindy from the evening beach walk. Hawthorne wrote it all down, and knew it was time to go.

He waved broadly as he stepped off the porch. Twenty minutes later, he was back in his hotel room, his laptop out. The first draft of the article didn't take long to write—maybe an hour. It was short. The young girl's story was certainly odd, but Peg seemed credible. Hawthorne was sure he could sell this to Ben. He went back over his notes and back over the article three more times. He struggled with whether to mention Devon in the article but concluded that raising her profile as an expert in such issues could only help her. He emailed it to Ben and followed up with a call. It took a little convincing, but Ben agreed to run it in the next morning's California section.

Hawthorne was satisfied. He could at least leave here with one byline. When he felt and heard his stomach growl, he looked at his watch. It was time to find some food.

❖ ❖ ❖

The view of the bay that evening was overrun with the lights of fishing trawlers. Hawthorne hadn't noticed them before. When the waiter took his drink order, Hawthorne asked about the boats.

"The squid are running," the waiter said, explaining that the trawlers came from as far away as San Diego and Alaska to get in on a good squid run, though the runs were fewer and farther between these days.

"The calamari is very fresh tonight," the waiter suggested.

"The wedge salad will be just fine," Hawthorne said. "Extra bacon bits please. Oh, and can you bring me a couple of rolls as well?"

"Yes, sir." The waiter said as he walked off.

As he sipped his drink, Hawthorne thought about his article and the information he now possessed; information that Devon had not yet received. A cliff. Palace Birdies. That had to be Rancho Palos Verdes, an area south of Los Angeles, that was surrounded by cliffs. He knew the area a little. It was out of his beat, but still in L.A. County. He smelled another story there, and he had the time. He didn't know Dr. Mindy, but that would come. The governor's announcement didn't seem imminent.

He looked at his phone and checked the time. After a quick scroll through his contacts, he pressed his thumb against a name and pulled the phone to his ear. It rang twice before being picked up.

"Boo Boo!" a woman's voice answered, stretching each syllable.

"I've told you to stop with that," Hawthorne responded.

"What's up, boyfriend?"

"I've told you to stop with that too," he said. "You work for the sheriff's department. This is not dial-a-date."

"Well, then how can I help you, sir?" the woman asked, now in a completely professional tone. The schizophrenic transition made them both chuckle a bit.

"Are you on the night shift tonight, Jordie?"

"You know I am," she replied, in a playful, sing-song tone.

"Can you do me a favor?" Hawthorne asked.

"You know I can't," she said, in the same tone.

"Come on!" Hawthorne insisted. "What the hell else do you have to do? It's just a little computer research."

"What's in it for me?" the woman asked.

"How about roses and red wine and a first-class trip to Tahiti?"

"Ooh, yeah," Jordie contemplated. "That does sound like a pretty good deal. Whatcha got?"

Hawthorne explained what he'd heard about Dr. Mindy. Jordie agreed to take a look and get back to him with whatever she found. Hawthorne thanked her and Jordie insulted his manhood. He thanked her for the insult. The wedge salad arrived just after he hung up.

❖ ❖ ❖

After dinner, Hawthorne walked back to his hotel. There was a damp chill in the air that he couldn't shake even after he was back in the room, so he hit a button on a small remote and started a fire in the gas fireplace. Kicking off his shoes, Hawthorne dropped onto the bed, grabbed the TV remote from the side table and started scrolling through the hundreds of channels with nothing interesting on them. He finally settled for an old rerun of *The Beverly Hillbillies*.

His phone rang a short time later. "That was fast," he said when he answered.

"Yes, well, I'm nothing if not efficient," Jordie said.

"I'm gonna let that go," Hawthorne responded with a half-smile. "Did you find anything?"

"Not on Dr. Mindy," Jordie said. "We don't have a record of anyone named Mindy living in PV, much less dying here."

"Well, hell," Hawthorne responded, taking and releasing a deep breath.

"There was a David Mendez that died here about four years ago," Jordie added. "He was found at the bottom of a canyon, not far from his house. Could that be the guy?"

Hawthorne went flush. "Did you say Mendez?"

"Yeah," Jordie answered. "Dr. David Mendez. I've got it right here."

"Will you send me the info on him?" Hawthorne asked, still not believing what he was hearing.

"Sure," Jordie said. "There's not much. The only contact listed is someone named Devon Mendez. Must be his daughter or something. She lives, or at least lived, in Westwood. I can give you the number that's in the file if you want."

Hawthorne knew it already but agreed anyway. "Yes, please. I owe you!"

"Indeed, you do," Jordie responded. "You know where to find me."

Hawthorne faked a laugh as he hung up. "Oh, hell!" he said after. The article was already in. He couldn't call it back now. Devon hadn't said anything about this. She was not going to be happy.

TWENTY

THE BREEZE ACROSS THE DECK WAS NICE. IT WAS LIGHT, AND cool and dry. Not far away, a light crackling fire burned in a small, rectangular fire pit encased in glass and embedded with small stones. It didn't provide enough warmth to cut the chill, but it added a welcome ambience for a cool Friday morning.

Colusa's table had a magnificent view of tall pines on the mountainside in front of him. Thirty feet below, a rushing river cut its way through a narrow valley. Aspen trees, which would soon be a glorious autumn gold accented the riverbanks. He looked forward to the color change.

Every deep breath brought cool, clean, pine-scented air into Colusa's lungs. He was dressed in a heavy, white, terry cloth robe, tied at the waist. On the table, a white porcelain coffee cup rested within the circular ridge of a small saucer. When the cup was filled, it contained black coffee, two sugar cubes, and precisely one teaspoon of milk.

Colusa examined the cup, and realizing it needed to be refilled, made a small gesture toward the house. A young man dressed in a starched blue uniform came over and attended to Colusa's coffee cup. "I'll take my breakfast now."

"Right away, sir."

Colusa had five newspapers folded neatly on his table. He read the same five papers each day, in the same order. He started with the *New York Times*, then moved to the *Washington Post*, the *Chicago Tribune*, the *Atlanta Journal-Constitution*, and finally the *Los Angeles Tribune*.

The young man laid a beautifully arranged plate of fruit, pastries, and scrambled eggs in front of Colusa just as he was picking up the *L.A. Tribune*. Colusa made his way through the headlines, most of which were repeats of what he'd already read. He flipped past the sports section. He could not have cared less about sports. He then came to the California section and began eating as he perused the various articles.

One in particular looked interesting and unusual: "Monterey Child Claims Memories of Past Life," by Todd Hawthorne. Colusa began the article with mere passive interest over breakfast. By the time he'd finished reading, however, his appetite had been replaced by the flush feeling of the blood running from his head.

"What the f—?" he whispered aloud. He jumped when the young man interrupted him.

"More coffee, sir?" the young man asked.

"No, I'm fine," Colusa said, waving the young man away. He rubbed a hand across his mouth and reread the article.

Kids dream. They dream by day, and they dream at night. Most of the time, the dreams are just that. But what happens when the dreams get a little too close to creepy for comfort?

That is what seems to have happened with five-year old Callie Schroeder of Monterey, California. From the time she has been old enough to speak, she has been talking about memories of a life she has never led, at least as far as anyone can tell.

'Her first words were Mama and Dada, like any child,' says her mother, Peg. 'But when she was three, she started having dreams about falling. I had no idea what to do. Her father died when she was two and I thought this was related to that.' But then, things became stranger.

'After Callie turned four,' Peg continued, 'she started

95

calling for a friend named Foot Foot. I had no idea what a Foot Foot was. It was not anything that came from our house.' Around the same time, Callie started talking about having another family. She said that she and her mother died in a car wreck when she was thirteen. In the child's chilling rendition, she could only hear her mother scream during the event. She says they hit the ground and died.

In the life before, the child's name was Claire, although present day Callie cannot remember the last name. She recalls that she lived by the ocean, but died in the mountains, where it smelled like pine. Her alleged death came on a day that her father made some important breakthrough at work.

The latest report from Callie apparently involves a man named Dr. Mindy, who perhaps lived in Palos Verdes, California, and was killed when a bald man with glasses pushed him over a cliff. There is no indication of what that event has to do with Callie's life, past or present.

While Callie's story is odd and fascinating, she seems clearly dialed into something above and beyond. Her mother has reached out to Dr. Devon Mendez, an expert in Los Angeles, for further study, but for now, one can only ask, 'Who was Claire, who was Foot Foot, who was Dr. Mindy, and who was the bald man with glasses who killed him?' Perhaps the answers to those questions will help us solve the riddle of Callie Schroeder.

Colusa couldn't finish his coffee. He simply stared at the paper. He had never heard of Peg or Callie Schroeder, and he didn't know anyone named Claire. But he did know Dr. Mindy. He knew him as David Mendez.

There was no way on the planet that this girl could possibly know anything about him and what he did. She was not out there that morning. No one was. He was too careful about that, or so he thought. Could he have missed something? The little girl did describe the event. Colusa was a bald man with glasses, and he'd killed Dr. Mendez. But then again, Monterey was nowhere near Palos Verdes. How could she have known? Colusa closed his eyes and began rehashing every detail of his actions that morning.

❖ ❖ ❖

The old man kept a meticulous routine. He left his house promptly ten minutes before sunrise each day, walked two blocks along the street and joined a dirt trail on the edge of a cliff as the eastern sky began to show some color. He walked for ten minutes along the trail atop the ocean bluffs, turned and retraced his route home. From Colusa's observations, neither the old man's neighbors nor anyone else on or across the street from the dirt path were active at that hour.

On that day, sunrise was at six fifteen a.m. Colusa looked at his watch and noted that the old man had probably just left his house. He shifted on the bench to give himself a better view of the area where the old man would first reach the dirt trail. A few minutes later, the man entered the trail right on schedule.

The information given to him said that the old man was Dr. David Mendez, and he was seventy-five years old. He was apparently some kind of scientist, not that it mattered to Colusa. He seemed in decent shape for an old guy, but definitely not an ass-kicker type. Colusa was certain he could get up close to this one without any problems.

Mendez had thinning white hair that was longer than that of most men his age, and at this time of morning, it was uncombed. He also seemed used to walking but had obviously been slowed in recent years by the affliction of old joints. He was wearing khaki pants pulled high over a light flannel shirt covered by a green windbreaker.

Colusa had been watching the man for several days. Earlier in the week, he'd picked a particular spot along the trail that passed very close to the edge of the cliff. Each day, he noted the amount of time it took for Mendez to cover the distance between the trail's head and that spot. Each day, it was about the same. On the day of the kill, when the old man was about one minute from the spot, Colusa stood and began walking toward him.

Colusa reached his chosen position and stopped when Mendez was about twenty feet away. He stood still and pretended to admire the ocean view. As Mendez walked by, Colusa abruptly moved to the left and stretched his right arm out. Colusa's right hand hit the old man square in the left shoulder and he squeezed in a fist full of jacket. Before Mendez could process the situation, Colusa pulled the old man toward him then gave him a hard shove.

Colusa was not a strong man, but he didn't need to be. He simply needed to catch an old man off guard and cause him to move about three feet to his right. He also had to take care that the old man did not grab him in a panic and pull him down too. Thus, Colusa's' push had to be quick and with enough force to take the old man off balance and drive him to the edge of the cliff. Gravity would do the rest.

Colusa's hit was perfect, and Mendez never saw it coming. The direct sideward impact on the shoulder caused Mendez' head to flop hard to the left. A powerful new momentum in the direction of the cliff overcame what little forward motion he had. Mendez lost his balance. His feet began to cross over one another. He tripped over a small bush and opened his hands, reaching outward desperately trying to grab onto something, but there was nothing there. Colusa anticipated this and began walking away, removing himself as a target.

Mendez made no sound as he approached the steep bluff, but his arms continued to flail as his right foot crossed behind his left. His right foot made another involuntary step to the side but there was no ground to stand on. By the time Mendez disappeared over the cliff, Colusa had reached the street. He crossed and continued walking until he reached the space between two houses. He ducked behind a bush and waited for the chaos to develop.

Minutes later, the scene was overrun with lights, and sirens, and people looking over the cliff. He walked out from between the houses unnoticed. His car was parked around a corner. He pressed a button on the fob, climbed in, and drove away.

❖ ❖ ❖

Colusa opened his eyes, convinced he had seen everything around him that morning and that there was no young girl out there. He didn't understand what was going on, but concluded that he didn't care about the how, he only cared about what and the who. If the girl knew too much, she was a threat—period.

The reporter and the doctor were threats too. They would have to go. Colusa didn't need anyone poking around in search of a bald man with glasses. But that could wait. Right now, he needed to keep the little girl from talking again.

Colusa gestured and the young man appeared. "I must leave for two days. Please pack me appropriately. The weather will be moderately cool."

"Yes, sir," the young man said. "Will you be needing help with your travel arrangements?"

"No, I will handle those personally, but I'll need my things ready within two hours."

"Absolutely, sir."

According to the arrangement, Colusa had three more days to complete the next phase of the plan, so he had some time. Colusa looked back at the article. He began thinking about how best to end Callie Schroeder.

TWENTY-ONE

MASTEN WAS SITTING AT HIS DESK FINISHING A LATTE WHEN he saw the article. He'd branched out this morning. *I should have stuck with coffee.* The latte was too creamy. Hands shaking, he placed the covered paper cup on his desk and rubbed his face. The story largely tracked what he'd heard in Monterey, except for the Dr. Mindy part. He hadn't heard that, and it was concerning.

Dr. David Mendez had once been like a father to him. The Los Angeles County Sheriff's Department never figured out whether he died accidentally or otherwise. They assumed it was an accident. He wondered if by Dr. Mindy the child could be referring to Dr. Mendez. He shook his head and scowled. *Fool,* he scolded himself. *Don't allow yourself to be sucked into this nonsense.* Still, he couldn't help but wonder.

He folded the paper and picked up his phone.

"Megan," he said when his assistant answered. "Do me a favor and see if you can find anything on a person named Dr. Mindy that once lived in Rancho Palos Verdes. He apparently died some time ago. No questions. Just let me know what you find ASAP."

Masten hung up and put his chin in the palm of one hand. His other five fingers tapped out a nervous rhythm on the top of his desk.

Masten's thoughts next turned to legal liability and all that comes with it. *The reporter used the child's name, for Christ sakes! And Devon's! Was Devon so reckless that she would put the university in such jeopardy? And what was she doing talking to a reporter in the first place? That was the last thing anybody ever needed.*

The lawsuit that was no doubt just around the corner would raise the profile of this whole affair well beyond Masten's comfort level. This needed to go away quickly and quietly. On another, deeper level, though, he wrestled with his need to speak with the girl again.

The ringing phone interrupted his thoughts. It was Megan. She couldn't find anyone with the last name Mindy living in the Palos Verdes area now, or at any time previously. Masten thanked her and instructed her to keep the matter quiet. "And get me Devon on the phone!" he shouted as he hung up.

His day had been derailed. It would consist of nothing but the article and the aftermath, and it would run long. He stared at his desk and continued the irritated tapping of his fingers. He made a snap decision. Tomorrow, he would head back to Monterey—this time, without an appointment.

❖ ❖ ❖

Devon was at her desk going over next week's lecture notes when Megan called her. Masten was immediately patched in.

"Who in the hell is Todd Hawthorne?" he shouted.

Devon was stunned. Masten had never yelled at her before. "I don't really know," she sputtered. "He's some kind of reporter. I met him a few nights ago in a bar." She heard how that sounded and started back-paddling. "It's not like that. We just sat next to each other and talked. Then we went our separate ways." She knew she was leaving out some of the story.

"Well, whatever you talked about certainly got him

motivated," Masten said.

Devon was confused. "I don't know what that means? What are you talking about?"

"Have you seen today's paper?" Masten asked, slowing his words like a parent scolding a child.

"No," Devon answered. "I don't read newspapers. I read the news online." She raised her eyebrows. *What the hell is going on?*

"Don't play games with me," Masten barked.

"I'm not."

Masten took a breath. He wasn't sure what to believe. "Your barstool buddy wrote an article about the girl we met in Monterey."

"What!" Now it was Devon's turn to yell.

"You heard me," Masten said. "Pull it up *online.*" He hung up hoping the contempt in his voice would hit the mark.

Devon put the phone down and sat for a moment, her eyes wandering around the office. She hit the spacebar on her keyboard, entered a password and clicked on a search engine. The article was on her screen in less than two minutes. She was slack jawed in less than two more. When she snapped out of it, she hurt a knuckle snatching her phone from the nearby table.

"You asshole!" she shouted when Hawthorne picked up. "Why would you do that? You used me!" she shouted. "I liked you and you used it against me! I'm an idiot, but you—you are a horrible person. Do you hear me? You are a loathsome human being!" Devon was shouting louder than she ever had in her life. "Now," she yelled. "I get to go try and undo this situation and see if I can salvage my career and that little girl's life! Do you realize what you've done?"

Devon hung up before Hawthorne was able to say a word. For the first time in her life, she didn't care how the message was received. She paced around her apartment, gritting her teeth so hard she could see her jaw muscles flex in the bathroom mirror.

Hawthorne had a tough hide, as was necessary in his business, but even he was taken aback by Devon's rant. He took a breath and hit the redial icon.

"Yeah," Devon yelled, still irate.

"Listen," he said. "I'm a reporter. I told you I was a reporter. I told you I get paid for the stories I write, not just for being on staff at the paper. Only a complete dumbass would talk to a reporter thinking that the conversation would stay just between them. Is that what you thought?"

"I thought you were a decent person who was genuinely interested in my work," she said. "I guess I was wrong. I guess it was just the martinis. I won't make that mistake again, Mr. Reporter."

"Devon!" he shouted. "This is what I do!"

"What is what you do?" She shouted back. "Find nice people and take advantage of them? That's a shitty line of work!"

"Oh, piss off Ms. 'I See Dead People.' Give me a break! Besides, I helped you! I raised the profile of your program! You should be thanking me!"

"Thanking you?" Devon shouted. "Are you serious? Can you be that stupid? You've ruined me! Wait! Wait! I think you are that stupid! You don't know anything. You write small time news articles about corrupt city council members, big deal! Here's a news flash for you Ace—Nobody reads them! It's no wonder you've never had a real story!"

The arguing stopped for a moment, then it started again.

"And here's the other thing I know," Devon said, still shouting, but with a palpable coldness that was not there before. "I don't ever want to see you again! You got that? Stay the hell away from me and stay the hell away from the Schroeders!"

With that, Devon hung up and continued pacing. She dreaded the thought, but she had to go back to Monterey and explain this to Peg in person.

Hawthorne stared at his phone for a few moments then walked to the desk in his hotel room. He opened the paper folder he received when checking in and pulled out the key to the minibar.

Twenty-two

WHEN COLUSA'S PLANE LANDED IN SAN JOSE, HE EXITED AS fast as he could, sped through the airport, and took the short shuttle ride to pick up his rental car. Traffic was heavy. It was, after all, California, where it seemed that everyone over here, had to get over there. And later in the day, everyone over there would have to come back to over here.

Once out of San Jose, however, the 101 opened up and Colusa made excellent time. He liked that. About thirty miles later, he slowed a bit as he passed through the small town of Gilroy. Colusa had never heard of Gilroy, but apparently, according to multiple signs, the place was the garlic capital of the world. Colusa enjoyed fine food and supposed that a town could do worse.

But it wasn't dinnertime when Colusa drove through, so the time between hello and goodbye to Gilroy was just a few minutes. He pressed forward and entered Monterey less than an hour later.

He'd been thinking about what had to be done and how it needed to be done. Killing was easy. Covering a killing was not.

And offing a five-year-old girl with some recent notoriety came with a litany of challenges. She couldn't just disappear. The whole country would come looking. He couldn't do anything that was obviously sinister; that would just reinforce her story and shine a light on some mysterious killer. *No thanks.*

It had to be an accident. But what kind of accidents do young children have? Drowning was a big one, but his research told him there was no water near enough for a young child to reach. There was always poison, but there was no way he could get into the house to set that up properly.

Colusa had no answers when he reached the house. He decided to watch and let the answer come to him. One option didn't take terribly long. A small gas meter near the garage of a neighboring house shined like a lighthouse on a dark ocean night. Explosions were his new thing, he guessed. He could do one more. And if he had to take out others in the process, well, that was that.

He spent about half an hour in his car pretending to fiddle with a map and feigning several arguments on the telephone. But he was mapping out the possible pipelines in his head. Colusa now had a good picture of the layout of the front yard of the house but saw no gas meter. He knew nothing of the back but expected that was where he would find what he needed.

He knew that driving up and down the street in front of someone's house was one thing. Hiking around the back was quite another. He pulled up a map of the neighborhood on his phone and studied the layout.

An hour later, Colusa drove to a neighboring street and parked. There was a narrow greenbelt that ran behind the house where the girl lived. He saw that as a lucky break. It was getting late, and no one was out and about, except one old man walking his dog. Colusa waved as the old man passed. The greenbelt was heavily treed, so he had plenty of cover. The house he was after was the third one in.

Colusa made his way down a small dirt trail canopied by pines. After several long minutes, he arrived behind the house. He recognized it from the color and the style of siding. The backyard, if one could call it that, was large. It had very little grass, however, just one terraced area. The rest seemed to be made of reddish gravel trails winding through manicured topiaries of short shrubs and various coastal oak, pine, and cypress trees. One of the trails led to a full-sized tennis court surrounded by a chain link fence coated with green plastic that helped it blend in better with the natural surroundings.

The bushes provided great cover. Colusa could lie behind them unnoticed for as long as he needed. He belly-crawled his way to the nearest shrub, and from there popped his head up occasionally to continue studying the lay of the land.

Just before the tennis court, the flat grassy area continued across the gravel trail to a smaller grassy area with a swing set. Behind the swing set, the manicured bushes curved around along the edge of the greenbelt. It was perfect.

He waited. And he watched. And he waited. By the time Colusa convinced himself that it might be safe to move forward, he had been lying on his belly, looking through the bushes, for another hour.

He saw no activity in the house, so he jumped up from behind the shrub and raced forward into the yard. A neglected juniper tree gave him just enough cover to go still and silent near the house, once again lying flat on his stomach. Decorative bulbs in trees and backyard lights gave him enough to see what he needed to see: the natural gas meter just beside the wooden frame of the back deck. The piping came up from the ground and went back into the ground, but that was okay. He didn't need much, and he knew which was which. He took a mental picture and had what he came for.

Colusa pushed up from his stomach into a sort of Balasana yoga position—ironically, he had to note, the "child's pose." The stretching it caused felt good. He lifted his body and moved onto all fours. He remained low under the juniper.

Colusa then crawled back across the lawn. When he was far enough away, he stood up as best he could and limped, half bent, back down the greenbelt. When he was almost at the end, a man's voice shouted, "Hey! What are you doing back there? Get the hell out of there!" The man started to approach, and Colusa picked up his pace. He made it to his car and sped away before the man reached him.

He wound his way through the neighborhood before crossing a main road and turning left onto a small road that led him to the valet lane of a high-end hotel. The building was a turn of the century Mediterranean villa, with a stark white stucco exterior and red Spanish tile roof. The inside featured fine imported marble, stunning stained-glass features, and richly finished woods. It was just Colusa's style, and it had the added benefit of being only ten minutes away from the little girl's house.

Once checked into his suite, Colusa walked down to the hotel bar. He sat down in a chair near a crackling fire and ordered a gimlet, made specifically with Hendricks's gin. Two young men sat on stools at the main bar. They did not notice him. At this stage of his life, however, he was used to it. Colusa couldn't recall one time in his life when he attracted the interested attention of another person. Such things were just not part of his reality. Perhaps that fact played a role in how he got to where he was, but it didn't matter now.

He finished the last bit of his drink and took a short walk around the hotel grounds. He checked his watch and thought through his plan. He had figured out a decent means. Now he needed to pin down the opportunity. He needed to know the girl's schedule.

TWENTY-THREE

COLUSA PARKED NEAR PEG'S HOUSE EARLY THE NEXT morning. Waiting and watching. He just needed an opportunity. The garage door opened as he sat, and a small SUV backed into the street. Colusa followed at a distance as the car made its way through the neighborhood. Peg stopped in front of an elementary school and got out with a young girl and an older boy. She took them both inside the school. Other parents were doing the same with kids of varying ages.

Colusa watched as two yellow school buses came in and parked beside the curb next to the concrete walkway into the building. He wondered why school busses and children were at school on a Saturday.

He sat and he waited, and he thought, and he watched the buses. Peg pulled away in her car a short time later, just before a group of older students came out of the entrance and cut a disorderly path toward the bus doors. After another half hour, the buses were loaded and pulled away. The area was then quiet.

An older couple walked by, and their dog hiked its leg on Colusa's tire. Otherwise, there was no activity on the street in front of the school. He knew that Callie Schroeder was inside. He saw her go. He'd never make it into the school though without ending up on the national news, so he continued to sit and wait. He rolled his windows down a little so he could better hear any noise or chatter that came from the front doors. As his eyelids grew heavy, he struggled between the varied shapes of the cumulus clouds he could see out the windshield and the darkness that activated the unrelated images in his brain.

Finally, he closed his eyes and laid his head back against the car seat. With the windows cracked, he felt and heard the gentle breeze blow through the coastal live oaks lining the road. He smelled the faint fragrance of a nearby wisteria vine. And against the otherwise silent background, he heard birds whistling their messages to other nearby birds. And he heard the other birds whistle their responses.

Colusa had just dozed off when his phone gave a short, sharp whistle. The contrast with the birds in the background was enough to awaken him. He looked down and read the text. His brain was still sluggish, so he read it again. It said what he thought it said. He had been given a green light for phase three, but he still had time. And he would use that time to fix the immediate threat.

He drew in a deep breath of the salty, sweet-smelling air then exhaled. The silence was broken by the inelegant sound of two more buses lumbering up to the front of the school. This time, the children boarding were young. Very young. Someone shouted for the pre-K group to collect near one bus and for the kinder and first grade group to gather at the other. It was Colusa's lucky day. He sat up in his seat and shook off the doze dust that had collected in his head. When the buses pulled away, he followed along. Close, but not too close.

The slow speed of the convoy allowed Colusa to take in the scenery along the way, including a marina with hundreds of white boats to his right. Some were large and others were small. Some were sailboats and some were luxury power cruisers. Some were just well-worn fishing boats.

Colusa had thought some about buying a boat one day. He

liked the idea of a catamaran. It would need to be big enough to have a cabin down below with wonderful teak finishings and a lounging couch out on the transom. Maybe he could keep a couple of deck hands around for company. The idea was nice, at least in theory.

The view of the boats began to disappear as the concrete wall to his right rose higher and higher. Colusa followed the school buses into a tunnel. Once inside, the cars around him began to honk their horns. It was irritating, like kids shouting in an empty room just to hear the echo. Colusa couldn't tell why the tunnel was there in the first place. It didn't go under any water. It just went under several buildings and maybe a park.

When he emerged a few minutes later, he could see the bay again. A large rock jetty protected another collection of boats. The road curved to the right then back to the left. A few blocks later, the buses stopped and made a sharp right turn, followed by a left onto Cannery Row. A waterfront park with hordes of people in black wetsuits carrying scuba gear caught his attention. That was not something he saw every day.

Colusa followed the buses as they made their way along the bay's edge. A couple of restaurants, hotels, and a small art gallery were nestled near an area with chain-link fencing that surrounded old concrete ruins of a fishing industry that had used the space in the not-too-distant past. He thought it odd to see such a developed town with multi-million-dollar oceanfront lots that looked as junky as a dressed up third-world landfill. The contrast was confusing.

Farther up the street, however, development took over. Here the street was lined with hotels, restaurants, and shops of all kinds—candy and ice cream shops, T-shirt shops, jewelry shops, a couple of general stores and, of course, the ubiquitous coffee shop. The road bustled with tourists trying to hit each one.

The buses finally stopped at a point where the straight part of the street ended and made a hard left. Colusa noted that Cannery Row ended at that point. He waited for a few minutes and watched as the kids began to get off the buses and collect in front of the building. The scene was chaos. With chaos, though, came opportunity. Perhaps a new means would present itself. He waited as long as he could before passing the buses and making the left. Even assassins had to find parking.

When he turned, he saw a blue banner paying homage to John Steinbeck hanging from a large wooden pole. At the next left, he saw a similar banner recognizing Ed Ricketts. He made another left into a parking lot, paid the fare, and walked around the block to the aquarium entrance where the buses were parked.

He loitered around for a bit, hoping to hear the child's name called, but he had no such luck. He decided to go inside and get the lay of the land. She was coming to him. He just needed to be patient.

TWENTY-FOUR

DEVON ARRIVED BACK IN MONTEREY STILL PISSED OFF AT Hawthorne. The early weekend drive sucked as did the rest of the circumstances. Her career was over. Nonetheless, she dutifully called Peg and told her she needed to meet as soon as possible. It was about Callie. Peg said she was doing some weekend catch up at her office and that she could see her when she arrived.

When Devon pulled into the parking lot, she found an open space reserved for patients of Monterey Ophthalmology Associates. She entered the building and didn't know quite what to do. There was no receptionist at the desk, so Devon called out. "Hello?"

Peg appeared wearing jeans and a white long-sleeved shirt. She pushed her thin glasses onto the top of her head. "Dr. Mendez," she said with more than a little concern in her voice. "Come back this way. We can talk in my office."

Devon followed her down the hall and into a small room with a desk and two plain chairs in front of it. Several anatomical eye models rested on two credenzas under her window. Various framed diplomas and certifications hung on the wall behind her desk.

"So, what's so urgent?" Peg asked as she shut her office door. She motioned for Devon to sit in one of the small, plain chairs, while she took a seat in the larger, more comfortable chair behind the desk.

"Did you see the *L.A. Tribune* yesterday?" Devon asked.

"No," Peg said. "I don't get any newspapers. I don't have time to read them. Why?"

"There is an article in yesterday's paper," Devon began after clearing her throat, "that talks about Callie and her experiences."

Peg cocked her head, confused.

Devon paused. "Peg, it identifies Callie by name. Hell, it identifies you by name. I promise you, Peg, I had nothing to ..."

"Wait, what?" Peg interrupted, razor sharp.

"Yes," Devon nodded, her eyes shifting between Peg's face and the floor. It was all she could do.

Peg sat motionless for a moment and began to shake her head. She pressed three fingers against her forehead as she continued to nod. She then jerked an open hand in Devon's direction.

"Who wrote this article?" she asked, her tone as sharp as before. "And how did they get the information? I thought our conversations were strictly confidential."

"They are," Devon said, still unable to focus directly on Peg's eyes. "The reporter got the information from you."

"What!" Peg shouted. "I never spoke with a reporter!"

"You did," Devon said. "You just didn't know he was a reporter."

"What?" Peg shouted again.

"There was a man that visited you yesterday," Devon said, now fidgeting with a pen that was lying on the desk.

"Yes," Peg recalled. "He said he was a colleague of yours."

"He's not," Devon said. "He's a reporter for the *L.A. Tribune.*"

Peg sat in stunned silence for a few moments. "Well, how in the hell did he get our information?"

"Um," Devon squirmed. "That's on me."

"What do you mean 'that's on you,'" Peg shot back. "What's

on you?"

"I met him in a bar. We were drinking and I started talking about my work. I mentioned Callie's case—though I didn't use any names! But the next day he played me to get just enough, I guess, to figure it out. Peg, I am so sorry."

Peg was fuming now.

"This is unbelievable!" she shouted. "So let me get this straight. My daughter is now the subject of an article in one of the world's top newspapers because of some school girl crush you have on a slimy newspaper reporter? Do I have that right?"

Devon stared down at her feet. She finally just nodded.

"And you say I am mentioned by name, too?"

Devon nodded again.

Peg's breathing was becoming more rapid, but she remained in her chair. She rested the side of her head against a fist and stared out the window. The room became silent—even more uncomfortable than before. She finally moved and threw up her hands.

"Well, what do we do?" she barked.

"I don't know," Devon said. "Where is Callie now?"

"On a Saturday field trip to the aquarium," Peg responded. "Why?"

"I don't know," Devon said again. "I just ..."

"I'll deal with Callie when I am done here," Peg said. "I think you have done quite enough. And the man you brought with you to my house—is he your boss?"

"Yes," Devon said.

"Well, I intend to speak with him as well. Understood?"

"Yes, ma'am." Devon looked down again.

❖ ❖ ❖

Hawthorne spent the better part of the morning emptying what was left of the mini bar. He hit it hard after the argument with Devon the day before. A brief consideration of the tab crossed his mind, but then passed as soon as he replayed the "never want to see you again" part of the argument. At one point, he decided that he couldn't possibly stay standing or seated any longer, so he lay down on the bed.

The bed started spinning. Or he did. Something started spinning, and Hawthorne felt the drinker's dash coming on strong. He rushed to the bathroom and knelt in front of the toilet. Vomiting was a little like putting on a wet swimsuit. Once one got past the initial shock, the rest wasn't so bad.

He rested on his knees, hugging the bowl, until the fluid in his inner ear stabilized. With two meals and an entire mini bar subtracted, he was finally able to raise his head to the height of the bathroom counter. The pink and orange splots of God knows what around the rim of the bowl didn't help matters, but he ignored them and made his way back to the bed.

The spinning was much better, but his conscience was not. He hadn't meant to cause trouble or ruin careers or lives. He just had a job to do. If he knew something, his job was to write about it. That's how he got paid, and that's how a free society remained free. There was no big conspiracy. He was a professional loudmouth, and he needed an article. He had been upfront about that. At least, he thought he had.

Guilt fought with his eyelids. Eyelids open led to a stressful place where he owed a couple of significant apologies. Eyelids closed took him to a peaceful place that joined fantasy and reality into an odd movie seen only through the brain and not the eyes. He eventually succumbed to the latter.

An hour or so later, a distant barking brought him slowly out of a dream where he was standing on the end of a long wooden dock watching a boat pull away. The folks on the boat were motioning for him to join, but he couldn't. He wanted to, but he couldn't. He didn't know why. As he stared at the boat, a small child beside him reached up and grabbed his hand. The two then turned and walked back up the dock. All the while, the barking continued.

When he managed to open his eyes, he could still hear the faint barking sound, finally realizing it was coming from a spooled-up sea lion in the bay, just outside his window. He looked around the room and took stock of himself.

REVISITED

The dream was still vivid and left him in one of those strange moods that some dreams can. It wasn't sad. It was nostalgic. It was comfortable, and he wanted to go back. He had no idea who was on the boat or where they were going, but he missed them. At the same time, he felt the comfort and satisfaction of having the child by his side.

Hawthorne didn't have that, but maybe he wanted it. *Was that what the dream was about? Who knows?* He lay in his bed and stared up at the small canopy that hung over the first couple of feet of the mattress. It was pink with floral patterns that were primarily the same pink, maybe a little darker, but also had touches of green and yellow worked in. Definitely not his style.

As his consciousness began to return to normal, he realized that his breath could probably cut through a steel beam. He lived with it for a few minutes, until he couldn't stand it anymore. He side-crawled to the edge of the bed and sat up. The dizziness was there, but short-lived.

Hawthorne put his head in his hands for a moment or two, braced himself against the nightstand, and pushed to his feet. His hand stayed in place on the nightstand until he caught his balance. He walked to the bathroom and took care of his laser breath.

Feeling much more civilized, he stretched out on one of the cushions in the corner bay window of his room. Cannery Row was three floors below and he watched people moving up and down the storied street. In the distance, the sea lion, or one of his friends, continued to bark.

The dream was still present and affecting his mood. He put his chin in the palm of a hand and looked out the window and up the hill that rose before him. That part of town wasn't beachy. It was mostly old tin warehouse-looking buildings surrounded by trees. He didn't know trees, but there were several different kinds.

No matter the view though, Hawthorne kept coming back to the dream. Not the specifics of it, but the way it made him feel. He had only one interpretation.

He walked to the nightstand and grabbed his phone, then

returned to the bay window. After a few deep breaths and some staring at the screen, he touched a number on his recents list. He looked at the sky as the number began to ring.

The call went to voicemail, which he knew was BS. She was there. He hit the hang up icon and touched the number again. The phone rang again. The result was the same and his response was the same. Devon picked up on the third try.

"What do you want?" she asked.

Hawthorne paused when he realized he hadn't thought any of this through. He didn't know what he wanted. Maybe he just needed to talk, and maybe for a long time.

"Listen," he finally said. "Please listen."

All he got in return was a loud sigh, but at least it wasn't a hang-up. Hawthorne made a face as he scratched his head. He started to speak a couple of times but just ended up sighing in frustration.

"I'm so sorry," he finally said. "I can get a little, ah, passionate about my work. I really didn't mean to cause problems. I didn't."

"Well, you did. My career is shot. My boss has to try and salvage what can be saved of the University's reputation and mitigate the legal exposure. My subject's mother doesn't want me to have any further contact, and I'm in Monterey on my own nickel. All in all, I'd say you caused a few problems. Wouldn't you agree?"

"Wait," Hawthorne said. "You're in Monterey?"

"That's what you heard in all of that?" Devon shouted. "You just don't get it, do you? A breach like the one you caused is a very big deal. You've basically ended years' worth of research and cost the University a shit ton of money in the process. Money they will no doubt come looking to recover from your paper." She enunciated the last two words for Hawthorne's benefit.

Hawthorne hadn't thought of that. *Was that true? Whatever.* As long as his information wasn't false. And Devon did give him the information. It's not like he stole it or made anything up, though he would have to take a liberal view of his meeting with

Peg.

"Where are you staying?"

"What?" Devon responded. *This guy is just not hearing me.* "Uh, the International or something like that. Why?"

"I don't know," Hawthorne said. "I'm sorry. I just want to help."

"I think you've helped enough." Devon's tone softened after a pause. "Look, the damage has been done. I don't have a clue how to fix it, and I don't think it's fixable anyway."

"I could apologize," Hawthorne offered.

"Next to me, you're probably the last person Peg wants to hear from right now."

There was a long silence on both ends of the line. Hawthorne stared out his window at the street below. Devon stared at a wall in her hotel room.

"Listen," Devon said. "I gotta go."

As she spoke, several big yellow school buses with the words "Monterey Peninsula Unified School District" written on the side passed under Hawthorne's window. "Well," he said, watching the buses, "for what it's worth, I *am* sorry. If there is something I can do, let me know."

"Yeah," Devon replied. "I can't imagine there is."

"It looks like there's some big field trip headed to the aquarium," Hawthorne changed the subject, not really wanting to hang up. "Several school buses just passed by headed that way. Those were the days, huh? Looks like fun."

"I'm sure it is," Devon said. "Callie is probably on one of them. Peg said she was going on a field trip." She cringed when she realized she'd done it again.

"Really?" Hawthorne almost yelled.

"No!" Devon shouted back. "What possible good could come from you talking to Callie?"

"I feel bad," he said. "I just want to apologize."

"Peg isn't there, and Callie doesn't know anything yet," Devon shot back.

"Even better," Hawthorne said. "I can catch her and explain in advance. I'll call you back later."

"Wait!" Devon shouted. "No! Do *not* approach Callie. And why would you call me back later?"

She was talking to dead air. Hawthorne had hung up.

"Shit!" Devon yelled as she slammed her phone down on the desk. "Shit, shit, shit."

She grabbed a room key and headed for the door. The aquarium was five minutes away.

TWENTY-FIVE

"ALRIGHT EVERYONE! MRS. ROBINSON'S CLASS, LET'S LINE UP right here." A young, blonde tour guide wearing a blue fleece jacket made an up and down gesture with both hands out in front of her. One side of her jacket had a white nametag with the word "Emily" on it. On the other was the small circular emblem of the Monterey Bay Aquarium.

"Single file, guys," a teacher instructed, as she walked down the line of students, gently forming them up. "Let's stay out of everyone else's way."

Devon watched the whole chaotic procession. She stood close by, looking for both Callie and Hawthorne. She spotted Callie. She didn't see Hawthorne. Callie was about five kids back from the front, holding hands with a friend.

"Callie and Sydney," Mrs. Robinson said. "You guys can team up again inside, but let's get in line for now, okay."

Both girls moved into the line.

"Now class," the guide shouted. "Before we go in, I want to give you a little history of the Aquarium, okay?"

Devon noticed that some of the kids heard the words, some

did not, as they were too busy looking around or whispering to one another.

"The Monterey Bay Aquarium is located on Cannery Row," the guide shouted. "Who can tell me why this is called Cannery Row?"

Only a couple of hands went up. The guide called on a boy near the back of the line.

"I thought it was canary, like the bird."

"No," the guide corrected. "It's cannery. Anyone else?"

A girl's hand went up.

"Did they make cans?"

"Nope," the guide said patiently. "This street used to be named Ocean View Avenue. A long time ago, back in the eighteen hundreds, Monterey was a whaling town. Fishermen would catch huge whales and use their blubber for fuel oil and their bones to make things."

"Eew," was the most common response, followed by a couple of "cools" from the boys. Eew was right, Devon thought, still looking around for Hawthorne.

"Then," the guide continued, "when the eighteen hundreds turned into the nineteen hundreds, fishermen started catching sardines. They caught millions of sardines and brought them here to be cleaned and chopped and put into cans. People back then, especially soldiers in World War One, ate lots and lots of sardines. And this building was one of the places where tons of sardines were put into cans. So, they called it a cannery. And since there were other places that put sardines into cans along this road, it began to be called Cannery Row. Pretty cool, huh?"

"Not really," one kid shouted back with a crinkled nose.

Ignoring him, the guide pointed toward a black, rectangular painting on the wall of the building with large white letters that read "Portola Brand Sardines." "This sign right here represents one of the brands of sardines that used to be canned here. Once we get inside, you'll see that the building is still a big industrial warehouse that has been turned into a bunch of cool fish tanks. And you will see huge schools of sardines! Who's ready to go inside?"

The hands came up now. With the help of Mrs. Robinson and an older boy at the back, Callie's class made it through the large, metal-framed glass entrance. Devon recognized the boy from the framed pictures in Peg's house. It was Callie's brother Max.

Devon kept her distance but followed the group inside. Everyone's eyes immediately focused upward on the life-sized replica of an orca hanging from the ceiling.

"Wow," they whispered.

"Okay, guys, let's all gather up here." The guide held up a hand and waved it side to side. "That is an orca, also called a killer whale. It's actually a dolphin, not a whale, but we will get to that in a little while. Right now, behind me here, are three old boilers that used to provide heat to the canning operations. There are no fish in there, but ... follow me this way." She held up a hand and beckoned with two fingers.

The group, Devon in tow, rounded the corner and immediately saw a huge, twenty-eight-foot-tall tank brimming with sea life and giant stalks of sea kelp.

"This is the kelp forest," the guide said. "It is open at the top and fed by water straight from the ocean. In this tank are things that you would find swimming around right out there in the bay."

A large gray shark with spots swam by. Several kids squealed. Others pointed and called out in delight. One kid, who probably needed more responsible parents, started humming the theme from Jaws.

As the kids stared at the glass and watched the endless activity inside, a diver wearing a wetsuit, mask, flippers, and a long hose extending to the surface, descended and began feeding the fish. He quickly became the most popular attraction in the exhibit. He was surrounded by more species of fish than the best marine biologist in the world could identify. The kids didn't care. They focused only on the endless movement.

The guide identified as many of the fish as she could and offered tidbits of information on each. She then made a "gather up" gesture with her arms and hands.

"Alright guys, we're going to move around the corner and

have a look at the kinds of things that live on a coral reef. Keep your eyes open for things you might recognize."

Devon watched Callie bustle along with her classmates. The guide led them to a large glass aquarium with an elaborate coral reef system inside. The reef was a busy place. Tropical fish of all kinds and sizes were swimming in every direction.

"Don't touch the glass, guys," Mrs. Robinson called out.

Max stood behind Callie. He put his hands on her shoulders, but she shrugged him off.

"Stop it!" Callie whispered as she twisted away. Devon had to giggle a little.

Embarrassed, Max simply stood with his hands in his pockets. He didn't know what else to do with them. The entire class worked to get a closer vantage point against the glass pane. Whoever was in front, wasn't there for long.

The movement and the dozens of species mesmerized and energized the kids. Everyone, of course, recognized Nemo the clownfish, and the kids' excitement level went off the charts for a bit. Once the excitement of fame wore off, however, they also noticed the blacktip reef shark, which was a hit, along with several species of strange cuttlefish, which all looked like miniature squids of varying shapes.

The line of kids then moved to the next room where they were met by a curious sheep crab pecking against the glass. A chambered nautilus propelled its way across the tank, sucking water in and blowing water out. When the nautilus cleared off, one kid spotted a large California moray eel lurking in a small hole in the reef. Its eyes were wide and intense, and its mouth rhythmically opened and closed in a way that would scare the hell out of anyone swimming near it. The sight was met with the expected squeals and pecking on the glass.

"Don't touch the glass, guys," Mrs. Robinson warned again.

Some kids listened. Most didn't. A smooth and quick movement caught Devon's attention. A man appeared from around the corner wearing black pants, a black shirt with a white tab collar, and a black jacket. He seemed particularly focused on Max. The man smiled at Max briefly and winked, then leaned his shoulder against the glass and crossed his arms. He cleared his throat and began to sing.

"When the eel's big and green, and it looks a-very mean, that's a moray.

With a-teeth big and sharp if he bites, a-you play a harp, that's a moray."

Max looked bemused as the old man laughed. The kids giggled and pointed. Mrs. Robinson and the guide simply looked at one another. Devon wondered if she should call someone. Dean Martin rolled in his grave. Devon watched as the still laughing old man walked closer and thrust his hand toward Max. "I'm Reverend Cloyden White."

Max returned the gesture with a weak, dead-fish handshake. "I'm Max," he said, avoiding eye contact.

"Max," the reverend said as he gave a solid bent elbow fist cheer. "That's a sturdy name. No doubt for a sturdy boy." The reverend gave an impish wink as he spoke.

Devon was taken with the man's accent. It sounded very Irish.

The reverend glanced to the left and right then leaned in toward Max as if he had a big secret.

"So, tell me, Max, what are you doing here? You're twice as big as the biggest child in the group." The reverend leaned in farther and held the back of his hand to the corner of his mouth. "Held back a bit, were we?" He chuckled at his own joke. Devon smiled at that one.

Max wasn't amused. "I'm here with my sister," he responded. "I get service points at my school."

"Ah, service points," the reverend nodded and contemplated. He raised an eyebrow and brought back the impish smile. "Can we cash them in for something good?"

"No," Max said, exasperated. "It's for extracurricular credit that helps with …." Max crinkled his brow. "I'm sorry, who are you again?"

"Good for you, Max," Devon said under her breath, trying not to be noticed.

The reverend raised his eyebrows and nodded. His mouth

turned down. "A spine, young Max, a spine," he said as he strolled past Max and patted him on the shoulder. "Keep that handy."

Reverend White then walked to the end of the exhibit, turned right and disappeared from view. Devon watched him go and shook her head. *What the hell?* She could tell Max was confused as well. She saw Max turn back toward Callie and work his way behind her again. Again, Callie shoved him off.

"Oh, Max!" Max and Devon both jerked their heads to the left and saw that Reverend White was peeking around from the end of the exhibit.

"You should really work on that handshake," Reverend White said as he winked and pointed a curved finger. "The meek may inherit the earth, but it's gonna be a while."

Reverend White then ducked back behind the exhibit and out of view. Max looked around, not quite sure what to focus on.

"Oh, and Max!" The reverend peeked out again. "One last thing. Mind your gas, lad."

Max looked down and behind himself, then back up again, confused and a little horrified. He hadn't done anything. The reverend was gone, but the echo of his laughter remained for a few moments. Max shook his head and moved in again behind Callie, with the same result.

Devon, still keeping her distance, walked to where the old man slipped away behind the exhibit. He was gone. "What in the hell was that?" she whispered. She stood for a moment then resumed her position at the outer edge of Callie's group. She had still not seen Hawthorne.

Twenty-Six

HAWTHORNE MADE IT TO THE AQUARIUM A FEW MINUTES before Devon. There were kids everywhere and he had no idea which group was Callie's. He didn't know if she was inside or still outside. He decided to check the former. He was sure he'd find her there at some point. He walked through the main entrance and stood in line behind several enthusiastic tourists. He swayed anxiously as he waited for his turn at the blonde-stained wooden desk. Once there, he pulled out a credit card and groaned as the nice lady swiped fifty bucks from his minimal assets in exchange for a ticket.

Entrance granted, he walked past the desk and looked around. The place was packed. Most of the kids in the entrance were pointing at the life-sized killer whale replica hanging overhead. Hawthorne stopped and looked at it, too. *Damn, those things are big!*

He continued through the crowd and turned right at his first opportunity. The sea otter exhibit caught his eye, and he watched as the furry creatures rolled, wrestled, and back floated around the exhibit. They were quite the showmen.

He continued down the wing. The things hanging from the ceiling were amazing. Above was a full-sized replica of a gray whale. *And I thought the orca was big!* Not much else was there, though, just a cafe, a gift shop, and a restroom. A walking bridge on the second level connected one part of the aquarium to another. Hanging next to the bridge was another large orca, but it seemed to Hawthorne that this one had a much happier look on its face.

He reversed course and pressed past the crowd by the entrance and made his way to a wing on the opposite side. The first thing to catch his eye on this side was a giant exhibit filled with extraordinarily tall kelp plants. The thick acrylic windows were paned with black dividers and looked to hold an ocean of seawater. The thing must have been thirty feet tall.

A school of sardines shot by in a flash. He thought it was ironic. Humble sardines built this wondrous place. He'd read enough to know that sardines and John Steinbeck put Monterey on the map.

Other creatures swam by including a large leopard shark that approached the window to look back at the tourists. Hawthorne's eyes were diverted from the shark when he noticed a diver in the kelp forest, tossing out fish parts to the collective occupants. The diver was swarmed by hundreds of fish, some colorful, some plain, but none of which Hawthorne could identify.

He turned his attention to the others looking at the exhibit. There were throngs of young school children, who had arrived on the buses. Still though, there was no sign of Callie. Or Devon. He knew she'd followed him.

He moved on after a few minutes, walking past a wall to his right and entering an area with several touch pools. That seemed like the right track. One of the tanks had sea plants with creeping snails and decorator crabs available to touch. A small placard identified each plant and creature.

Another tank housed several red sea cucumbers, a red abalone, and purple sea urchins in shallow troughs accessible to curious little fingers. Bat rays were in a deeper tank. Hawthorne thought they looked like alien space fighter craft out of a science fiction movie. The charcoal gray rays swam in circles around the perimeter as kids and parents dipped their hands in the water to feel the rays' smooth, but tough skin. Hawthorne still didn't see Callie or Devon.

Behind him, and across the atrium was a large, clear acrylic tunnel with a substantial gathering inside. As he neared, Hawthorne could hear the excited screams of the kids as large waves of water crashed over the tunnel and washed down into the tide pool outside.

He walked to one end and examined as many faces as he could. At last, he saw Callie sitting on a narrow concrete bench near the middle of the crowd. He scanned the area for Devon.

He walked into the tunnel, bumping past parents and kids, who were all looking up. About thirty seconds later, the next crash washed over, and the kids squealed again. He couldn't help but look up himself as he continued his way into the tunnel.

Hawthorne bumped headlong into a smaller man wearing a tan canvas jacket and a white ball cap with the words "Monterey Bay" embroidered in blue lettering with a small print of a gray whale. The man had clearly just purchased the cap in one of the aquarium gift shops.

"Excuse me," Hawthorne said. "I'm sorry."

Through his thin, black-framed glasses, the man's eyes locked onto Hawthorne's and stared straight through him for a moment. The man's expression was blank. After a couple of seconds, Hawthorne raised an eyebrow. The man had eyes like a shark. They were dark and cold and not a window to any kind of soul inside. The guy gave Hawthorne the creeps.

The man shifted his eyes away from Hawthorne and moved past without a word. Hawthorne turned and watched as he passed. He appeared to be alone. He was not holding the hand of a child and didn't seem to be associated with any of the children there. Hawthorne shook his head as the man disappeared into the crowd near the end of the tunnel. The next person to catch Hawthorne's eye was Devon. She was craning her neck, trying to see through the throngs of children and parents. Hawthorne quickened his pace. Devon saw him too and moved to place herself directly in front of him.

"Whatcha doin'?" she said in singsong voice, but not one that betrayed her irritation.

"Whatcha think I'm doin'?" Hawthorne sang back.

Hawthorne hadn't *seen* Devon since that night in the bar, and he had filled the gaps in his memory with constructs of his own mind, drawn mostly from the sound of her voice over the phone. He was not too far off, but he was off. Mostly, he had forgotten how she smelled. Even in this sea of humanity he could smell the delicate scent of tuberose and plumeria. She smelled like she had just walked out of a Hawaiian flower garden. Her hair was long and healthy, which he remembered, but he had forgotten how vibrant her eyes were.

"Todd," Devon said. "Seriously, you can't talk to Callie."

"I caused this," Hawthorne argued. "I'm going to try and make it right."

"Do you even know which one she is?"

"Really? There were pictures all over the house." The tone and look were unmistakable. *I'm not an idiot.* "She's sitting against the glass, just there," Hawthorne pointed to the exact place.

Devon realized that it was much easier to be angry with someone from a distance. Direct eye contact tended to smooth the emotional edges, especially when someone was looking for forgiveness. Her tone softened. "What's the point, Todd? What's done is done. You'll only make it worse. Just let her mother handle it."

As she finished her sentence, Devon and Hawthorne, like half of the room, jumped at the piercing and irritating protests of several fire alarms. It took several seconds before the alarm processed with the crowd, but soon the throngs were gathering in confusion in the common spaces of the aquarium. The parents with children held their kids near to them.

The children on the field trip were much less organized. Several guides began shouting their teachers' names.

"Mrs. Eubank's class! Gather over here!"

"Mr. Ritchie's class! Line up here!"

Devon was several feet and quite a few people away from Callie when the alarm went off. She lost Callie in the chaos. As she frantically looked through, over and under the crowd, she heard a voice call out, "Mrs. Robinson's class! This way!"

Devon saw a small girl start crying in the chaos. She watched Hawthorne pick her up and ask her something. A minute later, Hawthorne delivered the girl to her teacher. He patted the girl's back as he walked away. The moment was not lost on Devon.

Devon heard the call for Ms. Robinson's class again and followed the voice. She saw their guide standing near a wall abutting the kelp forest exhibit. She saw a panicked Max walking in that direction as well, looking at the face of every child he saw. The next voice Devon heard belonged to a man.

"Callie!" the voice called out. "Callie Schroeder!"

❖ ❖ ❖

Masten had just made it through the entrance of the aquarium when the fire alarm went off. He was already in a bad mood. True to her word, Peg called while he was driving and gave him more than an earful. He'd deal with Devon later.

It took a few minutes, but all at once people started filing out the doors. Bucking traffic, Masten pressed forward through the crowd. Most people seemed to be coming from his left, so he continued in that direction. An aquarium employee stopped him near the kelp forest and told him that everyone needed to exit the building. Masten lied and said he was looking for his family. The young man moved on.

Masten found it difficult to concentrate on anything with the lights flashing and the whining, grinding sound of the alarms screaming. Not long after the alarms started, they stopped. The silence was filled with a loudspeaker announcement that told everyone to exit the building while the alarms were being investigated.

Like everyone present, Masten's ears were ringing. He poked a finger in each and moved them around a little. When he removed his fingers from his ears, he heard a man's voice calling out for a person named Callie. He cocked his head slightly and heard it again.

"Callie Schroeder!" That got Masten's attention.

He began moving toward the voice but couldn't see the person who was calling. Too many people were hustling the other way around him. He moved closer to the sound, but he still couldn't see who was calling out to the child.

A tall, white-haired man in a black clerical outfit bumped into Masten on his way past.

"Sorry, lad," the man said.

"No problem," Masten grumbled as he continued listening and turning his head.

"Looking for someone, are we?" the priest said with a very distinct Irish accent.

Masten snapped around.

"Uh, my family," Masten lied, waving a hand.

"Who ya got with ya?" the priest asked. "I can see over most here. I'll help you look."

Masten was trying to remain casual, but he was growing impatient with the sudden, unwanted attention.

"Really," Masten said with a hint of testy in his voice. "It's okay."

The priest shrugged and insisted, "No trouble at all."

He put a hand on Masten's shoulder and started looking around himself. "What are they wearing?"

A clearing in the crowd opened and Masten caught a glimpse of Callie across the room near one of the tide pools. She was walking toward a man who was about eight feet from her and wearing a tan jacket and white hat. The man's hand was extended.

Masten suddenly heard another person begin calling out Callie's name. The hall had cleared out a bit, and Masten turned his head to look. He could see that it was a teenaged boy, also searching for Callie. He was waving his arms in the air, and his eyes were darting left and right as he scanned the room, yelling her name. He recognized the boy from pictures he'd seen at Callie's house. It was Callie's brother.

Max couldn't see Callie, who was around a corner from him, but Masten could see them both. He watched the boy put an open hand beside his mouth and shout Callie's name. He also watched as Callie drew closer to the man in the white hat. The reverend watched as well.

"Is this Callie part of your family?" he asked.

"No," Masten answered.

"Are ya sure, lad?" the reverend asked, pointing at Callie with his thumb. "You stopped looking around the second you saw her."

Masten jerked his head to look at the reverend, who was looking back with a grin. When Masten broke the stare and looked back around, Callie was gone. He turned his head back and forth for a second or two then looked back at the reverend. His eyes were wider.

"The girl walked off with the man who was calling her," Reverend White said, pointing in that direction.

Masten's eyes grew even wider.

"Is that a bad thing?" White asked.

"I don't know," Masten answered. "Where's the boy?"

Max was still calling out and Masten caught a view of him again. He brushed past several other people heading toward the exit and gripped Max by the shoulder. Reverend White remained in tow.

"Son," Masten asked. "Is your sister here with someone other than you?"

Max pulled away from the grip. "My sister?" he asked, half surprised and half skeptical. "How do you know my sister?"

Masten was curt. "I met her briefly at your house a couple of days ago," he said. "But I need to know. Is your sister here with anyone but you?"

"She's here with her class," Max said. "Who are you?"

Masten ignored the question. "Is her teacher a man?"

Max pointed at Ms. Robinson. "No," he said. "Her teacher is right over there."

Masten tightened his lips. "Come on!" he said, his tone urgent.

Twenty-Seven

"I WORK WITH YOUR MOM," COLUSA SAID. "SHE SENT ME TO pick you up."

Colusa hadn't spent any time around kids and figured that he would just keep it as vague as possible.

"Where's Max?" Callie asked.

Colusa's eyes shifted. "Max?" he asked.

"My brother," Callie said, somewhere between confused and suspicious.

"Oh, Max!" Colusa improvised, processing the information. He gave a quick chuckle and pointed toward the ceiling of the aquarium. "My ears are still ringing from the noise. Your mom said he was fine. She was mostly worried about you."

Callie took Colusa's hand. "Where are we going?" she asked.

"Right now," he said, "I just want to get you out of here, and make sure you're safe."

Colusa began to lead Callie toward the exit. The crowd grew as people gathered at the door. They were walking toward the main entrance when Colusa heard someone shout.

"Callie!" the voice called out. "Callie, come here!"
Colusa looked around and began walking faster.

❖ ❖ ❖

Masten and Reverend White followed Max. Max was searching for his sister. He approached a large desk that was labeled "Membership and Tours."

"Hang on," he said.

Max pulled himself onto the table and stood up. He looked around the area and saw Callie, about six feet away, with a man, headed toward the door.

"She's over there!" he called out. He then yelled for his sister.

The man started walking faster toward the doors with Callie in tow.

"Help!" Max yelled. "Security! He's got my sister!"

Max was pointing at Callie. His scream caught the attention of a security guard standing at the door, and several visitors headed toward the exit. Two of them were very near his sister.

❖ ❖ ❖

In the chaos that ensued after the fire alarm, Devon and Hawthorne lost sight of Callie. Not knowing Callie was being pursued, the two hustled toward the exit. They were just past the boilers when they heard a loud, shrill call for help. The unusual tone made them both look back. They saw a boy standing on a table yelling something about someone having his sister.

Hawthorne turned his attention from the boy to the line of people leaving the building. It didn't take him long to spot Callie holding the hand of the shark-eyed man in the white hat he'd bumped into earlier in the wave exhibition.

He flipped the back of his hand toward Devon.

"This way!" he shouted.

Devon followed Hawthorne as they ran around the crowd. The pushing and shoving near the door was obnoxious. Devon used the chaos to her advantage, taking the lead and clearing a path to the glass doors.

She and Hawthorne planted themselves in front of the doors, getting bumped and pushed by every passerby in the place, but still managing to set up a sort of checkpoint. A moment later, Colusa and Callie approached, making a brisk line for the exit.

"Right there!" Devon shouted at Hawthorne as she pointed.

Hawthorne put himself between Callie and the door as Devon pushed and shoved her way over. For the second time that day, Hawthorne stared into the shark eyes of the man in the white ball cap. Devon could feel her heart racing and her blood pressure rising.

"Hey!" she shouted, still swimming through the crowd. She was in full fight mode. "Let go of the girl, now!" she screamed.

Colusa caught a glimpse of Devon coming over the crowd. He slumped down and turned Callie back away from the exit. As Colusa attempted to retreat, Devon jumped toward him, swiping with a hand. She caught the edge of Colusa's white hat. Colusa scowled in response to the indignity and shot Devon an angry look.

The look had no effect on her. Devon pounced and managed to grab Colusa from behind.

The power in Devon's grip surprised and frightened Colusa. He pivoted to face her and shoved Devon backwards into Hawthorne. Still in fight mode, Devon used Hawthorne's body to regain her balance, but then immediately pushed him aside. The split-second delay provided Colusa the opportunity he needed.

"Come back here!" Devon leapt above the crowd trying to see Colusa. But he was gone as quickly as he had appeared. After a couple of jumps, she fell back onto Hawthorne again. Hawthorne was shocked by Devon's open rage.

"What the hell?" Hawthorne shouted, shaking now. "Are you trying to get yourself killed? That guy has the eyes of a psychopath."

"No," Devon responded still searching the crowd. "That guy has the eyes of a coward."

❖ ❖ ❖

With a firm grip on Callie's hand, Colusa hugged the wall of the gift store near the entrance and backtracked farther into the aquarium. He rounded the corner and made a beeline for a set of stairs just ahead. The stairs led to an elevated walkway that crossed over to a separate section of exhibits.

Colusa sped along the walkway, dragging Callie in tow. Callie was distracted by a large, happy-looking orca model hanging from the ceiling. She remembered seeing it when her class was on the lower floor. The orca, though, was now beside them. Colusa tugged on Callie's hand and yanked her along.

Max was still calling out for his sister. Callie heard her name and stopped and turned. Colusa heard it too and yanked on her again. Callie dragged her feet as she looked down and behind her, where she saw Max on the floor below. She waved at him with her free hand.

The motion caught Max's eye and he looked up.

"She's up there!" he shouted, pointing. Max took off towards the stairs, with Masten running right behind. Devon and Hawthorne heard Max yell and looked up. They too began running for the stairs. Reverend White simply stood by and watched all the sudden, frantic motion.

Colusa knew he was being pursued and picked up his pace. He was right at Callie's speed limit but tugged on her and told her to hurry. Callie didn't understand why a friend of her mother's would be so mean, but he was an adult, so she did her best to keep up.

When they had crossed the walkway, walls and structure forced Colusa and Callie to go left. They passed a stairwell leading down, and Colusa made a quick mental note. He was sure there was another, better way out, and that he could lose the others in the maze of exhibits and slip away.

The two turned right a little farther up and entered a small room featuring a turtle exhibit and a puffin exhibit. Callie had not been to this area with her class, so she was taking in all she saw as best she could. Colusa yanked her hand again.

He pulled her through another passageway, and they entered a darkened room with an enormous floor to ceiling tank that was labeled Open Sea.

Callie was mesmerized. Near the clear acrylic wall, a huge school of sardines swam in a synchronized, constant circular fashion, but the shape of the overall school was continuously changing, much like clouds change shapes in the sky. Beneath the school, several large tunas meandered back and forth with none of the sardines' organization.

A large stingray passed, followed by a larger hammerhead shark. Callie watched for a second or two while Colusa's eyes darted around, looking for the next best spot. He pulled Callie forward into an area around a corner that featured several kinds of jellyfish. That room was a dead end, however, and Colusa, frustrated, began making his way back the way he came.

Max and Masten reached the entrance to the Open Sea exhibit just seconds before Devon and Hawthorne.

"Jim!" Devon called out. "What are you doing here?"

"I should ask you the same thing," was Masten's slow, pompous response.

It took a moment for Devon to process the fact that Masten was standing next to Max. She guessed Peg called Masten just like she said she would, though she didn't understand what Masten was doing at the aquarium. Peg clearly told him Callie would be there, but she still wondered why Masten would come. She shook it off.

"Some guy has Callie," Devon said. "She's the girl you met the other day …"

"I know who Callie is," Masten interrupted, with a quick, raised eyebrow.

"Yes, sir," Devon apologized. "Of course."

"I believe this is her brother," Masten said, pointing at Max. "Is that right?"

"Yes, sir." Max nodded.

"What's your name, son?"

"Max Schroeder."

"Do you have any idea who this man is with your sister?"

Masten asked.

"No, sir," was Max's quick response.

❖ ❖ ❖

Colusa heard people talking and stopped. He looked at Callie and put an upright index finger against his lips. He then peeked around the corner saw the group standing in front of the only exit he'd seen. Colusa had boxed himself in. He pulled his head back and leaned against the wall, still gripping Callie's hand. His focus now was on trying to hear what was being said.

He wanted to get out quietly but knew the group wouldn't leave until they searched the area. Then he heard someone say those exact words. Colusa had no clean escape, so he decided to make a messy one. At least he would have the element of surprise. He reached into his jacket and pulled out a .38 caliber, snub-nosed pistol. He let go of Callie's hand and put his arm around her shoulder.

He thought about offing her right there, but the place was already crawling with first responders. He'd never get out— probably not alive and certainly not anonymously. He needed the girl for insurance.

Colusa drew Callie in close and put the barrel of his gun against her head. Callie tried to turn and look. Colusa used the gun barrel to push her head back around.

Callie began to shake. She didn't know the specific significance of a gun, but she now realized that the man was no friend.

When Callie started to cry, Colusa put his free hand over her mouth. He maneuvered around the corner with Callie in front of him and called out so that everyone saw, and everyone was clear about the hand he was playing.

"I want everybody back," Colusa said. "I'm going through that exit." He pointed to the only way out with the barrel of his gun. Then he put it back against Callie's head. "If anyone follows or anyone yells," he said, "the outcome is obvious." Colusa continued to hobble toward the exit holding Callie close.

"Very good," he said as the crowd opened up for him.

"Why are you doing this?" Devon shouted. She started to leap forward but Hawthorne raised an arm to stop her.

"Just stay calm and let us pass," Colusa said, ignoring the question.

Hawthorne and Devon moved aside to Colusa's left and Max and Masten moved over to Colusa's right. Devon looked across to Masten, who was studying the situation. Her eyes then cut to Max.

Colusa and Callie moved out of the Open Sea exhibit and off to the left toward the stairs. A few moments later, Colusa spoke, although no one could see him.

"Just stay where you are," he said. "Don't try to follow."

A long silence followed those words. No one heard anything more. The group looked around at each other for a minute or two, motionless except for their heads and eyes. When enough time seemed to pass, they all began to move out of the room. There was nowhere to go but the stairwell.

Glancing around at the others, Devon led the group down the stairs. Hawthorne, then Max, then Masten followed her. Halfway down, the stairwell made a ninety-degree turn to the right. Devon couldn't help but pick up the pace a bit in the transition.

When she reached the bottom, she gasped a little when she saw an unconscious man lying on the floor. A tall, white-haired priest was standing over him and had a protective arm around Callie. The others followed after.

"I think he must have hit his head on something," Reverend White said with a wink.

Max ran over and took a knee in front of Callie, checking her out as best he could. Devon stepped in behind Callie and put her hands on the child's shoulders. She dropped her head down to Callie's and asked if she was okay.

Masten cocked his head back and from side to side, as if he were trying to pop his neck. He looked at the man on the floor then stepped over him. He took another step and extended a hand to Reverend White.

"Thank you," Masten said. "It's a long story, but I am a dean at Griffith University. My young colleague here has some serious explaining to do, but this is clearly the university's problem, and I'll take it from here." Masten cast an angry look toward Devon, who took the look and passed it along to Hawthorne.

"Let me take these children home," Masten said, putting a gentle hand on both Callie and Max. "I have a lot to explain to their mother."

Devon stared at the floor and Hawthorne alternated between the floor and Devon.

"Go then," Reverend White said. "We'll clean up things here."

Masten led Max and Callie out of the aquarium, across the street, and to a parking lot around the corner. Without a word, they got into Masten's car and drove slowly away from Cannery Row.

❖ ❖ ❖

Back inside the aquarium, Devon, Hawthorne and Reverend White looked at one another uncomfortably for a long while. Reverend White finally broke the silence.

"You two carry on," he said. "I'll take care of this one."

He kicked a little at Colusa's shoulder as he spoke, and Colusa writhed at the stimulus.

"Thank you," Hawthorne said. "But I think we'll stay. I'll feel much better when I see this guy hauled away by the cops."

"Suit yourself, lad," Reverend White said.

A few minutes later, Colusa was fully conscious and cuffed. He was escorted out of the building by four armed officers and was on his way to the station for printing and booking.

"Not a bad day's work," Reverend White said as Colusa was frog-marched out of the exit. "I've earned a pint for much less. Care to join me?"

Devon and Hawthorne shrugged at each other and followed the reverend to the exit. They could both use a drink. A few minutes later, the three of them were in a restaurant, sitting at a table next to a glass window watching sea otters do the backstroke just a few yards away.

TWENTY-EIGHT

MAX AND CALLIE SAT IN THE BACK SEAT OF MASTEN'S CAR. Callie was still shaking from the encounter with Colusa. Max held her hand as he stared out the back passenger's side window.

Masten was quiet too. He entered the address Max gave him, drove past the large marina, through the tunnel, and turned on a street that passed a pretty park with a horseshoe-shaped lake. He was taking his time.

Masten hadn't really figured out what to do. On one hand, the information he heard at the Schroeder house and read in the article was chilling. Callie said several things that could have come straight out of his daughter's mouth. *How in the hell did she know those things?* He wanted to know more—more about Callie, and more about Dr. Mindy. He didn't buy Devon's cockamamie explanation, but something was going on.

On the other hand, Callie was five and needed to go home. The best course was to take her there. It was settled. For a minute anyway. But then it came back around. *What about the things she said?* Masten shook his head as he stared out the windshield. He let out an aggravated sigh and purposefully took a wrong turn. He needed more time to think.

According to Masten's phone, the house was four minutes away, seven minutes away, then ten. Max started to say something about the detour but kept silent.

Just take her home. Masten finally listened to himself, but now he was fourteen minutes away. He let the GPS recalculate then followed the directions back into the leafy neighborhood where they passed a small Presbyterian church. As architecture goes, the church was nothing special, just a plain, single-story, tan and brick building with a reddish, gabled roof. It apparently affected Callie though.

"Mister?" she asked. "Why do you want to blow up churches?"

Masten went pale. Callie was sitting behind him, so he couldn't see her well when he jerked his head around. But he could see Max and looked him square in the eyes. Max remained silent, looking confused. When Masten looked forward again, his eyes were on everything but the road.

"I don't know what you mean," Masten managed to sputter. "You must be thinking of someone else." He knew the response sounded lame, but an epic battle between panic and logic had begun in Masten's head. *There's simply no way.* He told himself to stay calm, and he was slowly starting to get there, when Callie spoke again.

"I miss Foot Foot," she said. "Do you still have him?"

With that, panic won the battle. Masten slammed on the brakes and stopped the car about a quarter of a mile from the house. He didn't look back and he didn't say a word. He lowered his head and stared forward. The street was not busy. No cars came or went at first, although he wouldn't have cared if they did. A car pulled up behind them and stopped. They had been sitting in the road for a long time.

"Hey, mister," Max said with a timid edge.

Max didn't get to finish his thought. Masten put the car back in gear and drove forward. He had to know more. "If you two want to see your mom again," Masten said, looking back through the rearview mirror, "you will stay still, and you will stay quiet.

Understood?" It was the only leverage he could think of.

Max and Callie looked at each other without saying a word. A big tear fell from Callie's eye, and she started shaking again. Max tightened his grip on her hand.

Masten drove past the Schroeders' house and circled around the block, leaving the neighborhood via the street that brought him there. He continued until he reached a main street that led him to a highway.

❖ ❖ ❖

Colusa never made it to the squad car, much less the station. Sunny climates didn't agree much with his skin. Depending on the time of year, the central coast of California could be cool, overcast, and foggy, or sunny and warm. Sometimes it achieved all in the same day. It was sunny when Colusa arrived, though, and he'd bought a small tube of lip balm infused with SPF 50 sunscreen.

He kept it in his back pocket, which is where it was when the officers frisked him. They had already taken his gun when they found the lip balm. One of the officers pulled it out, removed the lid and twisted the rough-edged extender at the bottom. The waxy column rose a little, then the officer put the cap back on and put the tube back in Colusa's rear pocket.

With his hands cuffed behind his back, and the officers holding each of his arms above the elbow, Colusa worked his fingers into his back pocket. He pretended that he was somewhere between struggling and uncomfortable, to distract from what he was doing.

He pulled the tube out of his pocket and felt for the lid. He removed it and rubbed the wax around the wrist of one hand. Then he grabbed the tube with his other hand and did the same thing for the opposite wrist. The combination of small hands and wax lubricant made it easy for him to free one hand from the cuffs. The cuff on the other side was ratcheted down too tightly. But Colusa now had two free hands with a slinging weapon dangling from one.

At that moment, no one would have known that Colusa was not a fighter. His life and livelihood were on the line in equal measures, and that brought a jolt of adrenaline and enterprise. He jerked his right arm back and out of the officer's grip, flipping his right wrist out as hard as he could, turning the loose handcuff into a small metal whip. The cuff struck the officer hard above the bridge of his nose. The cop's vision went blurry, and he fell to his knees, covering his face with his hands.

Colusa hit the other cop. It was more of a slap, but once again, the loose cuff swung out and caught the officer in the head, above his left ear. The second officer was bigger and didn't drop to the ground, but he did let go of Colusa and focused for a moment on the pain in his head. It was all the time Colusa needed.

He ran a few yards up the street past a dilapidated looking cabin with wooden stairs leading up to the front door. He saw a white sign with blue lettering that read, "Coastal Overlook." An arrow pointed in the direction of the bay. He turned and ran down the narrow alleyway. The building on his left was unpainted and unfinished and appeared to be constructed of old barn wood. The building on the right was a continuation of the much nicer white-trimmed, greenish gray structure that supported the sign.

Detail was generally Colusa's business, the aquarium being a rare exception, and even while running from the cops he noticed almost everything around him. The building on his left didn't extend very far back down the alleyway. He noticed a small courtyard of sorts behind it, bordered by two fences. The closest was a short wooden-framed fence with rectangular welded wire in the open sections, and behind that was a taller steel-and-wood-framed fence with chain-link mesh.

A cinder block wall bordered the opposite side of the area. The main features of the courtyard seemed to be a couple of rectangular concrete structures that were each partitioned off into about twelve or fourteen smaller squares. They looked like the ruins of some sort of old raised garden bed.

The courtyard and the building itself, really, seemed out of place to Colusa, like relics from another time. He ran past a small placard with writing on it. He assumed that the placard explained what all of this was, but he didn't have time to stop and read.

"He's down the alley by Ed Ricketts's lab!" He heard one of the officers shout.

Colusa reached the end of the alley and found himself on a wooden deck overlooking Monterey Bay. Below him were the rocks that created the great tide pools when the water was out. The deck, however, only went to the right, so he continued running that way. He saw that the deck was behind a hotel in the greenish gray structure. The short wooden-framed fence with rectangular welded wire continued around behind the hotel. Beyond the fence, fifteen or so feet below, was nothing but rock and sand.

A few yards farther up, there was a square hole in the deck, again bordered by the short wooden-framed fencing with rectangular welded wire. The cutout allowed hotel guests and passersby to view the waves, rocks, and tides below.

Colusa looked down at the rocks and sand and did a quick calculation. He then looked at the myriad windows and doors on the backside of the hotel. The easiest solution would be to head into the hotel and find a place to hide for a while. But he knew that the place would soon be crawling with cops and probably on full lockdown within the hour.

He made his decision. Before the pursuing officers rounded the corner from the alley to the deck, he threw a leg over the short wooden-framed fence. He entered the cutout in a corner, hoping he could shimmy down the large concrete support column to minimize his exposure to the fall.

The plan worked reasonably well. Colusa was able to grab the square column with his legs then do a fire pole slide most of the way down. He lost his grip about four feet above the entering tide and fell the rest of the way. He was bruised by the rock at the base of the column, but he was able to move under the deck and out of sight before the officers passed overhead.

He hugged the coastline under the hotel and a couple of adjacent buildings, staying wet and crawling over a great many large rocks, until he finally reached a sandy beach. He then tried to present himself as organized as he could and walked back up to Cannery Row. He was a few blocks from his car but chose a longer route along one of the much less populated streets to the east. He crossed the bustling main drag as fast as he could, relaxing a bit when the gawking population thinned out.

He arrived at his car in a foul mood with only the girl on his mind. He had her address and he vaguely recalled someone saying they were taking her home. That's where he decided to go.

❖ ❖ ❖

As Colusa approached the neighborhood, a car stopped in the middle of the road stalled his progress. Two tan brick walls capped with red clay Spanish roof tiles flanked the street into the neighborhood. A small black placard on the left wall read "Baja Mesa."

He waited behind the car, fighting the urge to honk and drumming his fingers on the steering wheel for a few seconds. The other car then began to move. Colusa followed the car into the neighborhood and noticed that it turned where his phone told him to turn. He saw three people inside, one man in the driver's seat, an adolescent looking person in the rear passenger side seat, and a small girl in the back seat behind the driver. They looked familiar.

A light bulb went on. The kids in the back were the ones from the museum. The girl he was after was *right there!* Colusa smiled and nodded. This was too easy. He eased off the gas and waited for the car to stop in front of the house. But it didn't. The car passed right by the driveway. Picking up a little speed, it followed the semicircular road around until it reached a straight feeder street, where it made a right. Colusa followed from a distance.

He made the same right and continued behind the car as it turned onto a larger street and onto a highway. Twenty-five minutes later, Colusa did a double take when he saw a large wooden cutout beside the road just outside Salinas. It was an old farmer with a white mustache and cowboy hat holding his lettuce in a suggestive way. A few minutes later, he was following the car onto the 101 headed south.

TWENTY-NINE

HAWTHORNE PICKED UP THE TAB. HE FIGURED IT WAS THE least he could do given the circumstances. The conversation at the table had been dominated by his apologies and remorse for writing the article and putting Callie in danger. Reverend White assured him that he had no way of knowing that a maniac would accost the child. White didn't judge Hawthorne at all for his ambition, even though Hawthorne made it clear that ambition was his primary motivation. White pointed out that the two things might not even be connected. Perhaps the man was just crazy. Hawthorne appreciated the consolation.

After a few drinks, Hawthorne concluded that even though he wasn't religious anymore, if he ever decided to go down that road again, it would be alongside someone like Reverend White. He seemed like a good guy, and he had a real big-picture vibe that Hawthorne appreciated.

When the waiter returned the small, black leatherette folder containing his credit card and the bill, Hawthorne signed and wrote in a generous tip. The reverend had, at least momentarily, lifted a weight from his shoulders.

As the three made their way to the front door of the restaurant, they saw Peg Schroeder run by on foot, headed towards the aquarium. Devon and Hawthorne exchanged quick, confused glances before darting out the door and following.

In the distance, they could see Peg speaking with animated gestures to one of the aquarium employees. They picked up their pace. A minute later they were standing beside her as she questioned the whereabouts of her son and daughter. Neither of them had been dropped off at school by the bus that had brought them to the aquarium earlier in the day.

"Oh, Jesus, Peg, I am so sorry," Devon finally chimed in. "Did no one call you? Dr. Masten took them home after the fire alarm and the other incident."

"What other incident?" Peg asked, still panting in a panic.

The glances that Devon and Hawthorne exchanged now were not confused, but full on *oh, shit.*

Reverend White jumped in and tried to diffuse the situation. "It's okay ma'am," he said. "It's all a bit of a misunderstanding and a grave lack of communication." He raised a disapproving eyebrow toward Devon when he said the last part. "Your children are safe," he continued. "We'll take you to your house."

"I have my own car," Peg snapped.

"We'll follow along," Reverend White said with a wink.

Peg didn't argue. She ran down the street, rounded the block, and got in her car. She exited the parking lot and headed home.

Devon's hotel was only a block away and she demanded, more than requested, that her car be brought around right then. The valet got the picture and returned in record time.

❖ ❖ ❖

Dr. David Mendez' Last Will and Testament was a bit of a mess. In one section, it said that he desired to leave all his earthly possessions to his only child, Devon. In another later section, it said that he desired to leave the scientific center he founded years earlier, the Southern California Institute for Advanced Research, along with all of Mendez' scientific files to his nephew, Steven Eddinghill. In that same section, a short paragraph left a fifty-acre estate he owned in Paso Robles, California, to his protégé, Dr. James Masten.

A brief note accompanying the will explained that Masten

should use his expertise in chemistry to find the perfect varietals of grapes to grow for local winemaking or to sell to the more established wineries farther north in the Napa and Sonoma regions.

As it turned out, Masten did neither. He didn't even know that he owned the place until quite some time later. Eddinghill and the Institute engaged in protracted litigation over the will. Eddinghill argued that the institute and all of its buildings, equipment, furnishings and files were his. The Institute argued that it was organized as a 501(c)3 nonprofit research organization and that no individual could own it. The lower court sided with the Institute, as did the Court of Appeals. Eddinghill ended up with only Mendez' research files and a meaningless title, Vice President of Special Projects.

Devon stayed away from the litigation. She had enough on her plate after her father's death. She inherited his house in Rancho Palos Verdes, the proceeds from a small life insurance policy, and the unenviable task of trying to find various bank accounts with very few records at her disposal. She knew nothing of the house and acreage in Paso Robles. Her father never mentioned it to her. He could be eccentric that way. But in any event, she didn't care.

Masten wasn't a party to the litigation either. The fifty-acre estate was an ancillary issue that was decided alongside the litigation between the Institute and Eddinghill. The first Masten heard that he was mentioned in Mendez' will was when he received a call one day from an attorney looking to complete the transfer of title to the small estate. He was quite surprised by the irony.

Masten had only been to the house once before, with his wife and daughter, at Mendez' invitation. Masten hated the house. The place was such a dump that his wife and daughter refused to stay there and demanded that he book them all into a nice hotel. Masten readily agreed.

Masten loathed the house even more now, but dilapidation wasn't the primary source of his hatred. He hated the house for what it represented—the worst day of his life. Then and now, he hated Mendez for leaving the place to him. He now owned the memory of that horrible day. He thought of declining the bequest, but a complex array of emotions beyond his comprehension wouldn't allow him to do so. He hated Mendez for putting him in that position. He also hated Mendez for suggesting that he take his family there. Had Masten taken his family anywhere else, his wife and daughter would still be alive.

From the day he inherited the house, Masten thought of calling a realtor, but he never got around to it. So, the dump was still his. The knot in his stomach grew and tightened with each mile, but the house was the only place he knew to take the girl where he could find out what he needed, undisturbed.

❖ ❖ ❖

When Devon, Hawthorne, and Reverend White arrived at Peg's house, Peg was already inside calling out for Max and Callie. She didn't receive a response. The front door was open, and the others walked in.

"What the hell is going on?" Peg shouted, looking at Devon. She never once looked at Hawthorne.

"I don't know," Devon said. "Let me call Dr. Masten. I'm sure there's an explanation." The call went straight to voicemail.

Devon's phone rang just as she was about to call Masten again. She recognized the number and walked out of the house and into the front yard to take the call.

"Devon," the voice on the other end said. "This is Steven."

Thirty

THE CALL WITH EDDINGHILL LEFT DEVON PALE. WHEN SHE returned to the house, she found Reverend White trying to reassure a very worried Peg. White did a double take when he saw Devon's face.

"What's the matter, child?" Reverend White asked. "You look like you've seen a ghost."

"Todd, can I talk to you for a minute?" Devon avoided looking at Peg.

The two stepped into the next room.

"We have a big problem."

"What?" Hawthorne asked, now looking worried himself.

"I just got off the phone with my cousin, Steven Eddinghill," Devon said.

"Okay?"

"I think my father is the Dr. Mindy that Callie mentioned," Devon said.

Hawthorne raised an eyebrow. "Why?" he asked.

"Well, for one," Devon said, "Mindy … Mendez? Those are pretty close. But the clincher is this. My dad was a neuroscientist. About five years ago, he was working on a secretive study on the brains of dead people. My cousin was his research assistant."

"Okay?"

Devon continued. "The study found that the subjects' brains both sent and received discrete electrical signals to and from some unknown, outside source. They even half-ass revived one guy who had been dead for three days."

Hawthorne recoiled. "That's way messed up!"

"It is," Devon agreed. "I didn't know anything about it. My father never mentioned his work much.

"But what does any of that have to do with the problem you said we had?"

"The problem," Devon said, "is that there was another scientist working with my father and my cousin. He apparently interpreted the results of the study as proving that there was a god, a creator or whatever. He wanted to release the information to the world. But he and my father disagreed about that interpretation, and my dad was so horrified by the whole thing that he shut the study down and locked away the data so it would never see the light of day. Less than a week later, the other scientist's wife and daughter were killed in a freak car accident not too far outside of Paso Robles."

"Oh, Jesus," Hawthorne said. "That's terrible, but ..."

"It was Dr. Masten, Todd," Devon said bluntly. "The other scientist was Dr. Masten. As in, my boss, Dr. Masten"

Hawthorne was dumbstruck. "I had no idea. That's horrible."

"The accident was horrible, and I knew about that, but there's more," Devon said. Her tone was now more stern than revelatory. "One year to the day after the car wreck, my father was pushed into a canyon in Rancho Palos Verdes and died. I saw the man who pushed him but couldn't describe him enough to help the investigators. They never figured out who did it."

"I'm so sorry, Devon." Hawthorne nodded along as he listened.

"The thing is, though," Devon continued, "When my father

154

died, Steven, my cousin, inherited all of his scientific files, including the ones involving their creepy testing. Right after my father died, the Sheriff's investigators searched his house, but when it came to the files, they didn't know what they were looking at. Nothing in the house seemed to be missing, so they let go of that angle."

"Okay," Hawthorne said.

"Stay with me," Devon responded. "I stayed at my dad's house the night before he was killed. I saw the whole thing from a distance. When I did, I ran to where my father was and left the front door of his house open. Things became chaotic, and I didn't return to the house until the next day."

Hawthorne nodded along.

"The thing is, I didn't remember that I had left the door open until a few days ago. That's another story, but anyway, I called my cousin and asked him to look through his files to see if anything was missing.

When he did, the files and data from the crazy weird study were gone."

"Did your cousin tell the police?" Hawthorne asked.

"No. It's been too long, and it was just a set of files." Devon answered. "The cops wouldn't care about that."

"Why would anyone want to steal files and data from a study like that?" Hawthorne asked.

"The question isn't why, Todd," Devon said. "The question is who. There were only three people on earth who knew about the study: my father, Steven and Masten. My father was dead. Steven inherited the stuff, so he wouldn't need to steal from himself. That just leaves Masten."

The logic hit Hawthorne like a semi-truck. "Holy shit!"

"Holy shit is right," Devon said. "And it gets stranger."

"There's more?" Hawthorne shouted.

"Today is Saturday, right?" Devon said.

"Yeah," Hawthorne responded with a tone of dread.

"Tomorrow will be the five-year anniversary of the accident that killed Masten's wife and kid. And the four-year anniversary of my dad's death."

Hawthorne formed the beginning of an F-bomb, but it trailed off as he thought.

"Devon," he finally said. "None of this makes any sense. The experiment stuff was weird. Cutting edge, maybe, but certainly weird. Then your father turns up dead and files turn up missing. Does that make Masten a murderer? Hell, this could just all be a coincidence. But the fact is none of it explains what Masten is doing with Max and Callie."

"Todd," Devon said with an apologetic tone, like a parent delivering bad news to a child, "Masten's daughter's name was Claire."

A light switched on in Hawthorne's head.

"But there's more," Devon said.

"Jesus, more?"

"Yeah. When my dad died, he owned a small vineyard in Paso Robles. He never said anything about it to me, but guess who he left it to in his will?"

"Your cousin?" Hawthorne asked, dreading the answer.

"Masten." Devon responded.

Hawthorne let the F-bomb form fully this time. It was loud, sustained, and effective, as any good bomb is.

Peg and Reverend White came running in from the other room.

"What?" Peg asked in a panic.

"Is everything all right, my boy?" Reverend White added.

"We have to go!" Hawthorne commanded. "Devon, can you find out where that house is?"

"I'm way ahead of you," Devon said, punching letters on her phone.

"Peg," Hawthorne said, in the calmest voice he could muster, "you need to call the police. They need to be looking for Dr. Masten. I imagine he drove his own car up here, but have them check rentals too, both out of Los Angeles and Monterey."

Eyes wide and confused, Peg nodded in agreement and picked up her phone.

"I don't think Masten intends to harm your kids," Devon said. "I think he may just need a nudge to bring them home. You should stay here in case he does. We'll let you know what we find out."

"I'll stay with you," Reverend White said.

"No, please go with them," Peg said.

She realized how terse her response was. On one level she didn't care, but on another, she didn't want to be rude. The man was simply trying to help.

"I'll be fine," she added in a much softer tone. "I appreciate your offer, but I really need to be alone for a while."

"As you wish, my dear," Reverend White responded. Facing Devon and Hawthorne he asked, "So what are we waiting for?"

❖ ❖ ❖

Devon climbed in behind the wheel of her rental car. Hawthorne rode shotgun, and Reverend White took the back. Devon entered the words 'Paso Robles' into the map on her phone and began following the directions.

"Shit!" Hawthorne yelled when they were barely out of the neighborhood.

"What?" Devon asked.

"Dammit!" Hawthorne reiterated his frustration.

"What?" Now it was Devon's turn to be frustrated.

"We didn't tell Peg anything," Hawthorne said. "We ran out and just told her to call the police about Masten. She doesn't even know we're going to Paso Robles."

"Yeah, we did," Devon challenged.

"No!" Hawthorne pushed back. "You and I talked about it, but she wasn't there. She came in after. She doesn't have any information to give the cops that's going to help them."

"Well," Devon said, "just call."

"Call who?" Hawthorne asked. "The cops? That won't work. We'll give our information to some operator, and it will take the rest of the year for it to trickle down, if it gets there at all. And I'm not calling Peg with any of this. We need to tell her in person. We need to turn around."

"Seriously?" Devon sighed.

"Yes, seriously," Hawthorne said.

Devon found a place to U-turn and backtracked her way to Peg's house. She parked on the street and turned off the car.

"You're up, champ," she said, glancing over at Hawthorne. "You started this. I think I'll just stay in the car."

Hawthorne looked over without saying a word.

"I believe we should all stay in the car," Reverend White chimed in. "Mrs. Schroeder was clearly done with us. I think you can give your information directly to the police when they arrive. I think she would appreciate that."

Devon and Hawthorne didn't disagree. They half nodded to one another and sat tight. Devon began to drum her fingers on the steering wheel. Hawthorne stared out the window. Hopefully, the police would be there soon.

THIRTY-ONE

MASTEN PASSED A GREEN SIGN INDICATING THAT THE NEXT five exits were for Paso Robles. He took Exit 231B, the exit for Fresno and Bakersfield, but he wasn't going that far. He stopped at the light at the end of the exit ramp then turned left onto Highway 46 heading east.

About eight miles down the road, Masten passed a winery housed in a Western-style wooden building painted a deep red. Adjacent to the winery was a prairie cottage, white picket fence and all, painted a bright yellow. He recalled talking to the owner about the fruit-forward bottles they were producing when he'd visited with his wife and daughter five years earlier.

About a half a mile farther, a dirt road intersected the main highway and Masten turned right onto it. On the left, a rusty chain link fence bordered his inherited property. A farm fence supported by red metal poles with white caps lined the right side of the road. A single, dead looking oak tree stood at the base of a hill in front of him.

Masten continued up the road, parked in front of the house, and got out of the car as a cloud of dust kicked up by his tires swirled for a moment then blew away in the wind. He noticed the distinct scent of musky sage coming from the blue salvia clusters nearby. He also noticed the silence. The wind was the only sound he heard.

He studied the small wooden house and was struck by its dilapidation. The low roof was bowed in spots and several of the dirt-encrusted windows were cracked or broken. Streaks of rust ran down the sides of an old air conditioning unit that poked through one of the front windows.

Masten walked to the rear driver's side door and opened it. He motioned for Callie to come with him. Callie looked over at Max, who looked more worried than Callie. Masten glared at Max then back at Callie.

"Do as he says," Max told her.

Callie got out of the car and stood next to Masten.

"You stay put and don't try anything," Masten said, pointing at Max. "Understood?" Masten glared at Max until he was convinced that the boy got the picture. When Max nodded in agreement, Masten closed the car door.

"Come with me," he said to Callie with a look and tone usually reserved for irritated school principals. Masten walked toward the house with one hand on Callie's back. Callie walked forward but kept craning her head back to look at Max, who was doing the same thing from inside the car. When they reached the house, Masten pointed to a patch of dirt next to the unfinished wooden porch and told her to sit down. "Don't move from there," Masten commanded.

Callie nodded and looked up at him, her eyes filling with tears. Masten stepped onto the front porch but paused when it sounded like a wooden plank might crack under his weight. He skirted that area and made his way to the front door, which was slightly open. Masten wondered if itinerant squatters had claimed the place. He knocked three times.

"Hello!" he called out. He waited in silence for a response, but none came. A moment later, he knocked again. "Hello!" He shouted a little louder. But still no one answered. Masten pushed the door all the way open and yelled again. He walked around the place to make sure there was no occupant somewhere else.

"Come on," he said to Callie, snapping his fingers. He stepped off the porch and made his way to the side of the house with Callie in tow. The side looked as run down as the front. There was no fence, no grass, no anything—just dirt and a few weeds.

The back of the house had more of the same dilapidation. They walked a few more yards out to the shed. "Hello!" Masten shouted. "Is anyone here? But the blowing wind was the only sound. Leading Callie back to the front of the house, Masten again stepped onto the porch. He poked his head inside the door and yelled one more time, then motioned for Callie to follow him in.

The inside of the place was stale and smelled of musty carpet. More than a few dead flies dotted the floors. The sound of the wind was faint now and Masten began to feel uncomfortable. A sudden chill ran through his body and goose bumps rose on the skin of his arms.

The only furniture he saw was a tattered cloth sofa in the front room, a small card table in the kitchen, and two metal fold out chairs at the table. He remembered why he wasn't impressed with the place when he visited before. He told Callie to sit down on one of the metal chairs and stay there as he looked around.

The house's single bathroom was dated, with octagonal pink tiles on the floor that continued halfway up the walls, where a dingy yellowish paint took over. A cheap off-white cabinet supported a cheap white sink. Dust and dead bugs collected in the tub.

An empty bedroom was across the hall. Its only features were a few feet of television cable poking through the mangy carpet on the floor and a glob of some kind of greenish goo on the wall. The only other bedroom was farther down. It was empty except for a bare mattress lying on the floor. Both bedroom closets were empty.

Masten motioned to Callie, and they left the house and returned to the shed. Two side-sliding doors met in the middle and were held together with a large, unlocked padlock hanging through the holes in each door's handle. He set the lock on the ground and pulled one of the handles to the side. The door began to slide. Masten let go of the door handle and reached both hands into the small gap he made. He pulled hard on the door, and it opened with a metallic scrape.

The floor of the shed was a solid concrete slab. There was a flat metal door on the ground. Masten pulled a string hanging from above and was surprised when a single, uncovered light bulb clicked on. *Why was the electricity still on?* A length of rope ran from a hook welded to the top of the cellar door and up through a pulley mounted overhead. The free end of the rope hung about halfway between the top of the shed and the floor. Masten grasped the free end of the rope and pulled. The heavy metal door opened.

Masten noticed a cleat welded to a metal brace on the wall of the shed, and he made his way over to it while pulling on the rope. When the cellar door was vertical, Masten twisted the free end of the rope around the cleat and secured the door. He walked to the edge of the open hole in the ground and peered in.

The light in the shed was just enough to reveal all of the steps and about a foot of the surrounding cellar floor. Beyond that it was pitch black. Masten searched for another light source but couldn't find one, so he reached for his phone and turned on the flashlight app. Even with that he could see only an empty floor.

Masten steeled himself and put his hand behind Callie. The two began descending the steps. When they reached the cellar floor, Masten thought he felt something brush across the back of his neck. He jumped back onto the lower step and spun in a panic as he brushed his neck and shoulders with his hands. In his tussle with the cobweb, however, he lost his footing and fell to the ground. He jumped to his feet and cursed out loud. His elbow and hip hurt, but he stood still for a moment and tried to regain his composure. His phone was lying a few feet away, the flashlight beam shining directly upward and revealing a light switch on the sidewall of the cellar.

Masten flipped the switch and the dark cellar lit up. He realized it had once been a wine cellar. It was about the size of an average bedroom. Three of the walls were covered with wooden cabinets filled with crisscrossed panels that created spaces for individual wine bottles. Most of the spaces were empty, but there were a few dusty bottles here and there.

A large oak barrel sat on its end in the middle of the cellar floor with two plain barstools on either side. The cellar was devoid of anything else. It was a simple wine storage space, kept naturally cool by being underground. It was also dusty and stale.

Masten told Callie to find a place and sit down. He didn't care if it was on a stool or on the ground. She chose the ground. He walked back up the stairs and closed the cellar door. He heard banging and screaming as he walked away.

"Let's go," Masten said to Max upon opening the car door.

Max followed the old man without saying a word. In the shed, Masten pulled the rope and opened the cellar door. Callie was sitting on a step near the floor, her face in her hands. She was crying. Max pushed past Masten as he ran down the stairs and knelt down in front of Callie, trying to reassure her that she was okay. He coaxed his sister off the step and walked her toward one of the stools. She clung to him with her arms around his waist and her face buried in his ribs. Max felt her tiny body shaking.

Masten grabbed an empty plastic bucket that was sitting against the shed wall and walked it down the steps. He stared at the two children for several minutes, but neither of them noticed. Callie was still crying, and Max's attention was on her.

Masten cleared his throat. "Listen," he said, "I need to go get some supplies. I'm sure you guys are thirsty and hungry. I'll figure out the bathroom situation when I get back. For now, though, use this."

Masten set the bucket on the cellar floor and turned to walk back up the steps. As he did, a loud crashing sound filled the cellar and the space got darker.

"What the hell was that?" Masten shouted as he jerked around.

He looked up and saw that the outside light at the top of the stairs was no longer there. The metal door was shut. He climbed the stairs and tried in vain to push the door open, but it was locked tight. Masten thought maybe the rope or the cleat had given way, but then he heard a scraping sound coming from the other side of the door. Somebody was there. He pushed again, but it was no use. He banged against the door and shouted, but that was no use either. After a few minutes, he sat down on a step and came to terms with the fact that he was now trapped in the cellar with the two children he kidnapped.

❖ ❖ ❖

Colusa had followed Masten's car from Monterey to the run-down house, hiding in the bushes while Masten was inside. He didn't know who the man was and wondered what the girl was to him. Colusa drew closer when the man took the girl down into the cellar. He made his move when the man took the boy down. Colusa closed the cellar door and shoved a short piece of wood through the handle and an adjacent metal hand-hold to block anyone opening the door from the inside.

The banging and shouting made it hard for Colusa to think. He re-checked the block he'd placed over the cellar door and left the shed. Looking around outside he saw mostly nothing. He had watched the man scour the house and the grounds. Clearly, no one lived here. He wondered who lived here before and why the man brought the girl and the boy to this place, but it didn't really matter to him.

He had almost accomplished his side mission and could complete it at any time, but he needed to think through the collaterals—the old man and the boy. Who were they, and how would this be seen? Murder, without suspicion of murder, was his profession, and this one required some thought.

Colusa climbed the steps to the house's front porch, avoiding the rotten wood, and strolled inside. He cased the house for a few minutes and, convinced he was alone, sat down at one of the card table chairs in the kitchen, staring straight ahead, tapping his knuckles on the tabletop.

He stood up after a few minutes. Restless, he started

rummaging through the cabinet drawers in the kitchen. He was a little surprised to discover there were still things in many of them. One had silverware. One had some old batteries, a small flashlight, a couple of screwdrivers, and some rubber bands. The last drawer was full of old papers. Colusa picked one up and read. It was a years old electric bill addressed to David Mendez. He felt a jolt as the name registered. A small hand-written note on the bill read "paid on 7/2/16 auto." He rifled through more papers. Most were simply collections of very old utility bills. The last one he picked up, though, was an old bank statement, also addressed to David Mendez, but the address was not in Paso Robles, it was in Rancho Palos Verdes.

Colusa stared at the statement for a moment. David Mendez was the old man he'd pushed over the cliff in Rancho Palos Verdes. He'd been hired to do that job by the same person who hired him to do the church jobs.

What in the hell is going on? He was standing in the house of a man he killed four years ago. He had three people trapped in the cellar and only knew who one person was. He walked to a light switch and flipped it. The lights came on. Colusa wondered how a dead man continued to pay his bills four years later. Was this a trap? He began to feel unnerved.

He took a breath and examined several of the old electric bills from the drawer. All of them had the hand-written note that included the word "auto." He looked again at the bank statement. Colusa noticed only the address before, but he now saw that Mendez' account was still flush with cash.

It took only a moment to realize that "auto" meant auto-pay. He noticed that none of the bills were more recent than July 2018. Colusa thought back and recalled that he killed the old man in early September 2018. September 4, to be exact. He recalled because he saw a news report the day after that Amazon stock had reached one trillion dollars. He was heavily invested in Amazon. That was a good day.

Colusa concluded that the electric bill had been drawing remotely out of the bank account, month after month, year after year. When Mendez was alive, he apparently wrote "auto" on his bills. But the bills kept paying even after he was dead. There was just no one to bring them into the house anymore. Since there was no mailbox, he guessed that there was a post office box somewhere in town that had probably started returning the mail to sender years ago.

Colusa rubbed his chin as he looked around the house. The corners of his mouth curled up when the self-congratulations began to set it. Murder, without suspicion of murder, was his game, and he was a master at it.

There was, however, the question of why he was here in the first place and who the other two people were in the cellar. He pondered the issue for a moment and recalled the article. He knew the role he played in the story, but who would have the motivation to kidnap a child and bring her to a dead scientist's house? Colusa though for a moment. Mom's dead, daughter's dead. Father's still alive. The answer became obvious to him.

After reading the article, the guy probably thought this five-year-old girl was his dead daughter returned to life. Colusa thought more. Dr. Mindy from the article, was obviously Dr. Mendez. Was the father mentioned in the article the same guy that hired him to kill the old man? He was, after all, the guy who lost his wife and daughter. But why would he want to kill the old man? Did Mendez kill the man's family? Was it about revenge? If so, why did the man want to destroy churches? How did the churches factor in?

Colusa didn't have enough information to answer those questions, and he didn't care. He was simply hired to do a series of jobs. He had finished two. He had two more to go.

The more he thought about it, the more certain he was that the man responsible for paying his fees was trapped in the cellar with the girl he needed gone. Did the man want her gone too? Colusa didn't know. The situation was delicate, but the article, combined with the present situation, reinforced his resolve that the young girl had to go. He had no idea how, but she knew far too much.

Colusa needed some time to think, but this run-down house was no place to do any serious thinking. He walked back through the closing of the cellar door and the entrapment of the three people below. The man, the moneyman, didn't see him. He couldn't have. So as far as that guy knew, some trespasser-hating hillbilly or the Zodiac Killer could have trapped him.

Colusa decided to let the situation marinate for a few hours. That wouldn't kill anyone, at least anyone he didn't want killed. He left the house and walked back down the road to his car. He drove back into Paso Robles and searched for yet another hotel room.

Thirty-Two

THE STEPS OF THE CELLAR WERE COLD AND HARD. MASTEN sat with his head lowered, rubbing his temples. After a few minutes, an odd feeling overcame him. He looked up to find Callie and Max both staring at him, their eyes wide with fear. Callie was shaking and tears streamed down her cheeks. Masten stared back, shifting his eyes between the two.

"Who locked us in here?" Max asked.

"I don't know," Masten shot back.

"I want to go home!" Callie shouted, still crying. "I want my mom!"

Masten looked at her and could only manage an affirmative nod.

"Why did you kidnap us?" asked Max, looking at the floor.

It was a good question. "I don't know," Masten sighed, uncomfortable now.

"So," Max continued, pressing the situation and the narrow limits of his own valor. "Are you going to hurt us?"

Masten's eyes shot toward Max. Both of them sat perfectly still. Masten didn't know the answer, and Max could tell.

"Look, kid," he said. "Right now, we are *all* trapped in this cellar, and we need to find a way out."

That didn't answer Max's question, and he looked at his sister, who was still crying. He fought back his own tears as he rubbed Callie's arms and shoulders.

"Look guys," Masten said, trying to defuse the tension. "I don't want to hurt you, but I don't want any trouble, either. Just stay calm and let's try and find a way out of here."

Masten couldn't tell if his words helped or not. Both kids were still terrified, and with good reason. They were a hundred miles from home, trapped in a cellar with a man who could not honestly assure them that this was going to end well. Masten didn't know if it was going to end well for him either, but the sad fact was he didn't really care. Whatever he had in Los Angeles was just a routine. It wasn't a life.

He did want to know the answers to his questions, though, and he had the girl right in front of him. He decided to press the advantage.

"Callie," he said, breaking the silence. "Can I ask you something?"

Callie and Max both looked over at him. Neither said a word.

"In the car, why did you ask me about the churches?"

Callie shrugged, her face blank.

"What about Foot Foot?" Masten asked.

He got the same shrug.

That's odd, Masten thought. *One minute she's crying over a stuffed animal she's never owned, and the next she doesn't even remember it.* From what Masten could conclude, the child's thoughts came and went at random times.

It was Max's turn to ask questions. "Who was Dr. Mindy?"

Masten did a double take.

"What are you talking about?" Masten snapped back.

"I don't know," Max answered. "My sister mentioned him. I was just wondering if you knew him."

Masten was beginning to wear thin. *How did these kids know so much?*

"I don't know anyone named Dr. Mindy," Masten said.

Max offered a blank expression and silence.

"I used to work with a man named Mendez," Masten blurted out. "He was a work colleague."

"Is he dead?" Max asked.

Masten could feel his hands begin to tremble. He looked down at his right hand and opened and closed a fist several times.

"He is," Masten responded.

"How did he die?" Max asked.

"He just died, alright!" Masten's answer came in sharp and just shy of a shout. "I don't want to talk about it. I'm sorry I said anything."

"You killed him," Callie chimed in without emotion. She was now staring directly at Masten. "You killed him after I died, but I still saw it."

Masten's face went ashen. His hands were visibly shaking. The conversation helped Callie stop crying, but it didn't bounce in the direction Masten had hoped. He stood up and took a few steps forward and had to brace himself on the wine barrel. He cleared his throat a couple of times, then finally managed to speak.

"Who told you that?" Masten asked Callie.

"No one," Callie answered. "I saw it." Callie delivered her response with a cool confidence that unnerved Masten.

"How could you possibly have seen that?" A little strength was back in Masten's voice, and his volume rose slightly. "I don't believe you. Someone must have told you."

"Wait!" Max broke in. "So, you *did* kill Dr. Mindy?" The question went unanswered as Callie spoke over the last of Max's words.

"You believe me," she said to Masten. "It's why you came to talk to me. I was Claire, before I was me. And just like we talked about, sometimes I remember things about being Claire, but not always. It comes and goes."

Masten's knees gave out. He controlled his descent to the floor by grabbing the edge of the barrel. He landed on his butt, still hugging the barrel's sides. His keys were pressing into his thigh from his pants pocket.

"You hired a man, the bald man, to push Dr. Mindy over a cliff," Callie continued. "You also wanted that man to blow up churches." There was a pause and then she asked, "Why do you want to blow up churches? Because of me? I don't want you to kill people because of me."

"Stop!" Masten shouted. "Just stop!"

Masten pressed his face into the wood on the side of the barrel, his eyes closed, and his lips pressed together. He looked like a man receiving the most painful shot ever given. But he didn't make a sound, and Callie had stopped talking. The cellar was silent for a moment. The girl really did know. And for some sick reason, she was tormenting him with the ghost of his dead daughter.

She had to go. She had to go now. Masten was a killer. He never dreamed he would be, but he had become a serial killer by any definition. He could do this. Killing a kid wouldn't be easy, but he convinced himself that he could do it and that it needed to be done.

He slowly rose from the floor. His hands scraped rhythmically against the barrel as he pushed himself up, and then farther up. The sound was a little like an old razor being sharpened on a leather strap. Once on his feet, he pulled the uncomfortable keys from his pocket, laid them on the barrel, and gave Callie a cold, fixed stare. He had never strangled anyone before, much less a kid, but he expected it wouldn't be that hard to do, at least physically. And what was the boy going to do? Stare at the floor?

Masten took a step forward. The room remained silent, but Max and Callie could see that the look in the man's eyes was different. They shot each other terrified glances and began to move.

The silence and movement were broken by a rustling sound scraping across the metal door overhead. All three looked in the direction of the noise. An imprint of the barrel was mashed onto Masten's cheek.

The sound continued. There were scraping noises, followed by clear footsteps on the metal door. They all remained still, listening. Then, the sounds stopped. Masten edged closer to the cellar steps, cocking his head to the side, trying to hear what was happening above. He heard nothing. He walked to the first step and stood on it, still listening. Nothing. He laid his body down on the upper steps and gradually raised his feet to the second step. Still nothing.

He pulled his legs toward him and pushed down on the second step, raising his body higher. Still listening, still nothing. Masten repeated the movement on the third step. He thought he heard something, but his breathing was blocking his hearing. He drew in a breath and held it, but there was only silence.

He exhaled and rolled over onto his back. A second later a loud, metallic gong sound echoed through the cellar. Masten jerked up quickly and banged his head against the cellar door. His hand jerked toward his injured forehead. As he writhed on the cellar steps, he heard the screech of the door beginning to open.

The daylight that shone in was like looking directly into the sun. Masten could see movement above but couldn't make out much else. The door groaned in metallic protest as it was opened, and the light became brighter still.

Masten was blinded by the light. He couldn't see anything through his squinted eyes, but he could hear just fine, and he heard a woman's voice yell.

"Oh, my Lord!" The word *Lord* was broken into two syllables. "What on earth are you doing down there?" the woman asked.

"Someone locked us in," Masten said. He was using the back of his hand to rub his forehead and shield his eyes.

"Us?" the woman said. "There's more of you down there?"

Masten pointed down the stairs.

"Are y'all okay?" the woman asked. "Who locked you down there?"

"I don't know," Masten said, raising himself into a seated position on a step.

Max and Callie could hear the conversation, but neither was sure what to do. Max glanced over at Callie, who was looking in the direction of the cellar door.

"I want to go home," Callie said.

"Me too," Max said in an urgent tone. He rushed to the bottom of the steps and leaned forward. "He kidnapped us!" Max shouted. "Call 911!"

The woman drew back and put a hand on her chest.

"What'd he say?" she asked.

Masten shot a look at Max then turned back to the woman.

In a whispered tone, Masten said, "He's talking about the guy that trapped us down here. We've been down here for a while."

"Well, by all means, y'all come out of there," she said.

Masten looked at Max and extended an arm. He then looked at the woman. As Max hurried over to Callie and helped her off the stool, he saw Masten's keys lying on top of the barrel. Glancing toward the door, Max slipped the keys into his pocket. He and Callie then walked to the base of the steps.

Masten gave them the "come on" gesture. Max helped Callie up first then followed behind her. The sunlight was overwhelming and each of them sneezed as they reached the top step. The woman extended her hand and helped Callie out of the cellar.

"Good gracious," she shouted. "You're just a baby! Are you okay, sugar?"

Callie said nothing but tucked herself in behind the woman.

"And look at you!" she said as Max emerged. "You're quite the young man, and you've sure taken care of ... is this your little sister?

"Yes," Max replied.

"Well good on ya," the woman said. She pressed her hand against Max's cheek and said, "You're a good brother." Max had been around enough old women to know the drill. He dropped his gaze and spun away, just as he'd done hundreds of times before.

Masten was last out of the cellar. He stood up and dusted himself off. "Thanks for opening the door," he said.

"Well, no problem, hon," the woman said. "So, what in the

world is going on? What's this business about kidnapping? Do you need me to call the police?"

Masten and Max exchanged a long look, and then Max broke it off. When he turned his head, he could see the car parked not far away. Max decided not to press the kidnapping claim. He had another plan.

Max looked around inside the shed to see if there was anything nearby that might be of use. At the far end, he saw an old lawn mower. A small red plastic gas can sat next to it. Farther around, on the sidewall, Max saw a couple of shelves made from wooden boards lying across metal braces. The shelves held a few old paint cans, a couple of bottles of things used to kill plants, a couple of bottles of things used to fertilize plants, and a large container of ant killer.

Closer to Max and not far from the shelves, a shovel and a wooden handled spading fork leaned against the shed wall. The spading fork caught Max's eye. It looked like a small pitchfork, with four metal prongs. Max took a step to his right, bringing him within a couple of feet of the tools.

"There's no need to call the police," Masten said to the woman. "I wouldn't know what to tell them. We didn't see the person that locked us in the cellar."

The woman cocked her head slightly. "Well, how in the world did he get you down there?" she asked.

Masten was growing weary of the questions. He didn't have any good answers. She was clearly curious and didn't intend to let it go. One way or another, this wasn't going to end well. He decided to try a little diversion, combined with a little truth and a few lies.

"It's a long story, but I'll start from the beginning," he said, touching his chest. "My name is Dr. James Masten. I was a work colleague of David Mendez. Dr. Mendez owns this house, or used to. These kids are my grandchildren."

Masten gave Max a menacing glare as he said the words.

"I hadn't seen Dr. Mendez in a while, and we were in town, so I thought I'd stop by and say hello. I didn't see him in the house, so we walked out here to check the cellar. We walked down the stairs and not a second later someone closed the door behind us and locked us in. We never saw who did it."

The woman stared at him for a second and nodded her head. She finally broke the silence with a sudden and perky gesture.

"Well, where are my manners?" She asked as she put out a hand. "My name is Verna Crenshaw. I live just up that hill over there. I came down when I saw two cars pull up. No one has been here in years. I thought maybe someone was trying to sell the place and get me a new neighbor, or maybe rob the place." She laughed at her own joke.

"Two cars?" Masten asked.

"Yes," she answered. "This one here, and another one that drove off before I could get here."

"Did you see who was driving that car?" Masten asked.

"No, I didn't catch him," Ms. Crenshaw replied.

"That must have been the guy that locked us in the cellar," Masten said. "What'd the car look like?"

"Just a car. Nothing special. It was blue."

Masten nodded and looked around.

He finally asked, "So, do you know Dr. Mendez?"

"No, dear," she said. "I knew of him, but I only ever met him once. He wasn't here much and when he was, he kept mostly to himself. He was friends with old Mr. Carnahan, who used to own the winery down there, but he died several years back, too."

When Ms. Crenshaw stopped speaking, her words finally registered in her own brain. She threw a hand over her mouth. "Oh, my goodness, dear!" she said. "You didn't know. You came here to see Dr. Mendez. Sweetie, I hate to tell you, but he died about four years ago."

Masten looked at the ground and tried to feign some level of surprise and sadness. After a few moments, he looked back up.

"I'm so sorry," Ms. Crenshaw added.

"Do you know what happened to him?" Masten pried, somewhat dreading the answer.

"No, dear. Mr. Carnahan was the only one around here who knew him, and he died first. I just heard through the grapevine that Dr. Mendez died, too. That, and watching the house sit totally empty for the last four years."

"Okay," Masten said. "That's too bad. I'm sorry to hear it."

Masten was not an actor, but he wasn't turning in a poor performance.

"Well, it was very nice meeting you," he said. "And thank God you found us and let us out. I can't thank you enough. I'd better get these kids back now."

Masten patted a pocket with his hand. Then he patted the other pocket. He looked confused for a moment and then remembered leaving his keys on the barrel in the cellar.

"I left my car keys down there," he said to Ms. Crenshaw.

Masten shot Max a glance. "Can you grab my keys for me?"

Max looked nervous and shook his head no.

Ms. Crenshaw looked over and saw Max's reaction. "Aw," she said, putting a hand on Max's shoulder. "I think they are sick and tired of being in that hole. I'll watch them for you."

Masten looked irritated but turned and walked down the steps. Max waited until he was sure Masten was at the bottom. He grabbed Callie by the arm, yanked her toward him, and began running toward the car.

"Young man!" Ms. Crenshaw shouted.

But Max was halfway to the car. He hit the button on the key fob and unlocked the doors. A moment later, he opened the driver's side door and pushed Callie in. He closed the door and locked it.

Masten was out of the cellar and almost to the car when Max hit the start button. Masten began beating on the driver's side window and pulling on the door handle as Ms. Crenshaw looked on in horror. Max threw the car in gear and pushed the gas pedal hard. Masten followed, beating on the car for as long as he could, but Max sped away.

He flew down the dusty road and didn't slow much when he reached the main highway. Max had no idea where he was or where he was going. Masten ran out of wind about halfway down the dirt road. He stopped and bent over, putting his hands on his knees, panting heavily. He raised his head in time to see the car disappear beyond the winery.

THIRTY-THREE

DRIVING INTO PASO ROBLES, COLUSA PORED OVER THE circumstances again and again in his mind. He was now certain that the old man in the cellar was the same man that hired him for this complex plan. Colusa knew what he had to do. There was no way to get to the girl without the old man seeing him. But then, if he killed the old man with the girl, he wouldn't get paid the remainder of his money, and payment, after all, was the goal.

He'd have to force the old man to pay before he killed him. Coercion and torture weren't in Colusa's toolbox, but he'd have to make do. He had enough gear with him to scare the hell out any normal human, plus, the house had a working phone. Once the wire was sent and the old man and girl were gone, Colusa would finish the job. He didn't want to just steal the man's money. Plus, the job was interesting, and he was more than a little excited about it.

Colusa slowed as he approached the turn for the highway that led to the house. He made the turn and accelerated eastward. He'd be back at the house in less than ten minutes.

REVISITED

The hills in the near distance were not covered in lush pines or snow or fascinating rock features. They were fairly plain, but oddly comforting. Perhaps it was the grape and olive vineyards that dotted them. Or maybe, he just watched too much television as a kid, and this was a common scene in many of his favorite old shows. Whatever it was, the view was sort of transformative.

An erratically moving car on the other side of the highway disrupted Colusa's trance. The car seemed incapable of staying in one lane or the other. It looked like a drunk driver on a speed bender—until the car passed him.

In an instant, he recognized the car from the house. Colusa couldn't imagine how they'd escaped from the cellar, but clearly, they had. He stepped on the gas and rushed to the next break in the median, made a quick U-turn and pushed the pedal all the way down. By the time he caught up with the car, it was at the Highway 101 intersection.

The car turned right into dense traffic heading north. Colusa followed, staying just far enough behind so as not to arouse suspicion. Even in traffic, the car was still all over the road.

❖ ❖ ❖

Max, while speeding down the dirt road in his kidnapper's car, shouted at Callie to get in the back seat and buckle up.

Callie did as she was told, crawling over the front seat and dropping into the back seat.

"Reach up toward the window and pull that metal buckle down," Max commanded.

Callie twisted a bit and found the buckle.

"Now, reach down across your lap and find the other part of the buckle down in the seat."

Callie found it and pulled it up.

"Good," Max said, glancing into the rearview mirror. "Now, put that metal piece above into the plastic piece from the seat and push them together until you hear a click."

"It clicked!" Callie shouted, looking up.

"Good," Max said, exhaling with relief. "Now just lean back.

Everything is going to be okay. I promise."

Max looked in the rear-view mirror. Callie seemed calmer as she looked out the window. The sky was bright blue, with a few puffy clouds floating along.

Max was trying to hold it together. He was driving faster than he'd ever driven in his life. His white-knuckle grip on the steering wheel resulted in a lot of correction and over-correction that took the car from one side of the lane to the other. He couldn't seem to keep the car straight, but he didn't care. He wanted to be as far away from the house as he could be, as fast as he could get there.

He'd paid no attention to his surroundings until he reached an intersection of the road with a major highway. Only then did he think about the fact that he had no idea where he was. The light at the intersection was yellow as he approached. He knew the red was coming. He had to decide, left or right. He pulled the car to the right. There was no particular reason.

After what seemed an eternity, the light turned green, and Max made a right turn onto the highway. He began to calm down as he drove, but he still had trouble holding the car on a straight path. He had no idea what his plan was, other than just driving away from the house and that psycho old man.

❖ ❖ ❖

The farther north they drove, the less traffic there was to contend with. The other cars seemed to fade away. Colusa watched from behind as the car worked to stay straight in the lane, improving a little with each mile.

The progression intrigued Colusa, and he wanted to check out a hunch. He moved into the left lane and pushed down hard on the gas pedal, closing the distance within a few minutes. A half a mile later, he was in a position to pass. Colusa continued accelerating and pulled alongside the blue car. He let off the gas long enough to match the other car's speed. He looked to his right and realized his hunch had been correct: the boy was driving the car. He didn't know what had happened to the old man, but the boy was at the wheel and the little girl, his target, was in the back seat, right behind the boy. They were alone.

The boy was fixated on the road and didn't seem to notice the car next to him. Colusa eased off of the gas and pulled in again behind the boy's car. He reached across the center console with his right hand and began rifling through a canvas bag in the passenger's seat. A moment later, he pulled out the .38 revolver he'd loaded earlier at his hotel. He liked revolvers. They had three fewer bullets than the old-school semi-automatics with nine-bullet clips, but they were simple, and they didn't jam. Plus, in all his years, he had never needed the three extra bullets.

In one coordinated effort, Colusa gripped the gun in his right hand and pushed the small lever to his left to roll down the right window. Once again, he gunned the engine and moved into the left lane. In a moment, he was next to the boy's car.

The boy was still focused on the road, but his control had improved. The car was stable and straight on the highway. Colusa matched its speed and watched the kid for a moment, then his eyes moved right. He could see about half of the little girl's head poking up over the back seat window. It was just enough.

He slowed a little to let his passenger's side window match up to the back window of the boy's car. The speeds of the two cars paired and he felt as if he were standing still, shooting at a fixed target. Keeping his left hand on the wheel, he raised his right hand and aimed the gun at a point just in front of the top of the girl's head. He needed to lead her a little because of the forward movement of the cars.

He pulled the hammer back with his thumb and began to put pressure on the trigger. He squeezed tighter, holding his target in sight. It was a straight shot. A split second later, the trigger caught, and the hammer came down.

❖ ❖ ❖

As he sped down the road, Max stared straight ahead, working to keep the car steady. His anxiety level was through the roof. Out of his periphery, he saw a sudden movement coming from the right shoulder of the highway. A gray streak darted in front of his car. It was a rabbit!

Max swerved to the right and slammed on the brakes. As he reached the edge of the gravel shoulder, the rear window exploded. In a panic, Max jerked the steering wheel hard to the left, causing the car to cross the left traffic lane and skid into the grassy median between the north and southbound lanes.

The grass was slick, and the car's leftward momentum brought the vehicle around until it made a complete one-eighty. Max still had his foot on the gas. He turned the wheel hard to the right trying to regain control. Then he jerked hard to the left, realizing that he was heading across the grass toward the oncoming southbound traffic.

The car responded and Max was able to straighten up, heading south along the edge of the grass and the highway. He eased his foot off the gas and the car slowed, but he pressed the brakes too hard, and the car swerved again on the slick grass. It came to a stop, sitting sideways across the median.

"Jesus Christ!" Max shouted. His entire body was shaking, and the adrenaline overdose made him feel lightheaded and nauseous. It took a few moments for his senses to come back to him. When they did, he could hear Callie screaming in the back seat. He turned around and saw that she was covered in glass.

"Shit!" he yelled and opened his door.

He scrambled out of the car and opened the back door next to Callie. He ran his hand across her head and felt small shards of glass embedded in her hair. He ran his hands across her shoulders and down her arms. He didn't see any blood. Her legs looked okay as well.

Callie was still screaming, but she didn't appear to be hurt. He gently tapped her face and called her name a few times. After a few minutes, her screams turned into sobs.

"Callie, are you okay?" Max asked.

She couldn't speak. Max repeated the question, but she still didn't answer. He let it go. She seemed scared as hell, but otherwise uninjured. Max stood up and buckled his hands behind his head. He took a deep breath and let out an enormous sigh.

His eyes turned to a set of blue and red flashing lights approaching from the north, accompanied by the shrill warbling of a siren. A few minutes later, the California Highway Patrolman parked his car on the grass not far away. The officer quickly exited his vehicle and ran toward Max, one hand resting on his gun.

The officer stopped running a few yards short of where Max stood. He drew his weapon, holding it with both hands, but kept it aimed at the ground.

"Is anyone else in the car?" he shouted.

"My sister!" Max yelled back. "She's five."

The officer examined Max for a moment and pulled his pistol level with the ground. He approached the car from the driver's side and craned his head to see inside.

"You stay put!" he yelled at Max.

Max threw his hands up by his shoulders and then let them drop.

The officer approached the car, like a cat examining a new toy. He looked into the passenger's side and saw only Callie, still in the back seat, then stepped slowly around the back and took in the shattered window. Walking toward the driver's side, the patrolman saw the open back door. He examined Callie for a second before continuing to the front of the car. When he had made his way around, he took a moment and checked out the median and highway in all directions.

Callie and Max were the only ones there.

"Come over here and put both hands on the car," the officer said to Max, still holding his weapon with both hands.

Badly shaken, and now more than a little confused, Max complied.

"Legs shoulder width apart," the officer said. Again, Max complied.

The officer holstered his pistol and began at Max's waist, patting down his left leg, then his right. He moved up the torso and then to each arm. The officer found nothing.

"Okay, you can turn around," he said.

He looked Max up and down for a moment.

"What the hell is going on, son?" the officer asked.

Max paused, then blurted in a panic, "We were kidnapped and locked in a cellar with the man who kidnapped us!"

The officer squinted and tilted his head. "Come again?"

"It's true," Max pressed. "We were trying to escape. I don't even have my license, just a learner's permit. But the car was there, and I had a moment, so we went for it. I don't even know where I am. I was just driving as fast as I could to get away from there. And then there was a rabbit and then the back windshield exploded. And then I thought we were going to die. Oh, God. I think I'm going to be sick!"

Max bent over and fulfilled his own prophecy.

"Jesus, kid," the officer said, his face wrinkled in disgust. "Let's move over here." He led Max to the front of the car and stabilized him against the hood.

"First things first," he said. "Are you okay?"

"I'm not injured," Max said. "If that's what you mean."

"How about her?" the officer asked, pointing back at Callie.

"I think she's okay," Max answered. "She's got glass in her hair."

"Alright," the officer said. "Stay here and let me check her out." He walked back to Callie and helped her out of the car. "Are you okay, sweetheart?" She didn't answer.

The officer looked her over from head to toe and didn't see any blood.

"Okay, let's come up here and sit down." He led Callie to the front of the car and helped her sit down on the ground.

"So, is this your car?" he asked Max.

"No," Max answered.

"Whose car is it?"

"I don't know," Max responded. "It's the car our kidnapper drove. Oh, God, I'm gonna be sick again!"

The officer took a deep breath and looked up at the white puffy clouds overhead.

"Alright," he said, trying to ignore the retching. "There is clearly a story here, and I imagine you guys need some water and a bathroom. Let's get in my car and we can head to the station and get you set up. Then we can figure out what's going on. Does that sound okay?"

Max and Callie both nodded in agreement, and the three began walking to the squad car a few yards away. The officer held Callie close, directing her with his muscular arm around her shoulder. Max followed a few feet back.

A second later, two shots dropped the officer to the ground. Both hit the officer in the ribs, just below his left arm. Both were mere inches from Callie's head.

❖ ❖ ❖

When the boy's car lost control, Colusa slowed to get out of the way and then saw red and blue flashing lights speeding toward the scene. He let the patrol car pass, continued about a half a mile farther, then made a left across the grass median, and joined the southbound traffic on the other side of the highway.

When he was about twenty yards away from the patrol car, he pulled onto the shoulder and stopped. He watched as an excited officer ran toward the scene with one hand on his gun. The officer drew his gun and took stock of the situation. Once the kids and the officer relaxed, the element of surprise was Colusa's. He decided to strike.

He dropped the wrong person, though. It was supposed to be the girl. He was frustrated. This never happened to him. He promised himself there would be no more mistakes.

❖ ❖ ❖

What Max lacked in bravery, he made up in survival instincts, like the rabbit he almost ran over. Before the trooper's body hit the ground, Max had grabbed Callie by the back of her collar and turned her around. The two ran back to the car as fast as they could. Max's instincts were telling him to crouch and stay low, but instead he followed his little sister, who had no instincts. Callie just ran like hell.

No other bullets came, but Max drove as if he were under attack. He crossed the median with a flying thump and headed north on the 101.

THIRTY-FOUR

"WELL, ISN'T THIS JUST THE BIG ADVENTURE," MS. CRENSHAW said, adjusting her stiff hair and sunglasses. "I haven't been anywhere in ages."

"Yes," Masten said, with tones of both defeat and sarcasm. "It's quite grand."

Masten leaned his head against the window and stared up at the small, cotton ball clouds in the sky. The shapes shifted as the high-level winds urged them along. One turned into a dog, and then into a butterfly. Ms. Crenshaw had a car, but she insisted on driving. He thought about just taking it, but an increasing body count was the last thing he needed. So, he rode along, and looked at clouds.

"You seem to have a lot on your mind," Ms. Crenshaw observed.

Masten did a slow head turn, a look of obvious derision on his face.

"Us small town folks notice everything." She shrugged. "Not much else to do."

Small town folks, Masten thought. He knew them well. He

grew up in a small town. If something felt different to them, they would never suspend suspicion. But, if something felt familiar, they would never suspend belief. Fact and truth never came into play. It was all about gut and opinions, with a heavy dose of stubborn to keep it going. He had no idea why this woman wasn't suspicious. Maybe she was. Masten looked across at her, then back.

"There it is!" Ms. Crenshaw shouted, pointing a finger toward the median. "I told you I'd find it!"

Masten raised his head and saw his car, looking quite the worse for wear. A man was lying on the ground nearby. Masten raised his body from the seat and craned his neck farther backward as the car moved forward.

"Slow up!" he commanded. "No, pull over."

Ms. Crenshaw obliged and stopped her car on the right shoulder of the northbound lane. As she did, the rear wheels of Masten's car began spinning in the grass and finally caught. The car jerked forward and turned left. It was now heading in the same direction as Masten and Ms. Crenshaw. When the tires gripped asphalt, the car continued left and sped right past them.

"Follow them!" Masten shouted. "Let's go!"

Ms. Crenshaw was an old-school Southern woman, and her high gear was about as fast as the viscous flow of the molasses she drizzled onto her biscuits. She pushed down on the blinker arm and carefully checked for oncoming traffic behind her, then slowly accelerated back onto the road.

"Oh, you're killing me," Masten muttered, rubbing his forehead. "Let's go!" he said, peeking out from under his hand.

Ms. Crenshaw shot him a look that said, *that's not very Christian.*

Masten didn't care. He shot an impatient look back and threw a hand toward the windshield. "Stay with them!" he commanded.

Out of his periphery, Masten saw another nondescript car parked beside the road across the median but paid it no attention. He was focused on staying behind his own car.

REVISITED

❖ ❖ ❖

The pace had stabilized. Masten told Ms. Crenshaw to hang back a little because he didn't want to panic the kids. Ms. Crenshaw was happy to help. The situation became more of a convoy than a chase.

"So, Dr. Masten," Ms. Crenshaw asked, "what's your story? I know what you told me, but what were you really doing with those kids, and what were you doing in the cellar?"

"Like I said, it's a long story," Masten sighed, looking up and out the window.

"Uh-huh," Ms. Crenshaw answered with more than a note of skepticism. "That little girl wasn't your granddaughter, was she? And the boy, he was no relation either, right?"

Masten turned and stared at Ms. Crenshaw. He began tapping the forefinger of his right hand on the armrest. The atmosphere in the car became very uncomfortable as Ms. Crenshaw awaited a response and Masten considered his options.

He chose his words carefully. "Believe me," he said, "the less you know, the better."

Ms. Crenshaw shot him a look without moving her head. Masten felt her discomfort and decided to try and disarm the situation.

"Look," he said. "The business with the kids is complicated. Very complicated. You should know that I had no intention of hurting either one of them, and I didn't intend for any of the rest of this to happen."

Ms. Crenshaw looked at Masten with an expression reserved for someone who had just perceived a foul smell. She began to wonder what this man was capable of and whether she had now become his hostage, too. Masten felt the doubt and looked out the passenger window. His uncomfortable ride just got longer.

"So, like I told you, I'm Verna Crenshaw," she said, in part trying to defuse the tension, and in part simply nervous chatter. "I was born and raised in Barnesville, Georgia. My daddy was a Baptist preacher, and oh, how he could stir up a congregation.

He really could. He kept his voice until his last breath, too. My momma stayed home and raised me and my two sisters and two brothers. They're all dead now. I was the baby."

"I'm sorry to hear that," Masten responded, trying to sound sympathetic.

"Thank you, dear," she said, "but they all lived long lives. They had kids, and grandkids, went to volleyball, baseball, basketball and football games. They went to birthday parties and graduations and even a wedding or two. A person can't ask for much more than that, can they?"

Masten couldn't respond. He didn't get to do any of that, and he never would. He turned his head and stared back out the window. *Five years on Sunday*, he thought.

"Well, anyway," she continued, "I married young. Me and the son of a big farm owner from down around Macon thought we were ready to take on the world. His name was Harvey Crenshaw. My maiden name was Beasley."

Masten continued staring out the window, not responding, but listening in spite of himself.

"Well, Harvey had big dreams, see," Ms. Crenshaw continued. "He was a good-looking man, and he was convinced that he could make it in pictures. So, we packed up our things and moved to Los Angeles. Being from a little town, I'd never seen such. Lord, what an adjustment. But after two years, Harvey hadn't got any parts, other than playing an extra fisherman in an old Chesterfield cigarette commercial. The star of that commercial, though, was that fella that played Mr. Kincaid on *The Partridge Family* a few years later."

Masten turned away from the window and gave a wry look.

"Yeah!" Ms. Crenshaw said with some excitement. "It's true. But that's all he ever got. We were dead broke and about to head back home to Georgia when Harvey heard about a job running a grape farm. Harvey didn't know a thing about grapes, but he sure knew how to farm. So, we drove up here, and he took the job on the spot. The rest is history."

"Where is Harvey now?" Masten asked, looking straight ahead.

"Oh, he died about fifteen years ago," she answered, wrinkling her nose. "Lung cancer. I guess those Chesterfields weren't so good after all. Those were tough days, but the farm owner, they call it a vineyard here, was good to me. He let me stay in the house after Harvey died, and in return I've been helping out with odds and ends, like bookkeeping, answering phones, and some light cleaning. It's been a pretty good deal. Harvey and I couldn't have kids, but the farm folks have become like family to me over the years."

Masten took it all in, then asked, "Do you ever think of going back? To Georgia, I mean?"

"Oh, no, dear," Ms. Crenshaw laughed. "My life is here now. I've been here too long. I may not have lost my accent, but I left Georgia behind a long time ago."

There was a long pause and then Ms. Crenshaw said, "So, now you know all about me, tell me about yourself. Are you married?"

Masten cut his head towards her with a raised eyebrow and then turn to look forward again.

"Oh, goodness dear, no" she said laughing. "I've been there and done that. I'm just talking. If you don't want to talk to me, that's okay. I told you about myself, but …"

Ms. Crenshaw's expression went from smiling back to neutral. She looked forward and drove in silence. The quiet lasted for several minutes before she began humming an old hymn, *God Be With You 'Til We Meet Again.*

Jesus, make this stop! Masten thought, then sighed. "I was married," he relented. "My wife and daughter died in a car wreck a few years ago. It was not very far from here, actually. It was a freak accident. Nobody's fault, but they're gone nonetheless."

Ms. Crenshaw put a hand over her mouth and gasped. "Oh, my dear Lord!" she said. "Sweetie, I had no idea." She reached over and put a hand on his arm. "I cannot imagine. I am so sorry. It just makes me want to cry."

"Yeah," Masten agreed. "Every day."

"Dear man," Ms. Crenshaw said shaking her head and squeezing Masten's arm tighter.

After a long moment, she continued, "Look, I told you my daddy was a preacher. I've been a believer all my years, and there is one thing I can tell you." She paused and turned to look Masten right in the eyes. "Your burden has a purpose. The Lord will reveal it to you when he's good and ready, but until then, know that he's looking out for you."

Masten winced. "With all due respect ma'am, the 'Lord,'" he made air quotes as he said it, "is the one who allowed my wife and daughter to die. So, I have no confidence that the 'Lord,'" again in air quotes, "has my back in the least."

In another time, Ms. Crenshaw would have gasped at the blasphemy, but she was old enough now to know that the plan she faithfully believed in came with a lot of loss, pain, and scar tissue. She had judged a lot over the years, but she couldn't judge this. She mostly just felt sad for the man.

They drove on in continued silence. Masten was done talking and Ms. Crenshaw couldn't think of any more appropriate questions. She wanted to know about his wife and his daughter and their life together, but she didn't dare ask. That would be cruel.

After several silent miles, Masten spoke again. "I spent my whole career as a scientist," he said. "Hell, even before that. From my childhood, I loved science. I loved the certainty, the reliability. Nothing was real unless you could prove that it was real, and then you could count on it, day after day. The Earth, the oceans, space, are all insanely complex systems, way beyond our present understanding, but they are all eventually explainable. We just have to get there. We have to catch up. At least that's what I thought. For thirty years, I was convinced of that."

Ms. Crenshaw took a moment to absorb the information.

"It does seem random, doesn't it?" she mused. "I'll tell you honestly, it's one of the most confusing issues we believers have to deal with. Something like that happens and we flat don't understand. Were we not good? Did we not pray enough? You know, just why? But that's where you just have to double down on your faith and trust in the plan."

Masten smirked, but still nodded absently. "My problem is," he rolled out slowly, "I don't believe in a creator. I *proved* that there *is* a creator."

Ms. Crenshaw crinkled her brow. "Do what, hon?"

Masten explained his research as simply as he could, then paused before he continued. "I sat in a church. I was in the front row, looking at the coffins of my wife and daughter." Masten cleared the tears from above his nose with his thumb and forefinger. "There were lots of people behind me," he said. "Friends, family, acquaintances paying their respects. The place was packed but silent and I could hear them whispering. And what I couldn't hear I could feel. Some people wanted to get out of the place and move on about their day. Some were looking forward to the food that people brought. Some focused on who they would talk to when the service was over. But nobody seemed to process my loss. Maybe they didn't care. Maybe they didn't have the capacity. I don't know. But that's when it hit me. Some animals, humans included, show a brief sense of grief, but all of them quickly just go on about their business. Your loss is yours to bear."

"Well, that's a little cynical," Ms. Crenshaw commented.

"Tell me it's not true," Masten responded. "You experienced it when your husband died. I know you did, and I know you know what I'm talking about."

Ms. Crenshaw raised her eyebrows and nodded.

"The other thing that hit me," Masten continued, more animated, "was that God, or whatever you want to call what is responsible for all of this, doesn't care, one way or the other. Kids die every day. Moms with kids die every day. Dads with kids die every day. The deaths happen in every manner imaginable. Car wrecks, crazy people, drownings, wild animals, you name it. All of these events leave behind a wake of indescribable suffering and pain for those who live. Where is the comfort? I've received none. Where was the protection? My wife and daughter received none. And as to the plan you talked about earlier, if the plan was to take my wife and daughter from me and leave me to walk this world alone and miserable, then

I'm out. And that god, he, she, or it—doesn't deserve anyone's support, worship, or faith. I think it's time people know this."

Ms. Crenshaw glanced over then back. The guy was starting to sound a little unhinged and she had no ready response. One would come to her if she thought long enough, but she didn't get that much time. The car in front of them swerved from its lane, and Max took the next exit. Masten and Ms. Crenshaw passed a large green sign indicating the exit was for Fort Hunter Liggett and Jolon Road.

Masten drew an uncomfortable breath. He knew the exit well. It was the beginning of the end of his life as he knew it. The thought of following the route initiated a small panic attack. The blood ran from his head. His lips pursed and twitched. His hands began shaking. And his right leg was bouncing up and down off the ball of his right foot.

Ms. Crenshaw, who was still pondering Masten's diatribe, didn't notice any of it. She took the exit and followed the car through a left turn, under a bridge, and onto a small, bumpy, two-lane road.

THIRTY-FIVE

WHILE THE OTHER TROOPERS WERE TRYING TO HELP THEIR fallen friend, Colusa moved his car about a mile farther south and stopped again. He needed a few quiet minutes. Idling on the shoulder of the highway, Colusa's mind raced as he thought about how best to address the new circumstances. Everything had changed in a short period of time. The solution he came to was not comfortable. It was not in his ordinary playbook.

He couldn't force payment from the old man because he no longer held him prisoner. He also no longer held the girl prisoner. She was a loose end twisting in the wind. One thing was clear though: to get paid the rest of his money, he would have to finish the next step, now. His work should have been easy, but he let the girl distract him. The constant surprises were wearing on his patience, and he wanted to get paid, so he decided to go ahead and do it. No more surprises.

The final part of the job was not going to happen the way he'd anticipated. He'd envisioned sitting beside a pool in an exquisite, ocean side hotel. He would be wearing a thick, white cotton robe, knotted around his waist, but open just enough to

194

catch the attention of some curious, passing pool boy. He would wink as he took a sip of his Bloody Mary. He would seductively pick at the bowl of grapes, melons, strawberries, and oranges as he dialed the numbers.

But the fates disagreed. The pool boy would have to wait until he was finished. They would meet, no doubt, but it would be under much less thrilling circumstances. Colusa picked up his phone and dialed a number. Then he dialed a second number, then a third, then a fourth. He didn't dial the last number. That was to come later, after the PDF document was released. He had no idea what the document said, and he didn't care, but it was part of the deal.

The point of pride for Colusa was that his last four calls would instantly be in the headlines. He grabbed the tablet from the passenger's seat next to him and accessed the wireless hotspot on his temporary phone. He pulled up a throw-away email account he'd created earlier and entered an email address into the "to" line, attached the PDF document he'd been given, and, without an entry in the subject line or any further commentary, hit Send. The phone and the email account would both be gone by the end of the day.

He leaned his head back against his seat and listened to the distant bellow of sirens swirling around the officer he'd killed a few minutes earlier. His thoughts turned to the doctor and reporter. Their day was coming soon. Colusa grabbed his tablet again and pulled up a search engine. Hawthorne's picture popped right up. Devon's took a little more time, but he found it. He recognized the faces. They were two of the people in the aquarium he saw when he tried to escape with the girl. Colusa wished he knew that information then, but he knew it now.

❖ ❖ ❖

Within minutes of Colusa's calls, first responders in St. Louis, Cleveland, Denver and Lubbock were frantically on the move. At that moment, each group knew only that a house of worship in their city had been destroyed, and that it was likely a multiple casualty event.

Reports of the explosions began coming in over the press wires. Television, newspaper and online reporters and producers quickly saw a bigger picture. The networks broke into their regularly scheduled programming. Television journalists from New York and Washington were being dispatched to the affected cities, while connections were hastily made with local reporters to bridge the gap.

Texts and emails flew back and forth between news outlets. All were obviously related to the explosions. The subject lines said so. The ambitious networks were looking for scoops: anything new that could help connect the dots. Sometimes though, it was better to stay cool.

In the frenzy of activity that had just beset the nation, most press workers wholly ignored routine message traffic that was not clearly related to the explosions. One, however, did not. Blythe Brookford, an older woman atop one of the major television networks, had seen it all. Her first big production assignment, at the ripe old age of twenty-three, was the Munich Massacre that happened during the 1972 Olympics. She had covered nearly every global event since. This one didn't move her needle much.

She was kept informed of new developments on the blasts, but there really wasn't much information to be had yet. So, she scrolled through the hundred or so unread emails she had received earlier in the day. Near the end of the list, she saw an email with the telltale paper clip symbol, but no subject entry. She wondered how this one made it through the company's spam filter. She didn't recognize the sender.

She could see that the attachment was a PDF document and wondered what it was, but she also knew that her network constantly received wackadoodle stuff from every kind of crazy out there. She decided to wait until she could have someone from IT check it out. She forwarded the email on. A call back came less than five minutes later.

"Boss, this is Barry," the man said. "The email is safe, and you're probably going to want to open it right now. Looks like our serial bomber may have reached out."

Brookford thanked him and hung up. She opened the document and began reading. She tapped two fingers against her lips as she read, but otherwise remained expressionless. When she finished, she raised her head, rubbed an index finger down her temple, then picked up her phone.

"Michal," Brookford said, "Can you find Mark and Rachel and send them up as soon as possible?"

"Yes, ma'am," was the response. "Right away."

"Thank you, dear."

Ten minutes later, the president of the network's news division and the president of one of the network's cable news subsidiaries were standing at her door.

"So, what do we do with this guy?" Brookford asked, handing each a copy of the document. There was silence in the room for a few minutes as they read.

"We have to put it out," Mark said. "If we don't, some other network will. You can bet he didn't just send it to us."

"He didn't send it to us," Brookford corrected, with a little smack. "He sent it to *me*. Why did he send it to me?"

Mark and Rachel looked at one another, the same unspoken thought running through their heads. A recent dead husband? A grandchild that never made it to two? Brookford had experienced both, but who could know with these wing nuts.

"I don't know ma'am," Rachel chimed in. "But we'll find out. In the meantime, I agree with Mark. We put it out with the caveat that it is totally unconfirmed at this point. But we need to be the ones to break it."

"Very well," Brookford sniffed. "Let Tyler know and load it onto his prompter. He can add it to the break-in. Make sure the unconfirmed part is added in as well. I don't want this guy giving us a black eye, understood?"

Both Mark and Rachel understood very well. Brookford was old school news. She had no tolerance for foolishness, and resented the hell out of the 24- hour news cycle that forced her to come up with "opinion and analysis" to fill the airwaves. Who gave a damn what some reporter thought about anything? That was not their job. At least, it shouldn't be their job. The same was true for all of the "experts." She thought that those folks needed to find real jobs. What was a "former federal prosecutor" anyway? She or he was just a lawyer that used to work for some U.S. Attorney's office somewhere.

Brookford dismissed the two and turned her attention to the televisions mounted on her office wall. She focused on the one in the middle. The progression didn't take five minutes.

"We have some additional breaking news," Tyler Maycroft read.

Good-looking and square jawed, Maycroft had blond, well-cut hair, going gray. He was middle-aged, well dressed, and in shape. He had a good ten years left before he aged out of the national news spotlight, but for now, he was well known and effective. His tone was of seriousness and authority.

"Our network has just received a document that is purportedly from the person responsible for today's bombings. Right now, we have no confirmation of who this person is or whether his or her claims are true, but we do want to share with you what was sent to us only moments ago."

Brookford nodded as she watched. Sometimes being on the edge meant stepping out onto the ledge.

"Again," Maycroft continued, "I want to emphasize that all of this is fresh, and we have not had an opportunity to confirm any of it, but here is what the document says, unedited and unabridged."

Maycroft cleared his throat and began reading.

"I know two things for certain: (1) a creator exists; and (2) it doesn't care at all about you. Somewhere deep inside, you know this to be true as well. It is obvious. It is right in front of us. Literally, in our faces.

Death runs rampant among us. All day. Every day. In every part of the world. You can imagine an infinite number of examples. I need not list a single one.

Sadly, people offer sincere prayers each day for their safety and for that of their loved ones. And yet, those same praying people continue to die each day. So do the ones they pray for.

Each person who died today prayed that they wouldn't. But they still did.

Some may argue that such events are part of a larger plan that we humans simply do not understand. I can assure you that is not true. There is no plan. I have now proven this to you. I have destroyed five churches in various cities across the country. Each of these churches had worshipers and faithful followers in them at the time. All of those worshipers are now dead. They were not saved. None were spared. Our creator did not care.

I killed these people of my own accord. This was not a random event. I was not told to do it by some voice in my head or from beyond. This was my plan, and mine alone.

If our creator will not save his own worshipers in the very place they gather to worship, then how can anyone seriously argue that it cares at all about anyone or anything? That point is now proven. It will be proven again. Our creator does not care. So why would anyone waste their time worshiping an entity that quite simply has no desire to return that affection?

And forgive me. I have put my second point in front of my first. There is a creator! The name we give it is reflective of us, not it. Creation has many parts that include many cultures and many histories. Each calls the creator different things, but we are all referring to the same entity.

Nonetheless, with the release of this short statement, I am including an extensive set of data that I was involved in gathering over several years. This data proves conclusively that each of us, without our conscious knowledge, receives information on a very distinct, electric micro-frequency. Each of us has a different one. In contrast, each of us, also without our conscious knowledge, is constantly sending information on a common, electric micro-frequency. The outgoing frequency is the same for all of us.

Together, these frequencies comprise what many refer to as our souls. They form consciousness. Information constantly coming and going. Memories, thoughts, emotions, experiences. None of these things are lost. They are being recorded. The creator wants to know every last detail of its creation. It is as if Renoir found a way to intrude on the Luncheon of the Boating Party. The artist crawls into his art. Our creator wants to know the pain of childbirth and the joy of holding a baby. It also wants to know the agony of losing that baby. It wants to experience all of its creation: all life, all death, and everything in between, from the ordinary to the extraordinary. Evolution is real, but it exists only to keep things changing so that the experiences are new.

We are mere vessels that communicate information. We are useless pawns. But we still feel the pain. And we feel it with no consolation, no numbing elixir, and no cure. We suffer horribly for no other reason than the creator wants to have an experience.

Why worship such a creator? Turn your backs on the being that has turned its back on us. The creator wouldn't spare its own worshipers in their houses of worship. Why spare the creator another moment of your time?"

"And that is the end of the document," Maycroft said, looking up at the camera. "Again, we want to stress that we have no information about it, other than to say that we received it, and it purports to be from a person claiming responsibility for the bombings. As soon as we learn more about this document and who sent it to us, we will let you know."

Maycroft then paused and listened to the voice in his ear.

"Right now," he continued, "I want to go to Katie Hass with our local affiliate in Cleveland. She has some additional information about the victims there. Katie, what have you got for us?"

❖ ❖ ❖

Verna Crenshaw followed the car down the road until it made a hasty left turn onto another road.

"Don't turn," Masten commanded, even though the command pained him deeply. "Just keep going straight."

"But I thought you wanted me to—"

Masten interrupted her. "We'll catch them up ahead," he

said. "That road curves around to meet this one. It doesn't go anywhere else. And if we follow them on that road, they'll know we're tailing them. Just keep going this way."

Ms. Crenshaw didn't like the sound of "tailing," but did as instructed. She glanced over when she heard Masten's phone whistle. He pulled the phone closer to read the text.

Five out of six, the text stated. *Document too. Early, but within window. You have my numbers. Six will follow when instructed after...*

The cryptic text made perfect sense to Masten and distracted him a little from the stress of the reunion with his surroundings. He owed the man money, and the man wanted it right away. He would set up the transfer as soon as he could. The account holding his wife's life insurance proceeds had been tapped twice before; once after Mendez was killed, and then again after the Mariner's Chapel had been destroyed. He didn't have the account information on hand, so the transfer would have to wait a few hours, but he didn't want to be that specific at the moment.

Masten turned on the radio, and poked around at the buttons, trying to find a news station. When a uniformed military guard in the road motioned for the car to stop, he turned the radio down. The delay was not well received.

Is there a problem? the next text asked.

There was more delay as Ms. Crenshaw fumbled through her purse for her driver's license. She finally found it. Masten handed his over and a few minutes later the two were waved through.

The next text he received was a series of question marks.

Masten responded once the car was back on the road. "Apologies. Going through checkpoint. Had to put phone down. Working on the rest. Back in touch soon."

Masten hoped that would buy him some time. He turned the radio back up and scanned for any kind of news. There was nothing on the FM side, and the car was not equipped with satellite, so he went old school, tapping a button and scanning the AM Stations. The digital numbers finally stopped changing when the radio reached 1130 on the dial. He heard a less than crisp man's voice say, "This is the KPRS Radio News Network."

The station identification was followed by a short piece of serious sounding, but oddly upbeat music. When that music ended, a different man's voice spoke over a muted recording of the refrain of a peppy country song about America. The song slowly faded away.

"And we're back!" the voice said. "You're listening to the Tom P. Hall Show, and I am the one, the only, Tom P. Hall. We're talking today about the various church bombings that happened across the country a short time ago. I think we're up to … how many, Donna? Four?"

A woman's voice chimed in and said, "Well, five, if you count the one a few days ago in Los Angeles."

"So, four or five," Hall continued. "And now we've received a statement from a guy who claims to be responsible. Have you guys heard any of this? Well, I know you have, if you've been tuned in here, and believe me, you should be, but let me go ahead and read some parts of it again for those just joining us."

As Hall read several portions of the statement, Ms. Crenshaw recognized the rant as the one she'd just heard from Masten not a half an hour earlier. Her eyes cut toward him before her head did.

"Just drive," he commanded, sounding now like what he was: a captor speaking to a hostage.

Ms. Crenshaw fixed her eyes forward and drove.

"Okay, Donna," Hall called out from the radio, "let's take our first call. We've got Donley from Ashford, Arkansas, on the line. What say you, good sir?"

"Yeah, thanks, Tom," the caller said in a thick drawl. "Listen, I think whoever this guy is, he's got several screws loose, you know what I mean? The ol' elevator don't go all the way to the top. It's being held together with duct tape and bailin' wire. I mean, the Lord said that we's all gotta face judgment day, and I'd ruther be a coon up a tree than have to stand next to that fella in front of the good Lord." There was an emphasis on the word *good*.

"I hear ya, Donley," Hall responded. "You know, I was

thinking about something my preacher said in church the other day ..."

Masten couldn't take anymore. He reached up and turned off the radio. They rode along in silence for a few minutes until Ms. Crenshaw couldn't take it any longer.

"Well," she said, in an ironic drawl of her own, "it looks like you've got the hicks all stirred up."

Masten shot her a confused look that seemed angrier than it was. He knew that she knew. He knew it when she looked over at him during the radio broadcast. *It was true*, he thought. *Small town folks do notice everything—at least everything immediately around them.*

And Verna Crenshaw knew that Masten knew. She pursed her lips and gnawed on the inside of her cheek as she continued to drive. The silence grew heavier.

"I'm not afraid of dying, you know," she finally said, looking Masten square in the eyes. "So, if you're thinking you've got something over me with that, you can think again."

She felt relieved having said it. Masten nodded, looking almost grateful that she shared.

"I'm not either," he said after a moment. "Hell, most days I wish for it. It just seems to be a hard leap to make in practice. But, dying, killing, I just don't care anymore. I'm fine with either."

Ms. Crenshaw opened her mouth to respond to the man's terrifying comment when Max and Callie suddenly emerged at a T intersection in the road a hundred yards in front of them.

"Slow up," Masten said. "See what they do."

She and Masten watched as the car turned left and continued up the road. Ms. Crenshaw was thankful for the interruption. She'd been about to tell Masten that she was not going to let him hurt those two babies. But now she knew that if she said it, he would just kill her beforehand. Verna Crenshaw had been around the block a time or two. She decided to show him rather than tell him.

THIRTY-SIX

"TRUST ME, CHILD," REVEREND WHITE SAID FROM THE BACK seat. "This will get us where we're going faster."

"But you don't even have a phone!" Devon exclaimed.

"Don't need one," Reverend White countered.

"My phone says that we need to take the 68 out to Salinas then down the 101 to Paso Robles."

"Your phone doesn't know what I know, child," Reverend White said. "Have a little faith. Turn here. The Cabrillo Highway is what we want."

Devon shook her head but did as the man said. "I hope you know a shortcut or something, because otherwise, this is going to take all year. The cops at Peg's already cost us a ton of time." Hawthorne nodded his silent agreement.

The drive quickly became very beautiful, but Devon was right, it was not the shortest way to Paso Robles from Monterey. It was the road one took to Carmel, then on to Big Sur, and to several extraordinary state parks at various points farther south.

Open ocean was on their right. The highway was well above the beach, though, winding its way along rocky cliffs. Sandy coves seemed to alternate with giant rocks out in the water. Here and there large cypress trees sprouted from the cliff edge or out of one of the wave-splashed boulders.

"It's magnificent, isn't it?" Reverend White observed.

Devon's response was somewhere between a hum and a grunt. She didn't move her head as she made the sound because she was focused on crossing a bridge that was so high above the creek and beach below it was making her a little dizzy. The reverend left it at that. After half an hour, the silence began to wear on Hawthorne.

"Does anyone mind if I turn on the radio?" he asked.

No one responded, so Hawthorne touched the power knob and turned the volume up a little. He scanned through a hard-core rap song, which he didn't consider to be music in the first place. Then he scanned through a channel where some guy singing in a falsetto was moaning and groaning about something. *I'd rather listen to the rapper.* He landed on another tune about having a beer on a beach. He liked that, but it didn't seem to fit the vibe of the drive. Hawthorne finally settled on a news station, adjusted the volume down a little, and slumped back in his seat. It didn't take long for the church-bombing story to come to the surface. Hawthorne sat up abruptly, exchanged a look with Devon, and turned the volume back up. After five minutes of coverage of the various explosions and their aftermath, the story moved to the written statement of the man who claimed to be responsible.

By now the bizarre statement had probably been read a thousand times over the airwaves, but it was the first time anyone in the car had heard it. Devon and Hawthorne went pale.

"Oh my God," Devon shouted, looking over at Hawthorne. "My boss is a psychopath! And I've known him since before I can remember!" She stepped on the gas a little harder, as if that would help somehow.

"So, what do we do now?" Hawthorne asked, more to himself than anyone else.

"We keep doing what we're doing," Reverend White said.

"I think this is one for the cops," Hawthorne replied.

"I think you're right," Reverend White answered. "The police are looking, but ...," he paused, "that doesn't mean we can't help too. An extra set of eyes never hurts a thing, and we have the side entrance covered from this road."

"What do you mean?" Devon asked.

"Well, if Dr. Masten is in Paso Robles and runs, there are major highways running north and south and then to the east. There's another two-lane blacktop that's a bit north of the city, and that's the one to be taken to escape all of that. And that road meets this road."

"Huh," Devon said, tilting her head a bit. *Maybe the old guy did have a plan.*

Then she thought again. "But you said this road will get us to Paso Robles faster."

"No," Reverend White drew the word out. "I said it will get us where we're *going* faster."

"Well, then, where's that?" Devon asked.

"The side entrance," Reverend White answered, in a tone that was part patient and part exasperated. "Like I just told you."

"Okay." Devon let it drop.

The car was silent for a few minutes, except for the radio, which provided continuous coverage of the explosions.

"This guy's going to burn in hell," Hawthorne chimed in.

"Sounds to me like he's already there," Reverend White responded.

"Well, yeah, but that's not what I meant."

"I know what you meant," Reverend White said. "I just find it funny that many people believe in some form of heaven and hell, but *only* in the afterlife. I don't believe that. I think the construction duties of heaven and hell fall to us, here. We can make one or the other, or sometimes both, depending on how we choose to act as human beings during our time in this world."

Devon glanced over at Hawthorne with raised eyebrows.

"Are you sure you're a priest?" she asked.

"I never said I was a priest," Reverend White shot back.

"Wait, what?" Devon almost shouted. "Then why are you dressed like a priest?"

"Now you're going to mock my wardrobe?" Reverend White asked. Neither Devon nor Hawthorne could see his face, but both heard the wry humor in his question.

"That's not what I meant," Devon said, unsure how much further to push.

"I am a simple servant," Reverend White said. "I am dressed like a simple servant. I don't need any further labels than that."

The car went silent again, but the radio played on.

"So," Hawthorne said after a while. "What's your take on what this guy said in his statement?"

Devon responded first. "I think he's batshit crazy! And I can't believe I never knew!"

"Sure, sure," Reverend White agreed, nodding along. "His pain and anger are clear, and his actions are regrettable, to say the least. But as to the rest, I wonder if he's really wrong?"

Devon looked like she just smelled rotten milk. "What?"

"Well, think it through," White said. "Death and suffering are indiscriminate. Sometimes we bring it upon ourselves. We often bring it on each other. Sometimes it just lands on us. Why is that? Why is it that the rain falls on the good as often as the wicked? Why *does* it seem that God doesn't protect his flock?"

"I think many would argue the opposite," Hawthorne responded. "People experience miracles every day. An inexplicably healed sickness. A near miss with a bus, or a baseball, or any number of other things. It happens all the time. Maybe there is a method or a reason we just don't see."

"Maybe," White conceded. "Or maybe it's just chance that we interpret as being part of some higher plan, or some reward for being faithful. The problem with that is that I've known many good and faithful people over many years who have not been extended such miracles. I think the issue is that people see and believe only what they want to see and believe."

"Yeah," Devon said, half kidding and half sarcastic, "you are definitely not a priest."

Hawthorne responded with an uncomfortable snicker until he heard Reverend White's full-throated laugh. Then he joined in.

"I am a humble servant, my dear," White repeated, still chuckling. "I am just here to help. Truly, though," he continued, "the problem is not with God. The confusion lies in our assumptions. And the answers to our questions will never be found until we back up and change those assumptions. Our questions and our doubts are based on a specific interpretation of God that we have inherited from those that have lived before us. But maybe they were wrong.

Despite our beliefs, no matter how strongly held, we are simply passengers on a ride, and we have no idea how the ride works, when it ends, or why it was put here in the first place. That's the thing that we need to come to terms with. Once we do that, we can stop beating our chests about what we believe, stop judging those who are different from us, and simply take care of one another on this ride. Only then will we start to see glimmers of Heaven."

"That's interesting," Hawthorne said as he thought about the reverend's words. "Do you really believe that?"

"I do," Reverend White said without hesitating. "And I think the poor man from the radio, Dr. Masten, has been maddened by the scratching of the surface. He seems to be under the impression that life on Earth is a right guaranteed by God, and when lives are lost God has turned on us. But if God is monarch of all, nature is the governor of our existence in this world, and nature has a much different perspective on the value of our lives here than we do."

This guy sounds like my physics professor, Devon thought.

"Hmm," Hawthorne grunted as he rubbed the back of a finger across his lips and nodded.

"*Eloi, Eloi, lama sabachthani,*" White said, almost in a whisper.

"My God, my God, why have you forsaken me?" Hawthorne responded in a similar whisper.

"That's right, Mr. Hawthorne," Reverend White said. "It's Aramaic. According to the Book of Matthew, Jesus spoke those words on the cross. Even the son of God wasn't spared his life on this Earth. Shouldn't that tell us all something? Perhaps there is a much bigger picture."

Devon shook her head. *This guy's a trip.* "What about Callie?" she asked.

"What about her?" White replied.

"Do you think she lived a life as another person before she became Callie?"

"Oh goodness," White said. "I wouldn't know. But would it make a difference?"

"What do you mean?"

"Well, it wouldn't change the laws of God or nature while she was alive, in whatever life. It wouldn't change the physical part of any particular life. Maybe it would affect the way subsequent lives were lived, maybe not. Mostly, it just bumps against some peoples' beliefs of one life followed by a heaven or hell or whatever in the afterlife, for what those beliefs are worth."

There was a long silence. The beauty of the coastal drive had become so continuous that it faded into the background. What once seemed special had become almost monotonous. Plus, the road had moved from the edge of the sea cliffs into a more mountainous area.

"How much farther do we need to go on this road?" she asked.

"Not far," Reverend White said, "maybe twenty more minutes."

Devon nodded and kept driving. A few minutes later, they passed a sign for the Julia Pfeiffer Burns State Park.

"Can we stop here for a bit?" the reverend asked. "I need to stretch my legs."

Devon pulled off the highway and into the park entrance. There was a self-pay station along the road just inside. The ten-dollar entrance fee was based on the honor system, as no ranger was present. Devon ignored it, justifying her decision by the fact that they would not be there very long. When the three got out of the car, each of them stretched and walked around a bit.

"May I borrow one of your phones?" White asked. "I need to check in."

"Sure, use mine," Hawthorne said, handing White his phone. "Say, we never did ask you, what church are you with?"

"Oh, it's an unassuming little place just a few blocks from the aquarium. It's a small, but lovely congregation."

"Wow!" Devon yelled. "Check this out!"

Hawthorne looked up and walked quickly down a path to join Devon. The path was a wooden boardwalk edged by a rustic wooden fence. To the left, a thin, but tall waterfall fell onto the sandy beach below. The beach was a compressed semi-circle with giant rocks gating each side. A large boulder poked out of the water a short distance out. Wind-blown Cypress trees grew out of the rocks that surrounded the small, green water lagoon.

"That's amazing!" Hawthorne said, admiring the view.

"Maybe one day we'll come to a place like this together under more agreeable circumstances," Devon teased.

Hawthorne did a bit of a double take and felt himself blush. Devon laughed out loud.

"Come on, stud," she said as she patted his back. "I think the kooky reverend is ready to roll."

Hawthorne followed Devon back to the car. Reverend White handed Hawthorne's phone back to him and climbed into the rear seat. Devon was still smiling as she pulled out onto the highway. Hawthorne sat in awkward silence.

"Is everything okay?" the reverend asked. "What'd I miss?"

"You didn't miss anything," Devon answered.

Reverend White didn't buy it, but let it go. "Well, not much farther now."

❖ ❖ ❖

Colusa thought for a few minutes about the text. He wasn't familiar with the area, but he knew the old man could not have gone too far. He wondered where a checkpoint might be. This was California, not North Korea. He opened the map app on his phone and pinched his forefinger and thumb together against the screen until he had an area to examine.

It didn't take him long to put it together. About ten miles

north was a road that led from the highway through Fort Hunter Liggett, a nearby Army base. Colusa pulled back onto the road and continued south until he reached the next exit, where he made a U-turn and rejoined the northbound lanes.

When he reached the scene he created earlier, Colusa had to slow down because the inside lanes in both directions were blocked by patrol cars. A young officer standing on a broken white line in the middle of the highway waved him through.

Like most drivers there, Colusa could not help but rubberneck in the presence of so many flashing, red and blue lights. An ambulance with all doors open was backed up near the trooper's body, which was covered with a yellow tarp that didn't quite hide the feet. There was a fire truck on the shoulder of the road and multiple patrol cars dotting the area.

Colusa slowed a little as he looked until the young trooper's motions became more insistent. He then pressed down on the gas and left the scene behind him. He looked around at the broad rolling hills covered with collections of trees interspersed here and there with patches of green grass with some tall brown grass in between the small groves.

The sign for Exit 252 told him where he needed to go. He took the exit and followed along the path of the other two cars that preceded him.

THIRTY-SEVEN

MAX HAD NO IDEA WHERE HE WAS GOING. HE TOOK THE EXIT off the highway because he thought he might be followed, either by the man who'd kidnapped them, or by the crazy bastard that shot at them, twice! *Who the hell was that guy?* Max had no idea. He just wanted off the grid for a while. Callie had fallen asleep in the back seat, exhausted from her hellish day.

Max had become more comfortable behind the wheel and was determined that he would drive all the way home if necessary. He knew he needed to call and check in. He imagined that his mother was beside herself at this point and he hated that, but he didn't have his phone with him, and he hadn't seen a safe place to stop. Right now, keeping himself and Callie alive and free was his priority. He would find a place as soon as he could.

The road stayed straight for a while then made a gentle ninety-degree curve around to the right, before straightening out again. He could see the mountain getting closer and could tell the elevation was rising. The landscape was changing from brown grass to green trees.

Max hadn't been driving fast since he left the highway, but

a couple of miles later he slowed even more when the road presented a few tight turns. As the elevation rose higher, he could see a deep canyon on one side, a rock wall on the other.

He slowed the car to a crawl when the road narrowed, and he began to experience one hairpin turn after another. He and Callie were now solidly in the mountains. Every turn brought a rock wall on one side of the car and dense pines on the other.

He grew more uncomfortable and nervous as the road edged closer to the side of the mountain but gasped after the next turn.

"Holy shit!" he shouted as he hit the brakes.

This stretch of road was terrifying. There was a wall to the right, and nothing at all to the left but a steep drop-off and a view of a distant green mountain rising from a sea of fog. There were no trees at the edge, and no guardrail. Max saw only a foot or so of patchy grass by the side of the road. The patch of green was all that stood between them and certain death in the form of a straight fall of several hundred feet. Max wanted desperately to turn around, but there was no way to do it.

He began trembling as he gripped the steering wheel, tears forming in his eyes. He stopped the car and looked back at Callie. She was still asleep, with the hole in the rear windshield above her as big as ever. The abyss loomed ahead, and Max, frozen, sat in the stopped car trying to gather himself. He couldn't tell how long because his intense fear wrecked his internal clock. It could have been five minutes, or an hour. All he knew was that at some point, a car pulled up behind him.

The movement of the other vehicle caught Max's attention in the rearview mirror. He watched the car stop behind him, his fear now flanking on two fronts. The first was the road ahead, the second arose from his dread of who was in the car behind him.

Max didn't know what to do. He didn't know if he was about to be shot or abducted for a second time. He imagined it could be both, or something worse. Max watched the car for what seemed an eternity. It didn't move and no one got out. The inactivity intensified his terror.

As the various scenarios played out in his mind, Max could

hear the engine of the car behind him revving up and down in a rhythmic succession, the open hole in the rear window amplifying the sound. Tears ran down his face. None of the scenarios he imagined were good. Max tried to process the situation but focused instead on his erratic heartbeat, and a panting rate that would match a dog on a hot day. He took a deep breath and tried to calm himself, at least a little.

All the while, the engine of the car behind him revved. The tenor sound of a car horn snapped Max out of his panic. He didn't respond to the first honk, so the horn came again. Max didn't respond to the second honk, either. On the third honk, the driver laid on the horn and held it for several seconds.

The obnoxious noise finally brought Max back. *Maybe the guy isn't trying to kill me, unless I don't move.* He eased his foot off the brake and allowed the car to crawl forward, pulling to the right as far as he could to hug the wall and put as much distance as possible between himself and the drop at the other side of the road.

The car behind him didn't like the pace and continued the incessant honking, but Max was driving as fast as he dared. He eased forward and rounded another sharp curve. Just after the turn, he saw an area of packed dirt off the pavement on the abyss side. The raised bank of dirt provided at least an illusion of protection from the void beyond.

The other driver took the opportunity and hit the gas, passing Max on the left. As he did, the girl in the passenger's seat hung out of her open window and gave Max a salute of sorts. She was yelling something at him, but he couldn't make out what she was saying. He had an idea, but he didn't care. That car was the least of his worries. Besides, he'd probably heard worse in the lunch line at school.

Max pressed on slowly. The hairpin turns kept coming, but the unprotected cliff was finally replaced by an area of dense pines. The rock wall sheltered oncoming traffic. The drop off was on his side now, but the trees obscured it. He felt a little more comfortable on this section of the road.

His confidence didn't last long. The next turn brought

another demon: fog. The rock wall had shifted back to his side of the road, and the abyss was once again open and obvious on the other side. It was a little different here though, with scrubby trees poking up from the steep mountainside below, and some sections had old, rusty guardrails.

The road was ascending again, and although the fog was light at first, in the span of a few yards, it became much thicker. Max slowed the car back to a crawl when he couldn't see more than a few feet in front of him.

He rounded another couple of turns and was relieved to see the fog thinning out. As he approached the next turn, however, the car began to sputter. Pressing on the gas pedal didn't help. The car died a few yards later. Max used what little inertia was left to pull it closer to the wall and out of the road.

He had no idea what was wrong at first. Studying the dashboard, he saw the fuel gauge was sitting below the empty mark. Max let out a groan as he slammed the back of his head into the headrest a couple of times. He hadn't thought about gas the whole time he'd been driving.

Max didn't know what to do. He was stuck on the scariest road he'd ever seen. He had no gas, and he had no phone. What he did have, however, was a traumatized sister sleeping in the back seat under a blown-out window. He was traumatized, too. The day, which had started out great, went to hell in a hurry.

He was tired of being chased, tired of being afraid, tired of being shot at, tired of driving on this god forsaken road, and while he was thinking of it, tired of being victimized and bullied generally. Max was just tired. His body's response to this revelation was to do nothing but sit there in silence for a while.

He had to admit the view was amazing. He'd never seen anything like it. The mountains and valleys contrasted with the fog in the distance, and the dense forests nearby made it look cinematic. But the road was scary—evil even. It felt to Max like the road was daring him to make one mistake. *Is the whole universe trying to kill me today?*

Max's musings were interrupted by another approaching car. This time, he tried to waive it around, but the car stopped behind him. It was farther back than before, so it was not as menacing or as loud, but still concerning. He rolled down his window and made a grand gesture of motioning the car on, but it didn't work. Max heard the engine of the car turn off. He rolled his window back up. *Oh, hell!*

❖ ❖ ❖

Verna Crenshaw wasn't having the time of her life winding around the dangerous switchbacks either. She wasn't a fast driver to begin with. She was the person who exasperated, almost to violence, every driver under the age of forty in Paso Robles. But she was proud of herself for managing to stay with the two babies in the car in front of her. She wasn't going to let anything happen to them. Nonetheless, she let out a huge sigh of relief when Masten told her to stop and kill the engine.

Masten knew exactly where they were. He had thought, even dreamed, about this place many times. He was bitter that the kid chose to stop the car in this exact spot. The drive over from the highway was bad enough, but this was adding insult to injury. He worked hard to quash both the extreme anger and hollow sadness he was feeling at that moment. He wondered how much these kids really knew.

Masten had distracted himself a little during the drive by examining the damage done to his car. Once past that, however, the anger resurfaced, and he wondered if there were other cars on the road nearby. He and Ms. Crenshaw had been passed by a couple of daredevils a few miles back, but that was it as far as he knew.

"Stay here," Masten pointed at Ms. Crenshaw, as he opened the car door.

"I'll do no such thing," she retorted, opening her own door.

Masten was irritated but took no action. He had other things on his mind. He walked from Ms. Crenshaw's car to the driver's side window of his own car, where Max looked back. The look of horror on Max's face affected Masten, but only for a moment.

He spent a few seconds examining the inside of his car, then rapped on the window with a knuckle. He followed the knock with a circular motion of his index finger indicating that he wanted Max to roll down the window. Max shook his head *no*. Masten gave an exasperated look and repeated his gestures, as did Max. Masten then walked around to the back of the car and leaned forward on the trunk.

"Hey, kid," Masten half shouted into the car. "I just want to talk."

"Why are you following us?" Max shouted back.

"Because you stole my car!" Masten answered.

It was a lie, Masten knew, but it was a plausible lie, and he could see that it made Max think for a moment. But Max was quick minded too.

"I stole your car because you kidnapped us!" Max argued back, his tired frustration loud and clear. "You trapped us in a basement, and I had no other way to get out of there."

That round went to Max and Masten's raised eyebrows showed that he knew it.

"Let me ask you this," Masten said, closing his eyes and rubbing his forehead with the fingers of his left hand. "Why did you stop here, in this place?"

"I ran out of gas."

Max's response was simple, innocent, and honest, and it hit Masten like a board over the head. *It wasn't pre-planned.* Masten placed his index finger and thumb against his mouth. He looked away for a moment, thinking. He looked back into the car and pointed at the broken back window.

"Is your sister okay?"

"Yeah, but she's tired and scared," Max answered. "We both just want to go home."

"Mmm, I don't know." Masten's response was cold. She's accused me of some pretty horrible things. I need to talk to her. Why don't you wake her up?"

Masten's demeanor was as terrifying to Max as the cliff at the edge of the road.

"Please, mister," Max said, "we really just want to go home."

Verna Crenshaw, who now stood behind Masten, had heard

enough.

"Sugar," she said to Max as she pulled a small subcompact 9mm pistol from the purse hanging over her shoulder. "Get your sister and take her back to my car. I'll take you home. I don't think this man will mind that much." Masten's eyes widened, and he put his hands up. Ms. Crenshaw winked and smiled. "You can take the girl out of the South, right?"

She held the gun on Masten while Max shook Callie awake. Callie had slept through a windy drive, a revving car engine, and a blaring horn, but awoke within seconds of Max touching her shoulder. Her long straight hair had become ratty during her nap. She sat up and rubbed her eyes. Max opened the back car door, but it took Callie a couple of minutes to get her bearings.

She crawled out of the car and saw Masten standing with his arms up watching Ms. Crenshaw.

"Come on, sweetie," Ms. Crenshaw said when Callie made eye contact.

Callie stood by the car rubbing the sleep out of her eyes, trying to process the scene. She looked at Max, then at Masten, and back at Ms. Crenshaw. She then took in the road, the rock wall, the rusty guardrail, and the chasm below.

"We're here," Callie said in a casual tone that didn't fit the intensity of the things happening around her.

Ms. Crenshaw's eyes shot toward Max, but she kept the bead on Masten's chest.

"We're where, dear?" she asked, turning her head toward Callie, but keeping her eyes on Masten.

"This is where I died," Callie said.

"I'm sorry, what?" Ms. Crenshaw asked, her eyebrows raised high.

"Remember?" Callie said, now looking squarely at Masten. "Our car was over there." Callie pointed to a spot across the road.

"There was a tire laying right there on the ground." She pointed to another nearby spot. "I was standing on the road beside you. You crawled up from the edge of that cliff there and were on your hands and knees, and then you rolled onto your back. Then I was standing right over you. I tried to touch your shoulder, but you didn't know I was there. Then I wasn't there anymore."

Masten's knees buckled, and he fell to the ground. He started sobbing. Ms. Crenshaw lowered her pistol, but just down to her side. Max searched the faces of his sister and Ms. Crenshaw, the back of Masten's head, and the surrounding scene trying to make sense out of any of this. Ms. Crenshaw could only shake her head. She raised her gun again slightly when a silver car, coming from the other direction, stopped several yards in front of them.

THIRTY-EIGHT

"CALLIE!" DEVON SHOUTED RUNNING FULL SPEED TOWARD the girl. "Oh, my God, are you guys okay?" Devon couldn't resist the urge to grab and hug the little girl. After a moment, she released one arm from Callie and held out a hand toward Max.

"Are you okay, Max?"

Max didn't speak. He started shaking his head no, but then contradicted himself with a shrug.

"Are you their mother?" Ms. Crenshaw asked, her pistol pointing at the ground.

"No," Devon responded. "I'm not. I'm just the idiot who started this whole mess. Their mother is back in Monterey, worried sick. We need to call her right now. Todd?"

"I'm on it," Hawthorne shouted.

"Well," Ms. Crenshaw drawled, gesturing toward Masten with her gun. "I don't know what you mean, but it seems to me that *this* is the idiot responsible for this mess. Are you with him?"

"No!" Devon answered, keeping an eye on the gun. "Well, he's my boss, but no, I am *not* with him."

Hawthorne and Reverend White approached the scene, both

casting curious stares at Masten, who was still on the ground sobbing.

"I talked to Peg," Hawthorne said. "She's still at the house with several police officers. They are going to reach out to the Paso Robles department and have them meet us here." Devon and Ms. Crenshaw nodded in agreement.

"I guess you gave this one a good scare," Reverend White said, still looking at Masten.

"I didn't do that," Ms. Crenshaw responded, referring to Masten's less than dignified position on the ground. "The girl said something about dying here and he dropped like a sack of potatoes."

"That's odd," Reverend White said "Well, anyway, we'd better get these kids ready to head home. The police will be here shortly." Reverend White held one hand out to Max and one out to Callie. "Let's wait back here, loves," he said, looking and sounding like the gentlest of grandfathers. "Max, my boy, I told you to mind your gas." The reverend chuckled as he started walking the kids back to Devon's car.

"Did you kill my father?" Devon asked, standing over Masten.

Masten looked up then dropped his eyes back down. He managed a slight nod. "I hired a man."

"Who?"

"I don't know. It was all anonymous. On the internet. The dark parts."

"Why?"

"I needed your father's files, and he wouldn't give them to me." Masten still couldn't look up.

"Needed his files for what?" Devon's tone was sharp, angry … sad.

"Look Devon. I'm a broken man. Kick me. Shoot me. Whatever you want. I know you're angry. I won't fight. I deserve it. But nothing anyone docs to me can huit worse than the pain I already feel every day."

Devon touched her mouth and looked up at the mountains across the canyon.

Masten raised himself up a little. "I wanted to do good at first. I did. But your father didn't believe. He didn't believe in what we found. You should know that I really did try to look after you. Maybe it was guilt. Maybe you we're all I had left. I don't know. It's no excuse."

Tears now formed in Devon's eyes. She tried to hold them back but couldn't. Through her sobs she said, "He was my father. He was all *I* had."

Masten nodded.

Devon took a deep breath. "Did the files have anything to do with the churches?"

Masten slumped back down and nodded again.

"Why?" Devon whispered. "You killed so many innocent people."

Masten rose to his hands and knees. There was a little more power in his voice. "He took my wife and daughter."

"Who did?" Devon asked.

"God."

Devon recoiled but said nothing.

"I had faith. That faith turned to knowledge. I *knew* what we found. We found physical proof of God. All I wanted to do was help, and he still took them from me. I needed the data from your father to show the world that God is real. I needed revenge."

Devon raised an eyebrow and looked at Ms. Crenshaw. She shrugged.

"My wife, before she died, never missed the Monday sunrise service at the Mariner's Chapel. She was devout. *I* was devout. We never missed in Santa Fe either, before we moved to Los Angeles. My daughter was born there. She was baptized in that church. My wife and I were married in that church. And God turned his back on me."

Devon didn't know how to respond. Nothing had happened in Santa Fe. *Was something more coming?* She looked around, wondering. "What about the rest?"

"They were random," Masten's voice was vacant. "They just proved my point."

"Why now?" Devon asked.

"The whole thing took some time to plan, but more than that, Claire would have been eighteen tomorrow. It seemed like a decent benchmark to make a point of a precious life lost."

Ms. Crenshaw shook her head, looking baffled, but remained at her post, gun at the ready by her side. Devon said nothing more. She turned and followed Hawthorne, the reverend and the kids back to her car. None of them saw or heard the car approach from behind.

❖ ❖ ❖

The first shot hit Verna Crenshaw just above the right shoulder blade. She dropped to the ground like the sack of potatoes she'd mentioned moments earlier. Colusa intended the shot to be square in the upper back, but the wind eddies created by the mountain wall and the valley in such close proximity carried the bullet a few inches up and to the right. He didn't care. He would aim the next shot a little down and to the left.

Colusa looked over the old woman's body and saw a man kneeling on the ground, his eyes wide with horror. He recognized the man from the cellar—the moneyman. He would deal with him last. The rest of the people on the road were now running toward a silver sedan about thirty yards away.

He moved forward past the man on the ground, who was squinting with one eye closed and holding one hand up in Colusa's direction. Colusa glanced down at him then moved on. He advanced past the blue car with the blown out rear windshield. He shook his head in frustration. *That should have ended this.*

The five people in front of him, including the girl, were now racing into the silver car and slamming the doors shut. The headlights and the yellow running lights flashed briefly as the car started. Colusa stopped and stood perfectly still. Through the windshield, he saw the faces he'd been studying back on the highway. It was the doctor and the reporter. Colusa smiled. *Three birds with one stone.*

He raised his gun, holding it with two hands. Colusa began

to walk forward. He put one shot through the center of the windshield straight at the reporter's head. He didn't like killing at a distance. He much preferred point blank. It prevented later surprises. But he could see that he'd hit Hawthorne square in the neck.

Colusa could see frantic activity in the car. He now wanted a shot at the doctor, but before he could take it, she turned around and leapt into the back. He'd come back to her. The front passenger door opened, as did the two rear doors. When he saw a tall, white-haired man rush out of the front passenger's seat and around to the back door, Colusa fired one bullet at the front car door. He wasn't trying to kill the man in black at that point; he just wanted him pinned down. Colusa strode forward.

In response to the bullets, Reverend White pulled the boy from the back passenger's side of the car and moved him around to the rear, pausing there for a moment, crouching as he worked his way to the other back door. The front driver's side door remained closed. When the young girl emerged from the car, Colusa decided he had a decent shot, and he took it.

He aimed his fifth bullet at a spot on the back driver's side door and pulled the trigger. The winds stayed predictable. The bullet pierced the middle of the door, leaving a sunken hole with no paint around the edges. Colusa watched the girl drop and the old man reach down after her.

He nodded with satisfaction. *Mission accomplished.* He wished he could have been closer, but he could see from where he was that it was a center mass body shot. He knew he was done when he heard the shrill scream of the boy call out the girl's name. It was now time to deal with the old man on the ground. Colusa turned and began walking that way.

❖ ❖ ❖

When Colusa passed him earlier, walking toward the silver car, Masten rose from the ground and crouch-walked to his badly damaged blue car. He watched the next shots play out from the driver's seat. The keys were in the ignition, but the kid was right; the car wouldn't start. He no longer had any doubts about the girl's claims. Somehow, in some way that he could never understand, his daughter had revisited him.

He never knew that in his darkest moments of shock, panic, and despair immediately following the incident, Claire was right there with him, trying to console him. The tears started flowing again and a wave of nausea came over him for even thinking about hurting the girl. She was Claire! Or at least some part of her.

Now she was in danger again and he had no idea how to help. If the damn car would only start, he would just run the asshole down. He looked over at Ms. Crenshaw, who was still unconscious on the road, but had her pistol firmly in hand. He opened his car door, ran over, and grabbed the gun.

Colusa fired his last shots as Masten approached him from behind, the gun held straight out in front of him. When Colusa turned, he saw Masten and raised his own gun.

"I've only got one bullet left, but you can have it." Colusa's voice was cold and smug.

Masten said nothing in response. He studied the man's face and realized it was time to kill the demon that he had conjured. Masten knew he had become a demon as well. He was now responsible for the deaths of hundreds of people. But at least he was a devil he knew. He had made choices, and he now acknowledged they were very poor choices that had ruined a lot of lives, just as his had been ruined, He would answer for that. Right now, though, he needed to rid the world of the devil no one knew.

Masten aimed the gun at Colusa's head and pulled the trigger. He heard only a metallic clicking sound. He pulled the trigger again. The result was the same. *Shit!* The gun was empty. The old woman had been bluffing all along.

Masten threw the gun down and raised his hands. He needed time. He was of no use to anyone dead right now. Colusa motioned his revolver toward his car.

"Get in," Colusa said. "You and I have some unfinished business."

A brief flash of motion caught Masten's eye as he looked at Colusa. Colusa saw the look on Masten's face and heard a sustained growling sound. By the time Colusa turned to look, Devon was only a few feet away, running full speed ahead.

Devon recognized the man. Black glasses. Balding head. She had no more questions and no more doubts. He was the monster from the cliff come to life on the mountaintop. She hit Colusa with her arms out and her right shoulder lowered, wrapping Colusa up and making full contact in the center of the assassin's chest. Colusa's legs flew up in the air. He landed back first on the pavement a second later. The impact caused Colusa's head to snap back and slam hard onto the ground, knocking him unconscious. Devon stayed on him, fists coming from the left and the right.

"You son of a bitch asshole!" She yelled with every punch.

Devon punched until Colusa's nose bled and his eyes and lips swelled up and turned purple.

"It's alright, Devon," Masten finally said, touching her shoulder.

Devon rolled off Colusa and sat on the ground, cross-legged, panting hard and crying.

"He killed my father." She said looking up at Masten. "And so did you! I should beat you senseless too."

Masten looked toward the other car and saw Reverend White standing over Max and Callie, his hands held in prayer. Max was alternating between pushing down on Callie's chest and holding her nose and breathing into her mouth at intervals.

"And now you've killed that little girl too!" Devon said between sobs.

Masten watched the scene completely frozen. He had no words. He was certain that whatever piece of his daughter he had experienced over the past week was now gone. Darkness started closing in from the periphery of his vision. He hated this place. He hated it more now than he did five years ago. This place took his family from him. For the briefest of moments, he'd gotten his daughter back, but had been too blind and angry to see it. Masten hated himself for that. But he was enraged at the fact that this place snatched Claire away from him a second time, and even more enraged that it was his own fault.

Masten heard sirens in the distance. The cops couldn't deliver the justice that he or the unconscious man deserved. He reached down and grabbed Colusa under each armpit and dragged him to Colusa's car. Colusa began to stir as Masten tried to lift him into the back seat.

"The cops are coming," Masten told him. "We've got to get out of here."

Colusa nodded and did his best to help Masten load him in. When Colusa was finally sitting in the backseat, he leaned his bloodied head against the headrest.

"Do you have the keys?"

Barely conscious, Colusa reached into his pocket and handed Masten the keys. Masten started the ignition and took a deep breath. The sirens were much louder now.

"Let's go," Colusa muttered.

"Yes," Masten agreed. "Let's go."

He put the car in gear and punched the gas, pulling around his own shot-up car and into the oncoming traffic lane. He continued forward, gaining speed, until he passed Devon's car with Reverend White praying and Max working to keep Callie alive. Masten moved back into his lane just as an ambulance passed, approaching from the other direction.

Masten pulled the steering wheel hard to the left, his foot still firmly on the gas. He scraped the side of Colusa's car on the same rusty guardrail that had done nothing to save his wife and daughter. The car left the pavement, crossed the dirt shoulder, passed across the tops of the scrubby bushes, and became airborne. For an instant, Masten felt the same butterflies in his stomach that Callie described on the day they met. He could hear Colusa screaming in the back.

❖ ❖ ❖

"What the hell was that?" one of the paramedics asked, as the car flashed past them and over the cliff.

"Jesus!" the other one responded. "Must be one of those days. I'll call it in, but those guys are gone. Let's see what we have up here."

The ambulance stopped just a few feet from Callie and three paramedics leaped into action. Hawthorne was still bleeding from his neck, and one of the EMTs laid him down and began treating his wound. Devon stood over them. The paramedic slowed the bleeding, but told Devon that Hawthorne needed immediate medical attention. They would have to find a way to get him out of there.

The paramedic then moved up the road to examine Ms. Crenshaw. She was now conscious, bloodied, and in a lot of pain, but her injuries were not life threatening. The single ambulance didn't have room for all three of the wounded, so Devon agreed with the paramedics that she would follow the ambulance and get Hawthorne and Ms. Crenshaw to Big Sur, where another ambulance would take them to the emergency room.

The ambulance reversed course on the narrow road and pulled away with Callie, heading back to the highway on the coast. Hawthorne and Ms. Crenshaw loaded into the back of Devon's car. Hawthorne lay across the seat, his heading resting on Ms. Crenshaw's lap. Max was still watching the ambulance weave down the road with his sister.

"Max!" Devon shouted. "We have to go. We'll be right behind them."

Max got into the car and Devon fired the ignition. She then realized that Reverend White was not with them. Devon cursed and got out. She looked up and down the road, but there was no sign of the reverend.

"Reverend White!" she called, then swore. "Reverend White!" she shouted louder.

There was no response. The only thing she could figure was that he'd somehow talked his way into the ambulance with Callie. She would check at the hospital. Right now, she had to move. She hit the gas and hugged the tail end of the ambulance all the way back to Big Sur. Wind whistled through the small, spider-webbed hole in her windshield.

The ambulance carrying Callie sped on to Salinas, where there was a hospital with a Level II Trauma Center. In Big Sur, Hawthorne and Ms. Crenshaw were loaded into other vehicles and taken to Salinas as well.

THIRTY-NINE

LIFE IS NOT PERMANENT, BUT THEN NEITHER IS DEATH. AS I watch the men and women working on my body, and see the others nearby, I am struck by the sadness we associate with dying. We miss each other terribly when we leave, or when they leave, but it's never the end. We see each other in between lives and then we circle back. It's never exactly the same, but we always circle back.

Maybe it's that person you lock eyes with on the street because you somehow look familiar to each other. Maybe it's a new friend with whom you feel an immediate, oddly strong connection. Maybe it's your new baby daughter having the exact birthmark on her leg that your grandfather had. You can see it every day if you look.

I've been here before, and I'm usually not here long. At some point soon, I will start to feel a familiar gentle push, like a breeze blowing a cloud in one direction or another. I never know the direction I'm being pushed. I just stop being here and start being someplace else.

Perhaps I will go back to being Callie Schroeder, perhaps not. I don't know. But it doesn't seem to matter. Wherever I end up, there will be pain, but there will also be joy. The journey and the growth seem to be the point.

I can feel the breeze beginning to blow. It's cool and light and reassuring. I have no fear or anxiety. If anything, I look forward to what comes next.

❖ ❖ ❖

"We've got her back!" the doctor shouted a moment after the third jolt of the defibrillator pads.

The machine to his left began beeping rhythmically after a terrifying period of nothing but a continuous tone. The screen was now showing strong spikes. It was just what the doctor wanted to see. He turned away from the table and wiped his eyes. He and the angels in scrubs around him had been frantic for the better part of an hour trying to save this baby. He did not want to have to tell another mother that she had lost her child.

The surgeon had repaired the damage to the little girl's lung and closed the bullet wound, but she had lost a lot of blood. This was a lucky day though. Her brother was close by and was able to donate enough of their shared rare AB negative blood type to get her through. Max was now in the next room sipping orange juice. He was the doctor's second stop.

❖ ❖ ❖

"Your sister's going to be just fine," the doctor told Max. "You saved her life. You're a hero." Max looked up, tears welling in his eyes.

The doctor patted Max on the shoulder. "I've already spoken with your mother," he said. "She's in with your sister now. Are you okay?"

Max assured the doctor he was fine. When the doctor left, Max took another sip of orange juice and thought about the fact that he had never been a hero in his life. That was a first. But it *was* his sister. Maybe sometimes we're pushed beyond our limits by love without limits.

Devon poked her head in and checked on Max. She was exhausted. She'd been shuttling between the surgical waiting room, Ms. Crenshaw's room, and Hawthorne's room. She told Max that Ms. Crenshaw was fine and would probably be released in the next couple of days. Ms. Crenshaw was lucky. The bullet had exited just a quarter of an inch below her right collarbone and the wound wasn't severe. The doctors worked their magic, but the damage was soft tissue only, nothing vital.

Hawthorne's surgery, she informed Max, had been more extensive. The bullet that hit him tore through neck muscle and lodged a small piece of glass from the front windshield just between the jugular and brachiocephalic veins. The bullet and the glass literally threaded a needle. The doctors were amazed that the piece of glass didn't end up severing something vital and killing him right there on the road. But Devon told Max, Hawthorne was going to be fine.

She ducked out of Max' room, walked down the hall, and took a left to the elevator bank. Two floors up, she exited when the doors opened with a soft ding, then wound her way around the labyrinth of rooms until she reached Hawthorne's. She knocked softly and opened the door.

"Hey, good lookin'," she said, trying to lighten the mood, at least for herself. Hawthorne was asleep when she entered, so he didn't hear the quip.

Devon paused a few steps in and looked at the man in the hospital bed. He was covered with a white blanket and had tubes running from his neck and nose. Various other wires were running from his chest into what was clearly a heart and breathing monitor. The bed seemed to contain more machine parts than human parts, and Devon pressed the back of her hand underneath her nose and against her lips. After a minute, she used the same hand to wipe away her tears. Walking to the edge of the bed, she touched Hawthorne's hand, at first just brushing against it, but then wrapping her fingers around his. She didn't squeeze. She just needed to touch him.

The monitor attached to Hawthorne was silent, but the screen drew a continuous mountain-like picture over and over as it scrolled right. An air conditioner kicked on blowing cool air into the room. It was the only sound she heard. A little while later, she let go of Hawthorne's hand and touched the blanket covering his leg. She left the room without Hawthorne ever knowing she was there.

Devon stepped into the hall and let the back of her head fall against the wall. Reverend White popped into her mind, and she raised her head. *Where the hell was he? Did I leave him on the road? No way. He was right there. Plus, he seemed to love intruding on people's situations. He was in the hospital somewhere.*

Devon decided to look for him, so she went back to the elevator banks, rode down to the first floor, and retraced her steps to the emergency room.

"Can you tell me if the paramedics who brought Callie Schroeder in are still here?" she and asked the attending ER nurse. The nurse directed Devon to a café across the street, where the now-off duty paramedics were grabbing a bite, and taking their time, before the long ride back to Big Sur. Inside the café, Devon saw two well-chiseled men and a very fit woman sitting in a booth. They were sipping water and finishing their meals.

Devon was glad they hadn't yet left. The three exuded hero vibes that would rival any Special Forces soldiers, but they were exceedingly polite when Devon approached them and asked if Reverend White had accompanied Callie to the hospital. The EMTs looked confused.

"No one rode back with us, ma'am," one of them said, pointing around the small booth. "Taylor and Hoff worked on the girl, and I treated the other two and drove. No one else was in our rig. We have another unit down there now with the Forest Service working on the car that went over the edge. We'll ask them to take a look."

Devon nodded, thanked them and walked away, thinking. She had looked. She had yelled. The reverend wasn't there. *He wasn't on the road. He wasn't in my car. He wasn't in the ambulance. The other car drove off the side of the mountain. He wasn't in that car! And the last car didn't go anywhere. No one was in it. So where did he go?*

Devon rode the elevator back upstairs to check in on the others again. She saw Peg coming out of recovery and heading toward Max's room. Peg looked at Devon briefly but continued on her path. Devon stayed outside. As she passed the door, Devon saw Peg was hugging Max without saying a word. Devon braced herself against the wall and studied the ceiling. She dreaded the encounter, but felt compelled to say something, though she didn't know exactly what. Peg apparently sensed the same meeting was imminent because she finally came out and stopped, facing Devon.

"I am *so* sorry," Devon said as she moved her head from side to side. There was no holding back the tears or the anguish on her face.

Peg stared at Devon for a moment then stepped forward and pulled her into a tight hug.

"There was no way you could have known," Peg whispered.

Devon cried into Peg's shoulder for a long while. Peg finally pushed her back a little and looked her in the eyes while holding her shoulders.

"How is your friend, and the woman?" Peg asked.

A nod *yes* was all Devon could manage at first, still through tears. "They'll be fine," she finally whispered.

"Good."

Devon pulled away and pointed at the door to Callie's room. Peg nodded. "She's going to be okay."

Devon broke down again. Peg ran her hand up and down Devon's back.

"I guess your boyfriend's a pretty powerful writer," Peg said, trying to break the tension.

Devon looked up, confused.

"He should finish the story," Peg said. "He should tell it all, so that people know. Make them understand how real all of this was."

Devon searched Peg's face for any kind of read on whether the woman was serious. Peg finally answered the question.

"I'm serious," she said. "He should tell it all."

Devon nodded, and Peg walked back into the hospital room to join her son. Devon's emotions were a complete swirl, but she knew marching orders when she heard them. She listened to very few people, but she heard Peg loud and clear.

FORTY

HAWTHORNE WAS BACK AT HIS APARTMENT IN LOS ANGELES recovering from his brush with death. Devon, who had driven him home from the Salinas hospital went to his place several times a day since. She even arranged to have his car brought back from Monterey. She knocked on the door for her mid-day visit, holding a small white paper bag. It took Hawthorne a few minutes, but he eventually answered.

"I've got chicken soup!" Devon said shaking the bag around a little.

Hawthorne smiled and then winced as he touched the white bandage on his neck.

"You really don't have to do all of this for me." His voice was hoarse as he motioned her inside.

"What, you don't enjoy my company?" Devon asked, teasing.

Hawthorne chuckled a bit and Devon helped him sit down at the small table.

"Oh, I forgot to tell you this morning," she said, pulling the soup from the bag and laying down a white plastic spoon. "I called the Big Sur Fire Department to check about Reverend White. No one saw anyone on the road there. So, I did some calling around to a few churches in Monterey, and no one has ever heard of a Reverend White. Don't you think that's really weird?"

"Yeah," Hawthorne said, before he had to clear his throat. He winced again when he did so and reached up to touch the bandage again. "I do."

He sucked a small amount of soup from the spoon and swallowed with caution. Devon noticed that his eyebrows rose as he swallowed.

"Just take it slow," she said. "You're getting better already, I can tell."

Hawthorne's look said *whatever*.

"You know," he said, still hoarse and changing the subject back to Reverend White, "he used my phone to check in with his church when we stopped at that state park. Look on the phone and see who he called."

"Well, now, that's an idea!" Devon exclaimed. "Very impressive, Todd Hawthorne. Where is your phone?"

Hawthorne didn't have the strength to emphasize that was what he did for a living, and instead pointed to a small desk across the room. "You can do it," Hawthorne said, sipping another half-spoon of soup. "I'm not exactly able to multitask right now."

"Are you sure?" Devon asked, drawing the words out and looking at him from the corners of her eyes. "What if I snoop? What other girls' numbers am I going to find on here?"

Hawthorne started to laugh and made himself cough. "Stop," he said through a lot of pain and a little laughter.

Devon smiled as she scrolled through the call log. She stopped smiling a few moments later. She stared at the screen for a couple of seconds then looked away.

"Alright," she said. "Just so I'm not losing my mind here, that was last Saturday, right?"

"Yes," Hawthorne nodded, contemplating the event. "A week ago, today."

"This doesn't make any sense, then," Devon said, flipping her finger up and down the screen. "Did you erase any calls?"

"No," Hawthorne responded. "I don't ever erase anything."

"Todd," she said as she looked up. "Only two calls were made from your phone last Saturday. The first was to 911. It was made at 5:12 p.m. The second was to a Monterey number, I assume that's Peg. It was made at 5:33 p.m. You made that call after we found the kids, right?"

"Yeah," Hawthorne said crinkling his face. "Let me see."

Hawthorne took the phone and examined it as Devon had just done.

"That can't be right," he said, puzzled. "I didn't call 911."

The two looked at each other for a moment, mystified.

"Todd," Devon said, looking a little pale, "Reverend White called 911 about thirty minutes *before* the shooting started. The paramedics arrived *ten minutes* after. And Big Sur is about *forty minutes* away."

Hawthorne was putting it all together, too.

"How could he possibly have known to do that?" Devon asked. "For that matter, how could he have known where the kids were going to be?"

Hawthorne shrugged and rubbed the back of his fingers against the bandage on his neck.

"Was he in on it?" Hawthorne asked.

"In on what?" Devon answered, beginning to get animated. "Two whack jobs offing themselves? He wasn't with them. He was with the kids. He got in my car with the rest of us when the guy started shooting. Then, when the ambulance arrived, he was just gone."

"I don't know," Hawthorne said. "It's weird, I guess, but in my line of work, I've seen stranger things. Um, I kind of need to lie back down. We can figure it out later."

Devon helped him from the table and over to his bed.

"I'm really not cool with this," he said, looking and feeling helpless as he crawled under the covers.

"Oh, I don't know," Devon responded. "I think I kind of like it. Maybe I need a key, so you don't have to keep getting out of bed every time I knock."

Hawthorne searched Devon's eyes for some sense of assurance that this was not going to end poorly for him at some point down the road.

"Maybe," Devon said, staring back, "I shouldn't have to knock."

"I've been hurt," Hawthorne whispered.

"I know," Devon whispered back. "I can see your bandage."

"That's not what I mean."

"I know," Devon whispered again. She could see the fear in Hawthorne's eyes. "Me too."

She carefully crawled across him and lay down, wiggling around for a moment until she was comfortable. When she settled in, she was on her side, spooning against him with one arm draped over Hawthorne's chest. She felt him swallow hard, then relax.

"Did you get your article in?" Devon asked.

"Yeah," Hawthorne whispered. "Thank you for the help. I've never written with a neck wound before."

"You finally got your big story."

"We'll see," Hawthorne said. "It's supposed to come out tomorrow. The governor's announcement would have been bigger news. I can't believe he decided not to run. Just out of the blue. There's definitely a story in there somewhere."

Devon's response was a monotone hum.

"I like naps," she murmured as she took a deep breath and then faded away.

"Me too."

In the quiet of the room, their breathing began to synchronize.

FORTY-ONE

EARLIER THAT SATURDAY MORNING, A GROUNDSKEEPER wearing faded jeans, a threadbare shirt, and a large straw shade hat walked through the garden at the Cathedral of St. James in Santa Fe. The rector had informed him that the water usage had been unusually high the previous month and asked him to have a look at the irrigation system surrounding the building.

The groundskeeper put the irrigation controller on a test cycle and walked from station to station examining the various sprayers, nozzles, and drip hoses around the building. Most seemed to be working normally. One, however, placed near a recently planted tree not far from the side of the cathedral, was not spraying at all. The groundskeeper noticed several other nozzles along that same line were not spraying any water.

He followed the smaller hoses back to their connection with a larger hose that ran along the ground beside the cathedral's foundation. A few yards later, he saw the problem. A splice between two pieces of larger hose had become disconnected, allowing uncontrolled water to spill onto the grass.

Once the controller was turned off, the groundskeeper

grabbed a few items from a tool shed and walked back to make the repair. Placing his gear on the ground, he knelt to dig up an additional portion of the hose. As he brushed away the dirt, he noticed a small orange brick on the ground tucked behind a shrub. The brick was clearly out of place, so the groundskeeper reached over and tried to pick it up.

The brick lifted but was connected to a thin metal wire. The man yanked on it a couple of times and realized he wasn't holding a brick. The object was hard, but soft enough that he could squeeze into it with his fingers. He laid it down and traced the path of the wire, which ran around the base of the building. Some distance later, the wire connected to another identical brick. The groundskeeper grew suspicious and went inside to tell the rector.

Twenty minutes later, a team from Santa Fe SWAT and an explosives unit arrived at the cathedral. Six bricks were located in all, each placed strategically around the building. The SWAT leader told the rector that if they had been detonated, the church would have been demolished. This, the leader explained, looked like it was intended to be included in the previous church explosions. The detonator was set and still active.

The rector crossed himself and re-entered the magnificent church. He knelt before the ornate altar under an elaborate cross and said a prayer of thanks. He had no idea why his church had been spared. He only knew that there had been a divine reason.

FORTY-TWO

PEG PUSHED THE BLANKET OFF AND STOOD UP, PRESSING THE palms of her hands against the back of her hips and stretching. The small sofa in the hospital room pulled out into a bed, but it was not comfortable. It didn't seem to bother Max much, though. She adjusted the blanket, so it covered her son.

Callie was sound asleep in the large, elevated hospital bed. The metal railings were raised, and Peg leaned against one as she checked on her daughter. Most of the tubes and wires had been removed, but there was still an IV line attached to the top of Callie's hand. The nurse said they would try to get Callie up and walking around later that afternoon, and if that went well, she would probably be discharged tomorrow.

Peg put on a robe and some flip-flops and tiptoed toward the door, trying hard to keep the backs of her shoes from slapping the bottoms of her feet. She eased the room door open then eased it closed when she was in the hall.

A passing nurse said good morning as Peg walked to a small coffee station down the hall, as she had done often in the past week. A short stack of newspapers lay on the counter next to the microwave. She pulled a *Monterey Journal* from the top, then noticed the *L.A. Tribune* beneath it.

The front-page headline read "Revisited: Have we all been here before?" The author was Todd Hawthorne. Peg skimmed the article standing at the coffee station. From her quick glance, it looked like Todd had hit it all and done a nice job. Peg was folding the paper and tucking it under her arm when she realized that another person was waiting for coffee.

"Oh, I'm sorry," she said.

"No problem at all," the man responded, nodding toward her newspaper. "It's really quite a fascinating concept, isn't it? I saw a TV piece on it this morning. Looks like it got picked up quickly. Gotta love the twenty-four-hour news cycle."

Peg smiled at the man and returned to Callie's room. Plopping down into one of the industrial chairs, she reread the article. Todd had recounted the entire story from top to bottom, starting with Masten and Mendez' creepy study and ending with the mountaintop scene that had nearly cost Callie her life.

Can any of this really be true? She knew Callie's perspective, and that was certainly very real, as evidenced by where she was and had been for the past week. But the continuous recycling of souls idea seemed pretty far-fetched. Still, the scientist in her conceded that there appeared to be at least some anecdotal data for it. *And,* she thought, *it's not any more far-fetched than the other things most people believe about death and what happens after death. But it would certainly take a different kind of faith.*

Peg stood up to check on her daughter again. Callie was still sleeping. She shook her head, wondering for the umpteenth time how anything like this could ever have happened to her baby. She thought too about her husband. She'd always been taught to trust in a higher plan. That was getting harder and harder.

Peg paced restlessly in bare feet for a few minutes, then sat back down and picked up the paper again. She drew in a deep breath then let it out. She folded the paper neatly and placed it on a counter-top near the sink in the room. She hated to throw out the rest of the news if someone else could read it later. But, she was finished with past life experiences. She hoped Callie was over it, too. One life was hard enough without even thinking about what may have come before or what might come next. The whole concept was exhausting. *Besides*, Peg thought, *no one really knows what comes next. It could be anything.*

FORTY-THREE

DEVON WAS SITTING AT HER DESK SCROLLING THROUGH emails when she heard a knock on the door frame. She looked up. It was Reverend White.

Devon was dumbstruck for a moment before she spoke. "Where have you been?"

"I've been around, dear."

"But on the mountain, where did you go?" Devon asked. "I looked everywhere. Asked everyone."

"I like to keep a low profile," he said with a wink.

Devon shook her head.

"Listen," he continued, "I just wanted to pop by and tell you not to give up. He's out there."

"Who's out there?" Devon asked, confused.

Reverend White pointed and winked again. "Ah, where would be the fun in that, dear?" he laughed a little as he backed out of the doorway. His footsteps faded as he walked down the hall.

Devon stared at the wall for a moment, then jumped from her chair and ran to the door. She looked left and right, but no one was there. She walked out into the hall and listened. There was nothing. She threw up her hands in frustration, just as her friend Ashley rounded the hall corner.

"Did you see that?" Devon asked?

"Did I see what?"

"A reverend in a black suit walking down the hall." Devon responded.

"Uh, no." Ashley dragged out the words. "Are you okay?"

Devon shook her head. "I'm fine."

Ashley crinkled her brow for a moment, then moved on. "So," she asked, "are you going to see Todd again?"

Devon smiled, moving on from the reverend as well. "Maybe."

"Maybe? That's all you've got?"

"We're taking it slow. It's complicated."

Ashley walked into Devon's office and sat down. "I think *maybe* you should uncomplicate it."

"*Maybe* I will," Devon said with a bigger smile.

"You're in love," Ashley responded, now smiling herself.

Devon looked away.

"Well," Ashley said, changing the subject, "I heard the Dean gave you the green light for continuing your research."

"She did!" Devon exclaimed. "Dr. Warnick went to her with additional funding from his benefactor."

"Who's his benefactor?" Ashley asked. "Definitely need a bottle of wine headed that way."

"No idea," Devon answered, "but she's all in, for whatever reason. I'm fully funded for several years!"

"That's margarita level good news." Ashley said. "Let's go celebrate!"

"I'm in," Devon said. "Just give me a couple of minutes."

Ashley sat in silence for a bit as Devon continued clicking things on her computer screen. When the wait lasted a little too long, Ashley broke in. "So, do you feel better knowing what happened to your dad?"

Devon looked up. "Not really."

"Interesting," Ashley mused.

"Honestly," Devon continued, "I just feel that much angrier. Or at least, I did. Then I saw this."

Devon slid a small, folded piece of paper across her desk to Ashley. It was a note, written in sloppy handwriting.

"The Dean found this when she had Jim's office cleaned out. I guess she thought I'd want it because it mentioned my name, or my father's name."

Ashley picked up the note and read. There were only three words at the top—*He will pay*. About a third of the way down the page, there was only one word—*Mendez*. The rest of the note listed out the names of twelve cities. Six had lines scratching through the names. Six did not. The six that were not scratched through were the cities where churches had been blown up, plus Santa Fe.

"My god!" Ashley said, putting a hand over her mouth. "This was his plan. He wrote it out."

Devon nodded. "I never have been able to figure out why Santa Fe was spared. It was wired to blow, just like the others."

Ashley shook her head. "He was crazy."

"He was angry," Devon replied. "And he let it destroy him."

Ashley looked up.

"Anyway," Devon continued, "I saw this and lost a couple of night's sleep, but then decided that it was healthier to let it go. I'm angry at Jim, of course, but I refuse to let him, or my anger ruin the rest of my life. I will not give him that power."

"You're an amazing woman, Devon," Ashley said.

Devon clicked her computer off and stood. "I'm an amazing woman who needs a margarita with her friend. Let's go."

Devon wadded up the note and threw it in the waste basket just before she turned off the light in her office.

EPILOGUE

WHEN THE CAR HIT THE GROUND, I IMMEDIATELY FOUND MYSELF out of my body and in this place. From here, I can see all my past lives, but the one I'm focused on is my life as James Masten.

There's nothing physical here. It's just consciousness—my consciousness. But it's a complete consciousness, and with that comes an inescapable review of who I was, measured against the powerful suggestion of who I should have been. It is a forced self-judgment that doesn't tolerate equivocation, argument, or justification. It is a mirror that reflects me, laid bare.

In that mirror, I see the deaths I caused and the lives I ruined. We are so interconnected as conscious beings that I see those events through the eyes of the people I killed and hurt. It is horrifying, and I'm ashamed. I'm also ashamed because I can see through the eyes of Claire, my daughter. I caused her pain and terror, and I will have to carry that with me forever.

I've not always been a bad person in my prior lives. In this one, though, I allowed my anger and bitterness to take over, and I chose the wrong path. I hope I get the chance to atone for my wrongs.

But there's also a peaceful comfort in this place. Even in the face of all that I've done. I can see Claire running along the beach, kicking at the sand, and disrupting nearby seagulls. There, they know her as Callie, but to me she will always be Claire. The knowledge that she has a long and happy life ahead of her before returning here gives me peace.

I can't see my wife. She's somewhere else, living a life as someone else. Hopefully it's a happy and fulfilled life. I wish I could see her, but I know we'll be together again, perhaps with Claire. One day, our paths will cross. We never really leave each other.

Acknowledgements

❖ ❖ ❖

I lost my precious wife of twenty-six years about six months after this book was completed. When I was writing, I had no idea it would be somewhat premonitory. I read it from a new perspective now.

The book took about three years to finish, although parts of it are much older. But all along the way, Jules was there. She was there for every edit, every change, every draft, and every re-write. Some of the words, sentiments and ideas come straight from her. I could not have finished this book without her intellect, input, and support. I have dedicated this book to her, but she also gets the first acknowledgement. Thank you, Sweetie!

My mother, J. Angelley Cobb, is next. A talented author in her own right, she took the laboring oar on all initial and final line edits, including one complete top to bottom re-write. She is a one-woman adverb police force, and I thank her for it. Sincerely.

I would also like to thank Amy at CopyRight Editing. Her work and input were invaluable.

I want to thank my friend of many years Jeff Hightower. He's a great attorney and a heck of a good beta reader. Thank you for your time, support, thoughts and input. *I like it a lot.*

A special thanks to my brother Rick Nelson. Your friendship and support mean more to me than I can say or write. You truly are my brother. Thank you for reading my book and providing your insight. I wish I could give you more on Reverend White, but I can't. Sometimes that's art. He jumped onto the page of his own accord and never left. Maybe he's a guardian angel. Maybe some other kind of manifestation. I don't know. I didn't plan him. As in the book, he just showed up.

Possible Spoiler Alert Warning:

I do want to say this, and spoiler alert in case anyone is reading the acknowledgments first, you may want to skip this part. But the chapter where Masten is telling Mrs. Crenshaw about the burden being his alone to bear is wrong in my *after the fact* experience. My family and I have been upheld and supported by a great number of friends and family. Thank you is not enough, but I don't know any other words. Thank you! You mean more to us than you'll ever know.

Lastly, thanks to everyone reading this. If you're all the way back here, I presume you've read, or are going to read, the book. Time is our most valuable asset and I thank you for spending some of yours with me and my imagination.

About the Author

❖ ❖ ❖

An avid reader of fiction his entire life, William O. Angelley's life has been decidedly *non-fiction* in nature, specifically as a practicing trial attorney since 1997.

He is a former Navy pilot and a graduate of the University of Texas School of Law. He has lived and worked as a lawyer in Texas, New York, California, and New Mexico.

While in undergraduate school, he was a volunteer and (sometimes) paid assistant for several medical researchers at the Texas Tech University Health Sciences Center, including a Histologist, a Rheumatologist, a Bio-Medical Engineer, and a Neurologist.

He currently lives near Dallas, Texas, with his children and several dogs and cats. This is his first novel.

www.AngelleyBooks.com

Made in the USA
Coppell, TX
13 March 2023